THE DEAD MAN STORY

MARTY CONLEY

ISBN: 978-1-68222-851-7 (Print)
ISBN: 978-1-68222-852-4 (eBook)

To my wife Barbara

SERENDIPITY:

When pleasantly surprising things happen because
of chance circumstances that are the result of human beings making
selfless connections which exist on the thinnest of threads.

CHAPTER ONE

Tuesday, September 2nd

I was afraid this would happen. I can't hold back a small burp that releases a disgusting, unmistakable smell. It's all my grammy's fault. Ever since she tried to kill me. Actually, she tried to kill my whole family. All of us. My brother, my parents, a bunch of cousins, and several aunts and uncles. No one died, but now I smell like fish.

A late-summer breeze sweeps down the river taking the fish smell with it. I've been coming to this spot along the river for as long as I can remember. The smell of the woods and river mixing together usually help me breathe a little easier. I can think of worrisome things until they seem small and harmless. Not today. The sky has lost its color and the river water has turned black. My neck creaks like the snapping of a twig.

"I can't believe summer vacation is almost over," Brady says.

A bird flutters out of the branches above and glides out over the water making several dips before flying straight downriver. I follow it as it seems to have nowhere to go, flying purely for the love of it. Brady sees it too and smiles. He's twirling a fat, shiny acorn between his bony fingers.

"This summer was way too short," Brady adds.

No one is making a move to go home, even though we've been here since right after breakfast this morning. We skipped lunch because if we went home to eat, we'd all be too lazy and tired to come back afterwards. Lunchtime was a few hours ago, and now I'm so hungry I'm thinking about eating the acorns I've been using to spell out my name, M-Y-L-E-S.

"I hate school," Kat moans.

Kat hates school but the reasons for her dislike are hard to explain. She's my cousin, although I can never remember if she's a first cousin twice removed, or a second cousin once removed. My mom and Kat's mom are cousins, so we're related somehow, and that's good enough for me.

"What's with you? You look like you're trying to twist yourself into a pretzel," Brady says, tossing me his acorn.

"I'm bored, that's all."

"You look bored, but that's not what I mean. You worried about tomorrow?"

"I don't know. It'll be alright I guess."

I look out at the river, stretched out like a shoestring. It's a swirl of unsettling activity. Tomorrow, the three of us will be starting seventh grade. My stomach tightens into a knot, and I twist my shoulders in response to the anxiety I'm feeling. My dad says I worry too much, and that's why I twitch. I've been fairly quiet with it most of the day, but now without warning, it's acting up.

I don't remember when my twitching started or why. My twitches come in ways I can't predict. They're like bad habits, impossible for me to avoid. I twitch the same way most people blink, or pass gas. Most of the time I don't even know I'm twitching until I've been at it for five or ten minutes. My parents were hoping I'd have outgrown it by now. Me too. Instead, it seems as though it's getting worse. The problem with anxiety is that after I weather one wave of panic there's often another warming up right behind it determined to push me over a cliff. It'll be a minor miracle if I get through this year without a meltdown. I had one last year in sixth grade that kept me out of school for a while.

I feel restless from too much sun and the dull familiar ache of boredom. Uncomfortable to the point of irritation I kick at Kat's feet. She's listening to music and ignores me. A second kick gets her attention, and she removes an earbud.

I love music but not half as much as Kat. "What are you listening to?"

"Just some hip-hop," she answers, her feet tapping to the beat.

Kat was one of the lucky ones who survived Grammy's attempt to kill us all.

We spend Christmas every year at my grandparents' house with my dad's entire side of the family plus Kat and her mom. Counting all my aunts, uncles, and cousins, there are something like thirty of us. My grammy has been making homemade eggnog every year since my dad was a kid. Only last Christmas the eggs were tainted and 22 of us wound up in the hospital with a bad case of food poisoning, something called *salmonella*.

My dad said I looked like one of those zombies you might find in the woods who'd been dead for two months, but was still walking around, somehow. He didn't look so hot himself. The only people who didn't get sick were my Uncle Joe's family, and Kat who doesn't like eggnog. Uncle Joe bragged to my dad that he and his kids never get sick because they all take a tablespoon of cod liver oil every day.

That's all my dad had to hear. The next day he ordered Chinese food and several containers of won-ton soup just so he could get his hands on a couple of those over-sized white ladles they give you. Now he makes me and my brother take a ladle full of cod liver oil every morning before we go to school. That means every time I burp I give off an oily, fish odor that anyone within three classrooms can smell. It's bad enough being noticed for my twitching, but then add a nasty dose of fish-breath and it's no wonder I have anxiety issues.

"What are you playing?" I ask Brady.

"A new game I downloaded last night. I'm trying to beat my high score," he says without bothering to look up.

I'm not big on gaming myself, it's too hard for me to sit still for that long. All that herky-jerky action on the screen sends me into a twitch-fest, and then I can't control the console in my hands. Brady on the other hand is a big gamer.

"Seems like we didn't get to do half the things we wanted to," Brady says.

"I got to do what I wanted," Kat says, an earbud dangling from one ear.

"Yeah, what's that?" I ask.

"Well, for starters I didn't have to go to school. And secondly, I slept a ton this summer."

"Sleep is overrated," I say.

"It's better than going to school," Kat says.

Brady looks up and appears to be done with his game. "Damn. My battery just died."

"That's what you get for playing video games for three hours." I sit up and try to uncoil the knot in my stomach.

"What do you say you tell us a story, Myles, as it's the last day of vacation," Brady says, putting his phone in his pocket.

I hesitate. Stalling for time while I try to think of something, my shoulders lurch with a twitch that's been itching to escape. Kat and Brady shift into more comfortable positions on the giant rock we're seated on. It's a car-sized boulder, smooth and flat on top, and sits at the end of a well-worn path cut into the slope of the river's embankment.

"C'mon man, tell us a story," Brady says.

It's not that I don't want to tell a story. I love to tell stories. And I'm pretty good at tellin'em. Might even say I'm famous for them. It's just that, sometimes, my stories get me into trouble. Like that time my brother Dennis was kidnapped. That was the story I told my parents, anyway. I thought someone had taken him while we were at Cracker Barrel having breakfast. The police even showed up after the manager called them. But it was my grandmother who found Dennis in the women's room where he was sitting on the crapper taking his sweet old time. He had no idea he was in the wrong room. Of course, my mother freaked out, and I was grounded for a month.

I don't know why I'm so good at telling stories, but once I open my mouth a curious mixture of imagination and falsehoods never fail to come together.

"I don't feel like it right now."

"What do you feel like doing?"

I rattle off a series of twitches.

I have a couple of twitches I do. I started with one, but over the years I've added a few new ones. My original twitch is what I call a *shoulder shrug*. I kind of snap my head towards my left shoulder and at the same time lift my right shoulder. It looks like I have a cramp in my neck and I'm stretching it out. Another one I do is an *eye-flutter*. I blink my eyes five times real fast. My newest twitch is a *rib crunch*. It's like I'm doing a sideways stomach crunch to fold myself in half. When I'm really stressed I'll fire off a sequence of twitches. Maybe two shoulder shrugs, followed by an eye-flutter, one or two rib crunches, then maybe two more shoulder shrugs. Then I'll repeat the whole thing again. I'm a mess and I know it. But there's not much I can do about it.

Hearing my stomach growl, I stand up. "You guys ready?"

"What's the hurry? We got all day."

"I gotta mow the lawn."

"Myles Walsh...Mr. Responsibility! Mr. Goody-Two Shoes!" Brady exclaims.

"Yeah, well, I'm hungry too."

"Hey, look." Brady says. He looks down at the edge of the riverbank where the water is lapping against a tangle of branches.

"What is it?" I ask, not seeing anything unusual.

"Down there, see it," Brady says, pointing.

I see it. A ghoulish head, trapped in the branches, is bobbing in the water.

"I'm gonna check it out." Unlike me, Brady is one of those thrill-seekers for whom nothing is too risky. He races down to the water's edge and

pries the head loose. It's a Halloween candy bucket in the shape of a skeleton skull. The whitish face is cracked in several places with grimy clumps of
river mud smearing its peculiar smile. Brady lifts it up. Black water pours
out of a hole where an eye once was.

"Look!" he says, showing off his treasure.

"It's junk. Just throw it away," I say. Brady ignores me and peers into
the skull's head.

"What are you looking for?" Kat shouts.

"To see if there's any candy in it. Myles says he's hungry."

Satisfied that the skull contains no candy, Brady flings the bucket
back into the river. It spins around several times in the swirling water. Its
one eye watches us as it begins to float away. Its voyage is short-lived, however, becoming trapped in the branches of some mangled-looking shrubs
along the river's edge.

I uncoil a round of shrugs and crunches. "C'mon, let's get out of
here," I yell to Brady.

Brady and Kat concede and we straggle back up the path toward our
bikes. Our hangout spot on the river is behind an old storage building about
the size of a large shed. It hasn't been used for a long time. Now it's just a
spooky-looking brick building with boarded-up windows surrounded by
tall, grassy weeds. The torn-up parking lot has become the neighborhood
dump. It's littered with discarded items such as broken bureaus with no
drawers, old boxy TVs with the screens smashed in, mattresses all ripped
apart, a filthy couch without any cushions, and all sorts of other things
people no longer want. Everything is sprinkled with broken shards of glass
that we tiptoe around.

We have the place to ourselves as no one else ever comes in here. A
chain is strung across the entrance that blocks cars from entering. A dis-
eased-looking sign hangs from the chain. The words KEEP OUT can barely
be seen because the sign looks like it's been there for a hundred years. On
the other side of the chain is a gravel driveway that runs about thirty yards

then hooks to the left and out to the main road. We always ignore the sign and ride our bikes around the chain.

We trudge up the path and enter the shadowy coolness of the woods. I turn and glance at the river. The water is swirling like it's in a hurry to get somewhere. I hear the faint chirping of a bird somewhere deep in the woods.

Our bikes are strewn on the ground right where we left them. We each grab our own bike and begin to walk up the gravel drive that leads past the brick shed to the main road. The autumn air is cool and the smell of acorns and pine cones wrap around me like a favorite blanket.

Kat stops. She's transfixed on something I cannot see myself. She twists around and looks at Brady and me standing behind her.

Then I see it, too.

It's about twenty-five yards ahead of us. A bag, half-obscured by the tall weeds in which it lays. A clear plastic bag, the kind you can see into. The bag itself isn't what catches our attention, though. It's something recognizable inside the bag that brings us to a dead stop. I can't tell what it is, the bag is too far away to notice any other details besides two brownish forms which stick out from the weeds.

We look at each other.

No one says anything.

There was no bag there this morning.

We've been coming here all summer. Dozens of times we've walked this path without a worry in the world. Seeing something that's out of place, even if it is in some sort of garbage bag, feels like an intrusion into our summer hideout.

"What do you think it is?" Kat says.

"I don't know," I mumble.

"We have to walk by there anyway, we may as well check it out," Brady says.

Walking with our bikes, we approach the bag. The closer we get, the more real those two forms are looking. My head is buzzing. One twitch bumps against another and soon enough a crowd of twitches have gathered around me.

At a distance of about ten yards from the bag we stop. Most of the bag is lying in waist high grass browned by the sun which hides what's in it. A small portion is extended onto the gravel path, and it is in this portion that the two forms begin to take a more familiar shape.

I can't believe what I'm seeing.

I screw up my eyes thinking my focus is somehow off. Up to this point neither the bag nor the brown, wooden forms have moved an inch, and I'm grateful for that. But that doesn't stop my heart from pounding so loudly that I'm afraid it'll wake-up what I hope is quietly sleeping.

"Whatever it is, it hasn't moved," I whisper.

"I don't like this," Kat trembles.

"Probably just some kind of joke," Brady says.

We tiptoe a little closer, and rest our bikes a safe distance from the mysterious bag, though close enough for a quick getaway if necessary. Brady approaches the bag first. Kat and I hang back waiting to see what will happen, expecting the worst. Is someone trying to scare us? Did someone come in here to dump something? If so, why'd they leave it in the weeds?

Questions flood my mind, but no answers come.

Brady parts the weeds like a skittery cat. I can feel the blood pulsing in my ears. And then he freezes.

"My gosh!" he gasps. His reaction startles me. He stares wide-eyed at the rest of the bag that Kat and I cannot see.

"What is it?" I ask in a voice that cracks, my mouth cotton-ball dry.

"You're not gonna believe it. Come see."

I have all I can do to keep my twitching from spiraling out of control. My eyes flutter, my shoulder muscles quiver, and my hands and knees are shaking. I must be bothering Kat because she turns and glares at me.

"It's okay," Brady says, then holds up his hands and relaxes a bit to prove it. "Man...this is unbelievable."

"What is it?" Kat whispers. Brady waves her forward and she steps in his direction.

I let out a sigh and look over my shoulder. The garbage-filled parking lot is a familiar presence that calms me. The mystery bag is probably just another unwanted item that's been dumped here. A bird flits onto the limb of a tree nearby and begins chirping a mournful tune. Focusing my gaze back onto the bag, I'm afraid its sad tune will wake whatever it is that is sleeping peacefully in the bag. My curiosity gets the better of me. Brady crouches down next to the bag, putting me at enough ease to walk over and see once and for all what this thing is.

I see it.

Things will never be the same again.

What we've found is something we aren't supposed to find. In a clear, plastic bag tied in large knot is a man.

A dead man.

He's an older man wearing a white sheet or a robe, I can't tell. His face is ashen and lifeless. I have never seen a dead person before, but there is no doubt in my mind that I'm looking at one now. Kat spins around, covers her mouth with her hands, and runs away without looking back.

The oddity of a man lying inside a bag on the edge of a gravel path numbs me. I struggle to breathe and to put sensible thoughts into my head as my twitching flares into full power. Brady inspects the contents of the bag. I take my eyes off the stone-faced man to check on Kat. She's standing near the entrance to the parking lot just past where the Keep Out sign is. As I peer back at the silent figure wrapped in plastic, I need to know that he is really dead. I can't shake the thought that this is just some over-the-top prank.

I scan the area around us in all directions for any sign of another person, or any sound or movement at all. Brady must be thinking the same thing, because he jumps up and spins around looking for any sign of danger. At first I think my twitching might have startled him, but he's looking all around as if someone is watching us.

Up until this moment I would have sworn that there was complete silence in these woods, but now that Brady and I are listening for any sound at all, all we can hear are noises. The sound of the soft breeze as it whistles through the trees, the lone bird chirping a frantic warning, and cars as they speed past on a road that's out of view. I pray for total silence, that's all I want to hear, but nature will not cooperate, she has a rhythm all her own and neither our presence nor the dead man's is going to change that.

"My gosh! Can you believe it?" Brady whispers.

"Who is it?"

"No idea."

"C'mon guys, hurry up, I'm scared!" Kat yells from the entrance. I wave to let her know that we're okay.

So far anyway.

"I can't believe this," I half-shout, feeling a little more confident that we're alone. That is other than the dead man in the bag.

"What do you think happened to him?" I ask.

"I have no idea. Do you see anything?"

"Like what?"

"Like blood"

My eyes dart the length of the deceased man. "I don't see any."

Kat shouts again, impatient for us to finish whatever it is we're doing. I turn and glare at her. I wonder, irrationally of course, if her shouting is also irritating the man in the bag. The pounding in my heart steadies and my twitching slows. I focus my gaze on the man's face. He seems to be older than my parents, but younger than my Grampy or Pappy. If I had to guess I'd say he's in his sixties. Was anyhow. His skin is a dull brown - like its color has drained away. He looks to be from India. Noticing the white sheet I figure it is a traditional robe of some sort. There are several strings of thick wooden beads wrapped loosely around his neck. He isn't real tall, or short, just average height. His hands are out of view as they have slid down by his sides. His feet, the two forms that first caught our attention, are bare, boney, and wrinkled.

I consider moving the weeds to get a better look, but just thinking about touching the guy, or even the bag, sends a cold shiver through me. I check the area around the bag looking for some clue to the man's identity and why he's been placed here when I see what looks like a golf ball tucked under the bag near his side. I use my fingers to roll it over to get a closer look. It's a ball of clumpy rice. That's odd.

"Look at this," I say to Brady, still afraid to speak louder than a whisper.

"What is it? Where'd you find it?"

"I think it's rice, it was right here." I point to the spot where it was lodged, then hand it to Brady.

Brady looks at me, confused about the purpose of rice at a death scene. "Was the guy eating lunch or something? Where's the rest of his lunch?" Brady says.

We look at each other, then at the lifeless man enclosed in the heavy plastic. For a moment I swear he's moved in some way. My courage, the little I have, is waning.

"I think I hear someone. I'm getting out of here," I say.

I glance up at the branch where the small bird was perched. The branch is vacant. An empty silence has replaced the bird's chirping.

"Yeah, let's get out of here, I don't like this," Brady says, then he heaves the rice ball far into the woods.

I stand up quickly, jarring the bag and the man inside, then scurry to my bike and pedal up the driveway towards Kat. I'm almost there when she yells, "Myles, can you get my bike?" I'm about to turn and ask Brady if he can do it when he goes whizzing by me on his own bike. Kat looks at me, her eyes pleading for help.

For crying out loud! Why me?

I pedal back to where Kat left her bike. The noise of loose stone crunches under the bike's tires. My eyes are glued on the bag, still afraid the man might wake up, and if he does, I figure he won't be very friendly about all this. The effort to walk with both bikes on the gravel is a clumsy one. I'm not comfortable being alone and near the dead man again. I pass within a few feet of the bag and then something I hadn't noticed before catches my eye.

A delicious terror grips me.

"C'mon Myles! Hurry up? Let's get out of here!" Kat screams.

"Hang on!" I yell back at her.

Without thinking or hesitating, I return to the dead man and poke a small hole in the plastic. I reach in and remove a mysterious item that captivates me. I walk away with my stolen treasure and then struggle with the chore of pushing two bikes at the same time.

"What'd you do, take a picture or something?" Kat says when I reach her and Brady.

"No, are you crazy?" I say.

"Hey, we should take a picture," Brady says.

"No way, that's gross!" Kat shouts.

"I'm not taking a picture, besides, I don't have my phone," I say.

"The battery on my phone is dead. Damn," Brady moans. "Kat, you have your phone?"

"I just brought my iPod," Kat replies. "Let's get outta here. We should tell someone what we found."

We ride our bikes around the chain that stretches across the entrance, then pedal out into a grey and strange afternoon like our lives depend on it. I look back to see if anyone is following us, but nothing stands out. A steady stream of cars rush by us in both directions on the busy road. I turn off Weston Drive onto Seymour Avenue. Kat follows me. But Brady just keeps on going towards his neighborhood, avoiding the trouble to tell us that he isn't coming to my house. A sense of safety floods me as soon as I see my house. Home never looked so good. I peel into the driveway and jump off my bike without breaking a stride. I reach the door and run in. Kat is just a split second behind me as we scramble into the house like a pack of dogs.

"What's all the commotion?" my mom hollers when we bolt into the kitchen.

"Mom!" I manage to yell, but I'm too out of breath to continue.

"What's happened?" she shouts as she stands up from the kitchen table. Her eyes dart from me to Kat looking for an answer.

I look at Kat, then gasp, "Mom, we just found a dead body!"

"Where? What dead body? What are you talking about?" Her mouth hangs open in disbelief.

"We were at the river and on our way back, by the chain that blocks the entrance to the parking lot, we saw a dead guy in a bag." The words tumble out. I'm well aware how how crazy this sounds. I search my mom's face for a sign of belief. I need her to tell me that what I saw was real.

"What? This better not be another one of your crazy stories, Myles." Her eyes are wild with doubt as she folds her arms across her chest.

"It's true mom. I know it sounds crazy, but we all saw him, and he was a real guy, and really dead. Ask Kat."

"Kat, is this true?"

"I think so. Whatever it was it looked real to me. But I didn't get a very good look at it."

"Just a dead body left randomly by the side of the road?" her voice squeaks with skepticism.

"Yes, but not the side of the road. It was more in on the entrance to the parking lot to the old public works shed. No one would've been able to see the body from the road."

"The poor man. He must have been hit by a car."

"He wasn't hit by a car, Mom."

"How do you know?"

"Because he was in a plastic bag. A clear plastic bag. He wasn't hit by a car," I say.

My mom hesitates a moment as she considers what to do. "You guys had better not be joking. You hear me?"

Doubt sits on my shoulder. I try to shrug it off but it doesn't budge. It's an ordeal to nod my head.

"Okay, I'll call the police."

Kat and I sit at the kitchen table and tell my mom more about what we found. About thirty minutes later the doorbell rings. It's the police. There are two of them, and they don't look too happy.

One officer is husky with bright red cheeks of flaking dead skin that looks irritable. He has the look of someone who doesn't smile very often. The other officer is shorter than me, all shiny and professional. His dark, probing eyes contrast with an otherwise pleasant-looking face. He's the first to introduce himself. "Hi ma'am, I'm Officer Lema and this is my partner Officer Mathias. We just came from the scene where you say your children found a dead body. Would you mind if we ask them a few questions?"

"Sure, is everything okay? Did you find the body?"

Officer Lema ignores my mom, places one hand on his hips, and smiles as he holds out his other hand to me. "What's your name, big guy?"

"Myles. Myles Walsh," I reply as I try to give him a firm handshake. I twitch a few shoulder shrugs as I try in vain to relax. The officer notices and gives me a look that I'm familiar with.

"You're a big kid. How old are you?"

"Thirteen."

"Wow, you are big. How about you?" he asks, turning his attention to Kat.

"I'm thirteen, too," Kat mumbles.

Turning to me he says, "You must be a football player, is that right?"

"Actually, I play hockey."

"Hockey. So you're a hockey player. Good. Good." His words are delivered deliberately, his eyes study mine.

"So Myles, I understand you and your sister and another boy found a dead body near the parking lot to the old public works shed, is that correct?"

"Yeah, Kat, she's not my sister though, she's my cousin, and my friend Brady, we found the body."

"What were you kids doing over there anyway? Really shouldn't be in there, you know."

"We we're just hanging out by the river, climbing trees, and stuff like that." The other policeman, Officer Mathias, takes out a small notepad and begins scratching away at it. Officer Lema, looks at me like he's sizing me up for a funeral suit. I thought we'd done something good, but you wouldn't know it by the expression on his face.

I do the best I can to describe exactly where we found the body. For some reason Kat acts like she has amnesia - all her answers are vague with no specific details.

"So, how do you know it was a real man? Did you actually see this person up close?"

"Yeah. We had to walk past him to get out to the road. We even went into the weeds to get a closer look."

"And you're positive, absolutely positive, that what you saw was a man, a dead man, inside a bag?"

I can feel my mom tapping her foot to an angry beat on the floor.

"Yeah, positive, he looked real, that's why I raced home and told my mom. I couldn't believe it myself." I sneak a look at my mom out of the corner of my eye.

She glares back at me.

"Is there something wrong, officer?" my mom asks. My neck flickers with confusion, and my shoulders groan with indignation.

"We're not sure yet," Officer Lema replies. He's making me nervous with all these questions. A couple of shoulder-shrugs muscle through my resistance.

I give the officer a detailed description of the dead man's appearance, though, he doesn't seem to believe anything I tell him. Nor does my mom.

"Well, what did you guys find?" my mom asks the officers.

Her question goes unanswered.

"Officer Mathias, how tall would you say this young man is?"

He clears his throat and sizes me up and down. "He looks to be about five foot eleven."

Officer Lema says, "That's what I would say. Five foot eleven." Finally, he addresses my mom. "We looked all over that area, ma'am, and didn't find anything. No bag. No body. We did find an area where some tall grass had been matted down. It appeared that maybe someone fitting your son's height and weight might have done that."

My mom clears the anger out of her throat.

My shoulders ache with plastic bags, white rice, brown feet, and death.

"But it's true!" I shout. "We saw it. A man in a bag, a real man, and he was dead!"

"And where's this friend of yours, this Brady?" Officer Mathias asks.

"He's probably at home," I say.

"Myles, if this is some kind of joke you better come clean right now, you hear me? I'm serious. Wait until your father gets home and hears about this. You and your stories!"

The tone of my mom's voice and the scowl on her face sets off a storm of twitches. Shoulders explode into shrugs, eyes crackle into flutters that strike rapid-fire, one after the other, and my head begins to pulse steadily, signaling that a headache is coming. The police must think that I'm some kind of bugged-out, screwball kid.

Of course they notice. "You alright kid? You seem nervous about something?"

My mom answers for me, explaining to the officers that I "have a condition." She knows when I'm ready to lose it, when I'm on the verge of a full-scale anxiety attack. That's when her compassion usually comes to the rescue, but at the moment she looks like she wants to kill me.

"It's alright ma'am, they look like good kids. But you kids can't be pulling pranks like this. You understand? What if there was a real emergency and someone was seriously hurt and we'd been sent on some wild goose chase?"

Officer Lema begins to walk back to the front door, then turns and says, "I expect better from a hockey player."

"I'm so sorry that we've wasted your time, officers. My son could shake a story out of his socks." She walks the police officers to the front door and stops to chat with them. I can't hear what they're saying, but can only guess that she's apologizing for my crazy story and nutty behavior.

I can't believe this.

We find a body, a dead man, and no one believes us. Can a dead body just up and walk away? If only I had some proof. Remembering my daring theft, I remove the dead man's treasure from my pocket. I cup it in the palm of my hand.

A ring.

Its intricate design gives it the appearance of an ancient artifact. The composition of its parts suggests a meaning that only the ring itself knows. And perhaps the unnamed dead man.

I am a stealer of rings.

My imagination is fired with thoughts that the ring may hold an important secret. A secret, which, for the time being, will remain with me.

CHAPTER TWO

Wednesday, September 3rd

Some people might say my family is boring, and I can't say I'd disagree with them. But one thing us Walshes aren't is snoozers. Every morning we're up with the birds. Not surprisingly, the whole family is in the kitchen when I pour myself a bowl of bran flakes. My dad places a shot glass on the table and slides next to Dennis. His silver hair is slicked to a shine bearing a mixture of plumbing odors and cologne that declares the day has begun.

About the shot glass.

My dad doesn't drink, but he does consume a small army of vitamins each morning. The shot glass is brimming with an assortment of colors, shapes, and sizes. Magic beans that he hopes will keep him alive forever.

"Don't forget your cod liver oil," he says, sliding the jar towards me.

"Dad, really, do I still have to take this?" He has no idea what grief this slimy fish oil causes me.

Before he can answer Mom says, "I wouldn't be complaining if I were you. Your dad and I aren't happy about the stunt you and your friends pulled yesterday. We haven't thought of a punishment yet, but you can't be making up stories, Myles, especially ones that get the police involved."

"I didn't just make up a story. Besides, today's the first day of school. The last thing I need is to smell like fish on the first day."

"Do you know how good cod liver oil is for you? There isn't anything healthier. You're lucky I go out and buy this stuff for you kids. You may not like it now, but you'll thank me later," my dad says.

Even Dennis, who doesn't complain about much, says, "I'm in high-school, how am I supposed to get a girlfriend when I reek like fish?"

Dad dips his lips into the oil. His eyes darken with a frown. When he finishes, he places the empty glass on the table.

"It's great that you take all those vitamins, and if you want to drink cod liver oil every morning and live forever, that's your business. But that shouldn't mean I have to drink fish oil for breakfast." I swear parents only have kids so they can tell them what to do.

Dad's about to respond when Dennis says, "Maybe we could just skip it this one time, Dad, being the first day of school and all?"

Dennis is a sophomore at Valley Tech, a trade school, and is in the plumbing program. He wants to follow in my dad's footsteps and become a plumber helping him in the business. He's been doing some jobs with my dad for a few years now and would quit school and start working tomorrow if he could. My dad won't hear of it of course, even though he can't wait to have Dennis working alongside him.

"Alright. This one time. But starting tomorrow, you take it every morning. No excuses. You hear me?"

Although riding my bike to school means I don't have to mess around with all that nonsense on the bus, like weeds pushing up through the cracks in the sidewalk, my thoughts keep flying off to worrisome things. What if I'm the only seventh grader who rides his bike to school? I lubricate my anxiety with a twitch that wrenches through my shoulders. I'd feel better if Brady or Kat rode their bikes too. But Brady's mom insists he take the bus, and Kat lives right across the street practically, so she just walks over. When I see a bike at the rack I'm relieved that I'm not the only bike rider. It's a Knapp Hotrock, an expensive bike. I wonder who it belongs to, but the owner is nowhere to be seen.

I stutter-step into McFarland Middle School, a pile of crumbling and faded bricks held together with spit and glue. It's home to more than one-thousand sixth, seventh, and eighth graders and sixty some-odd teachers. I have some of the teachers Dennis had when he was in seventh grade, so I know what to expect from them, plus my mom has warned them about my twitching. But one of the teachers is new, Mr. Curtin, and I'm worried about how he'll react when he sees me twitching out a few rib crunches.

One thing that keeps anyone from wisecracking on me is how much bigger I am than most kids. I wear a size ten shoe, the same as my dad, and I'm a full head size taller than most everyone else my age. Although I'm actually a gentle giant, most kids are intimidated by my size and strangeness.

"Good morning, welcome to A2," Mr. Curtin, my homeroom teacher says, greeting each person that walks into his classroom. Mr. Curtin is about my dad's age. He's a few inches taller than me, athletically built, with wire-rimmed glasses that frame bright green eyes. Kat thinks all teachers are nuts and out to get her. She'll be pleased to learn that this one is normal. So far anyway.

"Good morning!" His smile feels like a pat on the back.

I return his smile, nod, and walk past him into the room where many eager faces stare back at me. Although several other kids enter the room after me, Mr. Curtin's eyes follow me. Unable to relax, the muscles in my shoulders are as feisty as a bag of cats. Mr. Curtin's facial expression is one that I know well...one of curiosity and sympathy. Well, now he knows who I am.

We spend most of the morning in homeroom filling out tons of forms that no one will probably ever look at. I can feel my anxiety building with all these demands. Agitated, I'm fixin to twitch so bad and trying not to that I swear I could bite a nail in half. Nevertheless, a twitch frees itself from my shoulders. I can't tell if anyone notices, though.

Once the forms are done, the next order of business is filling out our schedules. All the other kids seem to be getting the hang of it and have their schedules mostly filled out, but mine is only partly done and I'm not even certain that what I've completed has been done correctly. Mr. Curtin walks over and sees the mess on my desk.

"What are you doing here Mr. Walsh, growing a garden? Your desk looks like a weed patch."

I learned a long time ago that staying organized is beyond my reach. He picks up my binder with rumpled papers sticking out of the sides. "How often do you water this thing?" A couple of kids snicker.

This prompts a flurry of jerky shoulder shrugs that get me an awkward look from several of my classmates. Unlike them, I need Mr. Curtin's assistance to finish my schedule. His easygoing manner, though, helps me smother the urge to twitch wildly. Next, we play a bunch of games meant to help us get to know each other better, including my favorite, 4-Corners. It's fun stuff and a nice, easy way to start the school year. I know it will be just another day or so and then the real stuff, the grind begins, but in the meantime this takes the edge off the anxiety I'm feeling.

When we finish the last round of our game, Mr. Curtin gives everyone their locker number and combination. My heart races and I fidget at my desk dreading what's next. For many of my classmates, a locker of their own is the pinnacle of seventh grade. That's because the cubicles we had in sixth grade offered no privacy. Our stuff would be taken all the time, never to be seen again.

"Just remember, left-right-left, and everyone should be fine. Let me know if you need help," Mr. Curtin shouts over our heads as everyone stampedes out into the hallway.

All around me lockers are flying open and kids are squealing and fist-bumping each other.

Not me.

Ten tries and I'm still no closer to opening my locker. I'm frustrated that I don't even bother trying to hide my twitching. I'm squirming out one shoulder shrug and rib crunch after another. Everyone is so preoccupied with their lockers, some kids have opened theirs multiple times, that no one seems to be paying attention to me. I'd gladly trade this trick box for my old cubby.

I give up.

I look for Mr. Curtin, but he's assisting someone else. The hallway is jammed with kids hunched over, weighed down with armfuls of big, heavy textbooks which they cram into their open lockers. Just when all hope seems lost, I see Brady. Although his homeroom is two classes down from mine, Brady is easy to spot wearing a hockey jersey for a team called the *Toothless Wonders*. A smiling mouth with a bunch of teeth missing adorns the front of his jersey. That's what I feel like doing to my locker - knocking the teeth right out of it.

I wave frantically to my friend. With Brady's help I relax just enough to finally open my locker after seven more tries.

After lunch period we rotate through each subject block to meet our other teachers. The math teacher, Mrs. Thompson, is funny and likes to tease kids in a playful way. I figure my twitching will give her plenty to tease me about. Mr. Agostino, the geography teacher, is real short and used to play college soccer. They each remember Dennis and remark how much I look like him. I don't think so. Dennis is a little taller than me, plus he's at least thirty pounds heavier. More of a linebacker to my quarterback. His face is square and tough-looking, while I remind people of a frightened dog with my droopy eyes.

Mrs. Glennon, the science teacher, is kind and friendly, with wheat-colored hair. I beg her to let Brady and I work as partners. She hesitates until I scrounge together a few twitches that gain her sympathy.

Brady's been my best friend for a long time. He's funny, loves hockey as much as I do, and he's never done or said anything disrespectful to me. He likes to tell jokes, especially *Your Momma* jokes. He's a prankster, too. But I don't think he could have pulled off this dead man thing. I had thought that maybe it was someone dressing up for Halloween, but that's still almost two months away. Plus, I knelt down right next to the man.

He never moved.

His expression never changed.

His face was grey. Cold stone grey.

I can't imagine Brady or an old man from India pulling a prank like that, but...then, what happened to the body?

"How sure are you that the body...the man we found, was real?" I ask Brady.

"Very sure." He says with a certainty I wish I had myself. "He was real, okay."

"How do you know?"

"I just do. Don't you?"

I squirm with a spongy shoulder shrug. "I do, but how come the police didn't find the body?"

"I don't know, maybe someone moved the body, or maybe they're covering something up. All I know is that it was a real man, and he was really dead. Besides, I went online last night and searched images for dead people," Brady says, with a smirk.

"What!"

"I did. You should check it out too."

"So?"

"So, there were all these pictures of dead people, you know - corpses. And I'm telling you, they all looked just like the guy we found. I mean they looked different, they were different dead people, but dead people all have this *look*. And the guy we found had the same *look* as all the dead people I saw online."

"What are you guys talking about?" the kid next to Brady says, leaning over and peering at Brady and me.

"Nothing," I answer.

"You were just saying something about dead people."

"Yeah, Myles's aunt is a nurse at the hospital and she was telling us last night about all the people who die there," Brady says.

"That's weird. Was it someone you know that died?"

"No, just random people. She has to fill out reports when they die, it's part of her job." It's obvious that Brady is enjoying this opportunity to tell his own story - a tall tale, no less.

"A report?"

"Yeah. Information the families need to give to the newspapers." Brady sounds like he's an expert on all of this. For a moment, I consider that he might be if he's been surfing the internet.

"Newspapers?"

"Haven't you ever read the obituary section of the newspaper?" Brady says.

"What's an obituary?"

"It's the section of the newspaper that lists all the people who've croaked recently. It tells about how they bit the dust, how old they were, and what they did when they were alive, you know, stuff like that."

"Well, I thought people go to hospitals to get better," the kid says. Clearly he's in the dark about how these things work.

"It doesn't work out that way for all of them. People die in hospitals too, you know," Brady says, getting all serious.

The kid shudders then turns his attention to his own worksheet packet.

"Did you check the paper or something? I didn't think of that," I whisper.

"I went on the website for the Caldwell Chronicle last night."

"Was there anything in the obituary about the dead man?"

24

"No. Not yet, anyway. I'll keep checking, though."

"Does your mom believe you? You know, about finding a dead body?"

"Not really. She thinks you put me up to this, that this is all your idea. Did your mom believe you?"

"No, she thinks it's just another of my crazy stories, that I'm making this all up as some kind of prank. So does my dad. They're thinking up a punishment for me."

"What are you gonna do?"

"I don't know. But, I know we found a dead body. No one else may believe us, but I know what we found."

"Think we should go back after school and see if we can find the body? It may still be there someplace. Maybe the police looked in the wrong area. I remember exactly where it was."

"You think that's a good idea? Aren't you creeped out from yesterday?" A double shoulder shrug and an eye flutter fumble out like spilled milk.

"It's no big deal to me. Oh well, I guess we'll never know who that guy was or what happened to him."

My neck and shoulders tremble with a feverish twitch. I reach into my pocket for the ring. Certain that no one is looking, I study its design. I have an unrelenting hunch that the ring was made for a purpose, one that may be unknown to me now, but has nevertheless embedded itself into my imagination.

When we rotate to English, Mr. Curtin gives us two more textbooks to bring home. That brings me up to approximately forty pounds that I'll have to lug home on my bike.

"Well, I hope everyone had a great first day. Who's excited about coming back tomorrow?"

If Mr. Curtin could guarantee that every day would be like this, playing fun games, even Kat would be excited to come to school. No one responds. Instead we sit there like a bunch of tombstones in a graveyard.

"I hope all of you, or at least most of you, feel like you know your classmates much better. We'll be doing a lot of learning this year working in small groups and that's much easier to do when you know and trust the people in your group. Today was a good start and you can expect we'll do more activities like we did today." Mr. Curtin moves around the room like a butterfly. Dipping, twirling, soaring, never really stopping at any one place for very long.

"Because you guys have been so great today we have enough time for a story. Being as I've learned a lot about most of you, this is a chance for you guys to get to know Mr. Curtin a little bit. The first unit we'll be covering is learning about stories, why we tell stories and why we love them so much. So here's a Mr. Curtin story. A true story by the way." He pauses at the front of the room. His stillness gets everyone's attention.

"Some of you may have figured out from the poster on the door that Mr. Curtin is a Yankees fan. But many of you may not know that Mr. Curtin is from New York. I was born in the Bronx, home of the Yankees and Yankee Stadium. My grandparents were born and raised in Ireland, but moved to the United States when they were in their late teens. It wasn't easy to find a job back then and when my grandfather first arrived in New York he earned money as a musician. He played the accordion in an Irish band. Eventually some friends helped him get a job working for the New York City Subway System. Now, there are two people that work on the train. One is the motorman, he's the one that "drives" the train. The other is the conductor. The conductor is the person that opens and closes the subway doors to let people on and off the train - this was my grandfather's job. Every now and then when the train was between stations he would leave his little compartment and get some fresh air, if you could call it that, by standing on the little platform situated between subway cars.

"Well, he was out there one time when a small particle of steel came off the track and lodged in his left eye. Ever get something in your eye? It irritates you and you can't help but rub your eye, right? Well that's what happened to my grandfather. He rubbed and rubbed that eye, even though my grandmother warned him not to. When it got so bad that he couldn't see out of it, and the other eye also started bothering him, he finally went to see a doctor. Unfortunately it was worse than he thought. He had waited so long to see the doctor, and his left eye was so badly infected, that the eye was lost. The doctor decided to remove the eye because he was worried the infection would spread to my grandpa's right eye, and then he'd have no eyes. Better to have one eye than no eyes, wouldn't you say?"

At this point, everyone, who's been fascinated with Mr. Curtin's story, begin to squirm in their seats, myself included.

Mr. Curtin continues. "After they surgically removed my grandfather's eye he was given a glass eye. When you'd look at him you'd never know one of his eyes wasn't real, that it was made of glass. It sort of looked like a marble, but instead of colorful swirls like most marbles have, this one looked just like a human eye. Now, my grandfather was under strict doctor's orders to keep the eye clean. You see, if the eye got dirty the infection could come back. So every night at bedtime, because he couldn't sleep with the glass eye in place, he'd take the eye out of its socket. The way he'd do it was like this."

Mr. Curtin takes his index finger and thumb and demonstrates how his grandfather removed his own eye. A loud shrill of oooohs! and yuuuuuks! and even a few coools! tremble through the room.

"Once he had his eye out he would place it in a glass of water with a cleaning solution to sanitize it. He'd usually place it on the windowsill above the kitchen sink. I'll always remember as a kid being fascinated watching my grandfather's eye bob up and down in a glass of cloudy water. It was really creepy, but cool at the same time, you know what I mean?"

"What did it look like when the eye was out?" asks a red-haired kid, Colin, who I don't remember having raised his hand in class once last year.

"Well, it looked like a cut or a bad sore except instead of being scabbed over, it was stitched up real tight. It had to be to keep the eye in place. Would be a problem if the eye just fell out and started rolling around on the floor while he was talking to someone, wouldn't you say?"

Several kids shout, "Did it hurt?"

"I don't think so, but my brothers and sisters and I thought it was awesome. I remember we'd all beg him to take his eye out. We'd say "Grandpa take your eye out, take your eye out, take your eye out!" He'd only do it after we'd nag him for about an hour or so, then just to get some peace and quiet he'd remove his eye."

"Did he just walk around like that with the eye out?" Kristina, the tallest girl in the class, asks.

"No, he had a black pirate's patch he'd wear whenever he took the eye out. Sometimes if it was late and we were up watching TV right before bedtime, he'd sit there in his chair with his pirate patch on - we all thought it was neat. The best memory though is when he was mad at us because we weren't behaving. Maybe we'd be running around the apartment playing. I had two brothers and one sister, so there were four of us, and like most kids we liked to play and horse around.

"That's fine to do in a house, but not in an apartment. People live below you and they can hear every step you take, and anytime we'd be horsing around it would get my grandfather all riled up. He'd worry about the neighbors complaining about the noise. When we'd be running around too loudly he'd pluck his eye out, and holding it between his fingers, he'd chase us around the apartment scaring the bejeezus out of us, yelling, "'The eye is gonna get you!'" Or "'You give me your eye and I'll take yours!'" We'd be running away from him screaming our brains out. Boy, was that fun."

This gets a nervous laugh from the class and an uncertain eye-flutter from me.

"It was especially fun when he'd come to visit and my friends would be over. My grandfather helped me make a lot of money one summer. You see, I'd bet some kids in the neighborhood that my grandfather could take his own eye out. Of course, no one believed me. They'd say things like, "'No one can take their eye out. It's wired into your head with veins, and muscles, and other things.'" I'd bet each of them five dollars that he could take his eye out and hold it in the palm of his hand. I'd go get my grandfather and say, "'Grandpa, show my friends how you take your eye out.'" Then he'd start digging and clawing with his fingers; my friends would all step back like they were ready to run for it just in case, and when he'd pluck it out, they'd all scream. He'd hold the slimy eyeball in the palm of his hand and show everyone - they couldn't believe it."

By now the whole class is totally grossed out and scared half to death. My desk is rattling and squeaking because I'm struggling to keep myself from twitching out of control. Luckily, everyone is so mesmerized by Mr. Curtin's story that I've managed to go unnoticed so far. I think, anyway.

"Even with just one good eye my grandfather would see everything. He'd watch us like a hawk making it almost impossible for us to start any trouble. My advice to you guys - keep your eyes open. Both of them. You never know what you might see."

Yeah, no kidding - like dead bodies in plastic bags.

"I see that everyone enjoyed that story."

The whole class agrees, and he gets no argument from me.

"We all have unique stories in our families. I had a grandfather who had a glass eye, but all of you have parents, or more likely, grandparents with interesting stories themselves. Your homework for tonight, yes, yes, I know it's the first day - welcome to seventh grade - is to interview an adult, preferably a grandparent and find out what your family's interesting story is. If there's one thing grandparents love, it's to get a phone call from a grandchild asking them about their childhoods - so go ahead and make those phone calls. Summarize their story in one or two paragraphs. No big deal. I just want to get a preview of your writing skills."

The final bell rings and Mr. Curtin shouts above the din, "Well, that's all I got and it's time to go. Remember, find an interesting story about your own family."

I bike home imagining that someone is watching me.

Someone with a missing eye waiting for the right moment to pounce on me.

Someone who puts people into plastic bags.

I tell myself this is impossible, and then realize that carrying an extra forty pounds in my backpack doesn't help my chances. So I do what any brave kid would do....pedal faster.

I make it home safely, but exhausted from the effort. The stress of the first day is with me when I walk in the door and I'm greeted by my mom who's more excited about my day than I am. She pesters me with the usual questions about teachers and schedules and other things. Then she asks about the new teacher, Mr. Curtin.

I perk up a little bit. "Mr. Curtin was cool. He told us a neat story about his grandfather who had a fake eye made of glass."

"Really?"

"He said his grandfather could take his eye out. He'd be holding it like this." I pinch two fingers together to show my mom, "and he'd chase Mr. Curtin and his brothers and sisters around with the eye."

"He could take his own eye out?"

"It wasn't real, it was made of glass. He said it was a true story."

"I seriously doubt it, but he does sound interesting. How about homework? Any paperwork? What do I need to sign?"

My mood darkens. "The only homework is for Mr. Curtin. We're supposed to interview a parent or grandparent about an interesting family story. Can I call Grampy or Pappy?"

"Sure, they'd love to hear from you and I'm pretty certain either one of them have a story or two they could tell you."

Mom is one of those organization freaks. Sometimes it can be a pain in the neck, like when she pesters me with a thousand questions, but other times it's helpful. This is one of those times. I have a folder full of paperwork and forms that have to be filled out and returned to school, and my mom will make sure everything is in order for tomorrow. It's one less thing I'll have to worry about. She asks a few more questions about friends then reminds me about my homework assignment before she's distracted with Dennis and his first day of school.

Any ideas I had about meeting up with Brady and Kat at the river are scrapped when my mom gives me a list of things she wants me to do. These include going over all the school forms with her and getting all my folders and things organized in my weed patch of a binder. Once that's done it's an early dinner and then we have to pick up Kat and bring her to hockey.

Kat's mom, my Aunt Betty, is a nurse and works all different shifts, and as my dad is the coach, we wind up bringing Kat to hockey most of the time.

Kat's dad isn't around.

He went out once to run an errand, pick up a gallon of milk or something, I'm not sure, but anyhow, he never came back. He just sort of, disappeared. That was about seven years ago.

My dad has coached our team the past two seasons, and uses our car time to catch up on things.

"Mom told me your first day of school went well, is that right?"

"It was alright."

"What did you learn?"

"Not much."

"Not much? You spent six hours in school and didn't learn anything?" he says, ribbing me.

"It was the first day of school, we just fill out forms and played some games. And we learned to open our lockers and stuff like that."

"Sounds good, but I'm sure you learned something. Kat, what did you learn today?" he says, looking at Kat in the rearview mirror.

"Uhh, I learned from my homeroom teacher, Mrs. Glennon, that you can't be successful in seventh grade unless you're organized."

"There you go. Organization is important, no matter what you're doing. You think I just decide what to do for hockey practice when we get on the ice? No way. I have a plan before we get on the ice, otherwise practice wouldn't be as productive."

Thanks Kat, I want to blurt. Now I have to think of something.

"My English teacher told us a story today about his grandfather who had just one eye. It was a good story."

"What did you learn from that?"

"It's better to have two eyes?"

Dad chuckles and shakes his head.

Guessing I should say more, I add, "He said we should keep our eyes open all the time, that way we don't miss anything."

Dad nods his head in agreement. "How did your teacher's grandfather come to have just one eye?"

"He said he had a job working on the subway and something got in his eye, and it became infected. So they had to take the eye out."

Shoot, I just remembered, I never called my grandparents for that story assignment. "For homework we're supposed to ask a parent or grandparent about an interesting family story. Does Pappy or Grampy have a fake eye?"

"Nope, all their eyes are real and so's the rest of them."

"Do you have an interesting story like Mr. Curtin's?"

"I've gotten a few black eyes over the years, but can't say any of them was serious. But did I ever tell you about the time I almost lost my right arm?"

"You almost had your arm taken off? I never heard that."

I sit up, anxious to hear a good story, especially one I've never heard before.

"It happened during my senior year in high school when I played for the football team. Our pre-season included double-sessions during the last two weeks of August. We'd practice early every morning at about eight o'clock until about eleven. Everyone would go home and have lunch then we'd come back around two o'clock and practice again until about five.

"I was a wide receiver and I went up for a pass and banged my elbow on the face mask of a defensive back. At first it just kind of stung real bad. So I shook it off and finished the rest of the morning practice. By the time I got home for lunch, though, it had swelled up real bad. The funny thing is, Grampy happened to come home for lunch too. That's something he almost never did. I showed him my elbow, which at that point I couldn't straighten out at all. The swelling extended a good four or five inches from my elbow." My dad bends his elbow and holds his other cupped hand about five inches below it to show the extent of the swelling. I imagine it was a gruesome sight.

"The whole thing looked quite deformed and Grampy was convinced that I had a compound fracture, so off to the emergency room we went. After I explained what happened to the doctor and he took and viewed an x-ray, he told me that the ding from the face mask had caused a blood clot. What we thought was swelling, was actually a big sack of blood that had backed up at the corner of my elbow. It would need to be drained. And, he warned me, it was going to be very, very painful."

I grimace imagining a five-inch sack of blood hanging from my dad's elbow. My shoulders fidget with a queasy twitch. "What did they do?"

"The doctor explained that he was worried about the clot moving to my heart. He didn't have time to numb it with novocain. He told me, "'You need to know, son, that this is going to be very painful. Are you okay with that?'" "'I guess so,'" I answered, as if I had a choice in the matter. I was strapped face down on a hospital bed. One of the nurses placed a rubber guard in my mouth, to prevent me from biting down on my tongue. A typical reaction when people are experiencing incredibly intense pain. I've heard of people who've bitten their own tongues in half, and he didn't want me to do that."

"Oh, my God!" Kat screeches from the back seat. She's a rough-and-tough hockey player on the ice, but a bit squeamish when it comes to blood and other things.

"It gets better. He hung my elbow, with the sack of blood, off the side of the table I was strapped to. He instructed the nurses to make certain that the rubber mouth guard stayed in place. They wheeled in a stand and stood it in front of me. Dangling from the stand was a large plastic bag. It was empty with a clear plastic tube coming out of it. Next, he sat in a chair and using a razor blade, he sliced open the sack of blood. I could feel every centimeter of the razor as he made his incision. I chomped down with all my might on that rubber piece. Instantly, a spray of blood splattered the wall in front of me. A nurse quickly placed the other end of the tube into the bloody sack. Then all the blood just drained up through the tube and filled the large bag. And that was that."

"Geez, dad, that's gross."

"It's a good thing Grampy decided to come home for lunch that day. Who knows what would've happened if the clot hadn't been cleared."

"But how did that almost cost you your arm?" I say.

"The doctor warned us to be looking for any symptoms of infection. My parents took his advice seriously. You see, earlier that year, during the winter, a kid that I grew up playing hockey with had cut his knee from another player's hockey skate. The game was in some small town in the boonies. The kid's name was Greg Holmes.

"Unlike me, he was taken to some country-bumpkin hospital to have it taken care of. A few mornings later, his parents were upset because he was still sleeping and he was gonna be late for school. They went into his bedroom to wake him up and discovered that he had died during the night. They found out later that he had gotten what's called *staph infection*. Somehow he had contracted the infection when he cut his knee. Staph infection can be deadly. No one knew he had it. It killed him."

Is that how the man at the river died? Maybe he had a contagious disease. Is that the reason he was stuffed into a plastic bag and dumped like yesterday's trash?

"Did you get staph infection Uncle Brian?" Kat asks.

"I did. Everything was fine for a few days, but then my whole arm became sore, just pulsing with pain. It turned yellow then green. I knew something wasn't right. My parents, remembering what had happened to Greg, rushed me back to the hospital. The doctor put me on antibiotics and kept me under close observation until the infection cleared. I was lucky. Greg, unfortunately, was not."

My dad stops. His thoughts wander off to another time and place. I'm told that he was very good - good enough to play college hockey, but he started working as a plumber right after high school. I wish I could've seen him play when he was younger and still believed that there was a jersey with his name on it and a sheet of ice waiting for him in the NHL.

The hockey team we play for is the Bulldogs. Kat and Brady are both forwards, but they usually play on different lines. Me, being the coach's kid, I get moved around more than a piece of meat at Market Basket, meaning I play wherever my dad needs me.

We practice twice each week and the best part are the locker room shenanigans before we get on the ice. My dad usually has to come in more than once to remind us that practice is starting soon and we better be ready when the ice is ready. When I see Brady walk in and dump his bag down and slump onto the bench without joining the fun, I suspect that Jake has been giving Brady a tough time again.

Jake is Brady's older brother. He's one of those kids that get some kind of cheap thrill from bullying around a smaller, younger brother. There's not much Brady can do about it. Jake's in high school, is bigger and wrestles, so he can take Brady anytime he wants.

Brady is coat-wire thin, all skin and bones. You can see every rib in his body and other bones I didn't even know people had. He's good at saying things that get under Jake's skin, but that usually results in Jake putting Brady into a headlock or throwing him down to the ground. Brady's complained to his parents, but his dad isn't around all the time to keep a watchful eye on Jake, and when he is, he's got his head buried in his laptop. Brady's mom cares, but she doesn't seem to do much about it.

Because we're late, as usual, I'm not surprised to see my dad come into the locker room. But instead of scolding us for fooling around too much, he has an important announcement.

"Listen up. I have great news for you guys. In November, Thanksgiving weekend, we're going to Lake Placid to play in the Can-Am Tournament. For those of you who may not know, Lake Placid was the site of the 1980 Winter Olympics and that's where the greatest moment in the history of American sports took place. The United States hockey team beat the Russians and went on to win the Gold Medal. And that's where we'll be playing. Hustle up. Practice starts in two minutes."

The locker room buzzes with excitement. "I've probably seen *Miracle on Ice* ten times!" I say to Brady.

"Can you imagine playing on the same ice where Eruzione scored that game-winning goal?" Brady exclaims, fist-bumping me.

"This is awesome! I can't believe I'm gonna play in Lake Placid!" I shout.

I was barely two years old the first time I put skates on. Actually, Dennis had the skates on before me. My parents brought Dennis, who was six, to the rink to learn how to skate. But when Dennis went out on the ice for the first time, all he did was scream and cry. He carried on so much that Dad took him off the ice and didn't know what to do with him. He'd just bought all this equipment and paid for the program. It all seemed like a waste. Then he looked over and decided he'd put the skates on me and get me out on the ice.

I loved it.

The problem, though, was that once Dennis saw me having fun he started crying again, this time because he wanted the skates back and wanted to go out on the ice. So, once more my dad had to change the equipment, this time taking it off of me and putting it back onto Dennis. Naturally, I started crying. After that, my dad went out and got me my own set of hockey equipment.

Even though I was only two years old, Dennis and I learned to skate together, and I've loved hockey ever since. But Dennis gave up hockey when he enrolled at the Tech and started working with my dad. He's found what he wants to do.

Unlike most things, hockey comes easy for me. A hockey rink is my sanctuary. When I lace up a pair of skates I become a different person. The twitch-free me. The real me. On the ride home I find out that I've been offered a chance to play in an invitation-only All-Star game while at Lake Placid. It's a showcase game featuring the best thirteen and fourteen-year old prospects in New England. Apparently, my size and speed have gotten the attention of some prep coaches, including the coach at Saint Michael's Prep. They're the four-time reigning high school state champs; they're practically a hockey factory, producing more college players than anyone else around. That's where I hope to play.

CHAPTER THREE

Thursday, September 4th

I wake up feeling anxious. Yesterday was a free pass. Even though fig-uring out my schedule and how to open my locker was nerve-wracking, it's nothing compared to the grind of real classes and homework. Not to men-tion the pressure of tests, quizzes, and worst of all, writing assignments.

"By the way, Myles, your father and I talked it over last night and we've decided on your punishment."

I was hoping they'd forgotten about that.

"We think it's only fair that you apply yourself in school this year - that you stay focused on doing your best. You're a smart kid and we know you're better than a 'C' student. Our expectation is that you get all A's and B's for the first term - otherwise they'll be no Lake Placid. You can go. You can hang out with your teammates when you're there - but you won't be able to play in the tournament games. At this point, we're undecided about the all-star game. That's up in the air. Also, needless to say, there'll be no more monkey-business between now and then. You hear me?"

"That's not fair!"

"It is fair. School is important. There's no way you're getting into Saint Michael's with a bunch of C's, no matter how good a hockey player you are. Plus, you have to learn, Myles, that you can't go around telling crazy stories and playing jokes. Sometimes they backfire and people get hurt."

"But..."

"I don't want to hear it. We're serious about this."

My shoulders sag under the pressure of expectations. My stomach boils with fear and uncertainty. I'm one of those students for whom nothing is easy. It's not that school's impossible. I manage okay, thanks to my mom's help, and get mostly Cs with an occasional B. Staying organized and on top of homework and writing assignments and other projects pushes my anxiety button big-time. That's my biggest challenge - avoiding a meltdown.

Adding to my anxiety, round two in the cod liver oil fight goes to my dad. I get no support from my mom. She conveniently disappears when my dad slides the jar over and watches while I choke down the putrid yellow oil.

The upside of gagging down a huge ladle-full of fish oil every morning is I must have the cleanest, healthiest teeth in the town of Caldwell. I brush them for a full five minutes after I take the cod liver oil, hoping the smell of clean teeth coated with toothpaste will mask the puddle of fish oil reeking in my stomach. The problem, however, will come later when my stomach begins digesting the oily mess. Then everyone in my class will be victimized by the side effects - a silent and powerful smell that makes everyone think they're at a fish market. Which they're not. And as I've learned over the years, no one wants to be at a fish market at eight o'clock in the morning. Nor do I.

The whole ride to school I try my best to burp out all the cod liver oil I can. It works once in awhile. Actually, it's worked only once. One morning last year I was on my way to school and I was burping as fast as I was pedaling. Next thing I know I had a stray cat following behind me. When I got off the bike to chain it up, the cat stretched its paws up onto my leg and wouldn't stop meowing. I had to tell the little beggar that no matter what it smelled, I didn't have any fish. But that didn't stop it from pacing back and forth outside the classroom window all morning.

As usual, I can't force a single burp on the way to school; that means only one thing - I'll be dropping fish oil bombs all day. Great, just what I need.

When I reach the bike rack, I figure I've solved the mystery owner of the bike I saw yesterday. It belongs to Jogesh, a short, chunky kid with a round, friendly, face framed with brainy-looking glasses. He lives in the same apartment complex, Cedar Gardens, as Kat, though in a different building.

Inside, I spot Brady. He's wearing another hockey jersey, this one is for a team called the *Jawbreakers*. Its logo is a guy getting a hockey stick smashed in two pieces over his head. I feel like that's what my parents did to me this morning.

"What's up?" he greets me.

"Just so you know, my parents have told me that if one more monkey-business thing happens I won't be able to go to Lake Placid. That means we need to watch what we're doing. The worst part, though, is I'm also on academic probation - just one 'C' in a class and Lake Placid is toast."

"Man, that's totally severe."

"You can say that again. I'm already stressed about school and grades."

"You gotta learn to relax, my friend."

"Like that's easy for me. Do you know how important Lake Placid is to me? That All-Star game is my chance to show the Saint Michael's coach what I can do. Just one lousy test grade and it's bye-bye Lake Placid. Bye-bye All-Star game. I'll be royally pissed if I can't play."

"Well, then, you can kiss Lake Placid goodbye, because you my friend, are never gonna get a 'B' in English. And that fish-breath of yours isn't gonna help, either."

It's already started and I haven't even burped yet. I want to step inside my locker, close the door and stay in there all day. That is if I could only get my locker to open. Once more Brady helps me, and not wanting to be near me for one second more than he has to, he quickly scoots away to his homeroom.

Just as I fear, near the end of science my classmates get their first whiff of cod liver oil. It would be easier if we were doing a lab and using chemicals or something that I can use as an excuse. Instead, we're in our seats and Mrs. Glennon has us organizing apps and folders on our iPads for an assignment that she handed out at the start of class.

Claire, a brown-haired girl sitting in front of me, identifies herself as the first victim when she tries to wave the smell away. The odor of skanky fish oil wafts helplessly out of me. Trying to swallow my own fishy burps is useless. I twirl my tongue inside my mouth. The comforting flavor of toothpaste has been replaced by the unsettling taste of cod liver oil. Just breathing fans the stench all around me, making things even worse. Nothing I can do now but stop breathing, and I'm seriously considering how I might do that. Instead, I squeeze out a few eye flutters, twist my shoulders a half-dozen times, and stretch my legs. Claire turns around and glares at me, clearly annoyed. I glance around the room. I can't sit still, and I can't relax. Suddenly the kid sitting next to me blurts out, "Hey! It smells like fish in here!"

His outburst gets Mrs. Glennon's attention. "Excuse me, Cam?"

"Sorry Mrs. Glennon, it's just that I smell fish." Cam is the football version of Brady. He wears Patriots apparel to school everyday, and knows me from elementary school. This isn't the first time he's made a point of making me the unwanted center of attention.

"I do, too," Claire chirps, then turns around and looks directly at me. As mean as the expression on her face is, it's nothing compared to mine.

I want to kill my mom.

Claire's expression changes from anger to sorrow when she notices me twitching like a fish with a hook in its mouth.

Just when things couldn't possibly get any worse, they do.

"Alright," says Mr. Curtin, "I need everyone to hand in last night's homework. Just pass it up to the front row."

Damn! I forgot to write down my dad's story from last night. Mr. Curtin was the only teacher to give homework on the first day of school. With all the excitement about Lake Placid, I forgot to write it down.

Now my mom is going to kill me.

I slump my head into my arms which are folded on my desk. Powerful twitches rumble from my stomach up through my shoulders. My head pulses with sharp spasms. A cod liver oil bomb flares up so unexpectedly that it stings my nose and waters my eyes. The smell leaks out with a mind of its own with no hope for a safe return. I'm twitching so hard that I'm dangerously close to falling apart.

I feel a hand on my back and sense Mr. Curtin's voice. He leans in close and I hear him whisper, "Myles, are you okay? Do you need to see the nurse?"

I shake my head. I hear Mr. Curtin's feet shuffle away. When he clears his throat and addresses the class I feel myself spinning towards the edge of a cliff. Voices murmur around me.

"Let's get everyone settled down, I have a quick assignment I need to explain," announces Mr. Curtin.

"Is this about tonight's homework?" Jogesh says.

"No, this is something different. I'll explain in just a few moments. Who wants to hear a Mr. Curtin story?"

The thought of listening to another of Mr. Curtin's stories gives me a blast of much-needed fresh air. The tension in my shoulders slackens. My free fall slows. The sharp spasms in my head subside into a dull fog. Although I still feel queasy, my stomach is calming down. I lift my head and do my best to act normally. I hear the scraping of chairs and desks as everyone gets comfortable, ready for a good story.

"This is a true story by the way. This happened a long time ago before I married Mrs. Curtin. I went to college here in Boston and after I graduated my first job was working as a paramedic - you know, those people you see working in ambulances. For my training I was assigned to an ambulance crew in the city. We'd respond to all kinds of medical emergencies: people who'd slipped and twisted an ankle on the sidewalk, kids who'd swallowed money thinking it was candy, people hurt in car accidents - things like that. You know what I'm talking about?

"Then one day, early, on a freezing-cold February morning we got a strange call. Some people living in a high-rise apartment building smelled a bad odor coming from a neighbor's apartment. In the city one smells all kinds of things - but these people had never smelled anything like this before. It was the worst smell they could imagine. Even a few apartments away, it made their eyes water and their throats burn. They'd banged on the door where the smell was coming from for a while, but no one answered. They were worried that something had happened to the elderly man who lived alone in the apartment.

"They notified the building manager and when he got into the apartment he discovered the most gruesome sight imaginable. It was so gruesome that the when the police arrived they didn't want anything to do with it. They said it was a job for paramedics - so that's when we were called."

"What was the smell? Was it week-old fish?" Patriots-boy asks.

A few people laugh. I slide down in my seat.

"I'm getting to that. Well, for starters, we could smell the odor everyone was complaining about as soon as we entered the lobby. It was so bad that I started dry-heaving in the elevator. It only got worse when we arrived on the floor where the apartment was located. It smelled like something nasty had been cooking for a long time. Too long. Two policemen we're waiting for us - they looked awful - like they'd been throwing up. We walked down a narrow corridor that led into the main living area of the apartment, and that's when I first laid eyes on the elderly man. At least what was left of him."

"What happened to him?" Brady asks.

"Well...it looked like what happened was that he'd been looking out the window. From his apartment there was a nice view across the rooftops and out to the Charles River. Directly underneath the window was the radiator - you know - the big cast iron thing that heats up the place. Like most elderly people, they get cold easily, so he had the heat cranked up all the way. The radiator was sizzling-hot. It must have been 100 degrees in that room. While he was leaning on the window sill enjoying the view, he must have had a major heart attack. For those of you who've never had one before, a heart attack is incredibly painful. The old man must have collapsed and he became pinned between the window sill and the sizzling-hot radiator.

"All I could imagine was the poor man suffering in massive pain and fighting for his life as he was slowly cooked and char-broiled by the radiator. Most of the skin had melted right off the guy. His muscles had been cooked to the point that they'd blackened and would crumble when you touched them."

"That's disgusting - that's gross - that's awful." The whole class is revolted by Mr. Curtin's story. I thought I told crazy stories! Someone raises their hand and actually has the nerve to ask if the guy was dead.

"Of course he was dead," Mr. Curtin says.

"I saw a dead body once, Mr. Curtin. It was in a coffin," says Patriots-boy, snickering.

"If you're gonna see a dead body, Cam, that's a good place to see one," Mr. Curtin replies.

Brady, all revved up by Mr. Curtin's story asks, "What did you do?"

"That was the tricky part. You see, the guy was mostly 'stuck' to the radiator, like a piece of barbecue chicken when it gets stuck on a grill. I hate to say it, but we had to scrape the guy off the radiator. He came off in small, flaky pieces. It took a long time. The worst thing I've ever had to do."

"Why are you telling us this Mr. Curtin?" Kat asks.

"That's a good question and there's a good reason. You see, I learned that the old man had lived in that same apartment for most of his life, more than fifty years. But none of his neighbors really knew who he was. They didn't know anything about him. We had to notify the next-of-kin about the man's death, but he had no known family. I don't think a single person showed up for the funeral. Even now, many years later I think of that poor man and his unfortunate demise and wonder who he was. What did he do for work? What kind of life did he live? Did he ever marry? Did he have children? Every person's life matters. Everyone has a story.

"You see, our lives are a story. All of us. We each have a story. And we live out our story everyday. I've often wondered what his story was."

Mr. Curtin stares directly at me. I squirm under his glare. A side crunch and an eye flutter ripple through me. Mr. Curtin's eyes stay on mine for a moment longer, then they scan the rest of the faces that stare back at him disbelievingly.

"But, that leads me to our assignment. I've given you the start of a story, what I want you to do is finish it. I want you to write that dead man's story. Who was he? Where did he come from? Why was he living alone? Did he have a family? Did anyone miss him? You decide and write the rest of the story. This writing assignment will count as a double-test grade. Don't worry though, you'll have a month to complete it. I've already loaded the rubric and other details onto your iPads."

The bell rings, half scaring me to death. I look over at Brady. His face is screwed up with a grinning mouth and cagey eyes. I'm not surprised, this morbid dead-guy stuff is just his thing. Not me. Tension returns to my shoulders. A flurry of rib crunches does little to ease the nausea in my stomach. I wish Mr. Curtin had told us this story after lunch - now I've lost my appetite.

Everything has gotten more complicated.

A dead guy. Angry parents. A crazy teacher. A writing assignment.

The feeling that I'm about to slip off an icy edge stays with me all day. The last of the cod liver oil was mercifully burped out in Mr. Curtin's class, but I sure got some funny looks from my classmates during math and social studies. I head straight to my room when I get home. My head is pounding, I'm exhausted, and I still feel nauseous. To say it wasn't a good day, would be an understatement. All I want to do now is close my eyes and sleep.

Shortly after I collapse into bed I hear the garage door open, meaning my mom is home early, something she does the first week of school. She knocks on the door. Not waiting for a response she opens it and peaks in. She hesitates a moment then walks in and sits next to me on the bed.

"Tough day today? Want to tell me what happened?"

I shake my head and bury my face into my pillow. Her fingers stroke my hair.

"Did something happen in school?"

I twist with a ropey shoulder shrug that causes the bed to heave and squeak. "It's not fair that I'm being punished for something I didn't do. Brady and Kat saw the same dead body I did, but their parents believe them; they're playing in Lake Placid. Plus everyone at school thinks I smell like fish. I hate that stupid cod liver oil."

"Ahh, the cod liver oil. You know your dad wants you to take that everyday, it's good for you."

"Well then Dad should take it, he can drink the whole bottle if he wants. But why do I have to take it if I don't like it?"

Mom sighs. "I'll talk to him and see what he says. I'll see what I can do. But with school, Dad and I just feel that you can do better. It's great that you're a good hockey player and you want to play in college someday, but without good grades, I'm talking A's and B's, that's not gonna happen. This is a good way for you to learn an important lesson about pulling pranks and improve your grades at the same time."

She runs her hand through my wavy hair. A clump falls into my eyes and she pushes it aside. "Everything else alright?"

I don't answer. I just shrug my shoulders.

"How are you doing with your homework?" she asks, still tussling my hair.

Figuring I've achieved a small victory with the cod liver oil, I decide not to let her know about the missing homework. What she doesn't know won't hurt her. Arguing with my mom right now would be like diving into the octopus tank at the aquarium. It's better that she feels guilty about making me go to school smelling like a bucket of dead fish.

After complaining about all the homework I have to do, I roll onto my side and rest my head in my hand. A sign of surrender. But I can't even do this without a shoulder twitch interrupting my protest.

"Your science homework sounds interesting. All you have to do is find an object and write a list of five observations?"

My shoulders slip with a flimsy twitch.

"Maybe you could head over to the river to find something." Mom lays her hand on my shoulder and gives it a squeeze. My shoulder stiffens. I don't want to be at the riverbank alone.

My parents once took me to see a doctor about my twitching. He gave me these breathing exercises to do whenever I feel stressed, but they don't help much. I tried journal writing too, after my mom read some stuff online about anxiety, but it doesn't really help either, mostly because I don't like writing. It's not easy trying to figure out exactly what makes me feel edgy. I don't know why I feel anxious. I just do. Today though, I know exactly why - a simple case of homework overload. Gratefully, there's no hockey practice tonight, so I have extra time to get it all done. A lazy rib crunch causes the bed to squeak and reminds me that I have to get moving.

Once my other homework is done I text Brady and Kat to see if they want to work on our science homework together. Kat texts back that her mom won't let her leave the house. Brady texts back that he can make it and he'll meet me at the riverbank. I know he's itching to check it out again. The riverbank isn't my first choice, but as long as he's gonna be with me I feel safer chancing it. Feeling more relaxed, the urge to twitch gently slides away.

When I turn onto the gravel path I see Brady's bike at the edge of the woods. But there's no sign of Brady. Everything is quiet until the sound of my feet scraping on the gravel sends a squirrel darting across the path near where we found the dead man. The tall grass is matted down like an empty bed that's just been slept in. I don't understand how a dead body can just disappear. Little does the dead man know what trouble he's caused me.

Figuring Brady has claimed the best spot on the rock for himself, I head down the path towards the embankment.

The rock is unoccupied.

The sound of river water lapping the shoreline draws my attention. I'm half-expecting to find Brady face down, his back hunched out of the water - drowned. Instead, I'm startled when I hear someone sliding down the path. It's Brady. He bursts through the bushes then leaps onto the rock, landing first on one foot, and then the other. He stands in front of me with a wide, beaming smile. It's just the type of showman entrance one expects from Brady.

"Whassup dude?" Brady declares.

"Where'd you come from? You scared the heck out of me!"

"I was just hanging out up there, scoping things out."

All summer we'd lived in trees. I'm a good climber but I mostly stay in the lower branches, the ones that are thick and solid. Even Kat climbs a few branches higher than me. Brady climbs until you can't see him anymore. There are a bunch of trees along the riverbank with branches big enough to sit on comfortably and kill an entire afternoon on. Those are the ones I like most.

"What'd you got there?" I see that Brady has something in a plastic grocery bag that he's holding.

"My airsoft gun."

"We're supposed to be doing science homework," I remind him.

Brady scoffs. "That'll take five minutes. That leaves plenty of time for a game. Even brought extra guns, and goggles, for you and Kat." Brady suddenly realizes that she's not here. "Is she coming?"

"Can't make it. Her mom is making her do all her homework."

"Yeah, right. I bet that doesn't last more than two weeks."

Kat can get into these funky moods when she doesn't want to do any schoolwork. Aunt Betty has to practically drag her to school sometimes. I've never really talked to her about what happened with her dad, but I suppose it's hard with him gone. It's just Kat and her mom in a small apartment. That's why she spends so much time at my house. And here at the river.

"What's up?" It's Kat, standing there like she's waiting for a bus, listening to her iPod.

"I thought you had to stay home to finish your homework?" I say, surprised.

"Yeah," she responds.

"Did you get it all done?" I say.

"Nah," she answers, grinning like an alleycat.

"What did your mom say?" Brady asks.

"She doesn't know."

"Know what?"

"That I'm not there." Her wicked grin spreads into a devilish smile.

"You're crazy. You're gonna get in so much trouble," I tell her. But Brady is more right than me. Kat and her mom may fight a lot, and not just about homework, but nothing ever seems to change.

"You at least planning on doing your homework?" Brady says.

"Sure. I'm gonna do my science homework first."

I know she doesn't mean it. She hops up onto the rock without a care in the world.

When we play airsoft wars we usually stay close to our hangout spot on the riverbank. There are enough trees to provide easy cover from any surprise assaults or bushes to conceal oneself. Brady's the reigning airsoft champion. He has a knack for climbing trees quickly and without being seen. Perched high above he just waits until Kat or I pass by below him, then he picks us off with a few sniper shots. One of the disadvantages of being big is I climb as gracefully as an oversized bear. Every time I climb a tree someone always sees or hears me and then I'm an easy target.

Instead I bury myself the best I can into a thick brush of honeysuckle. Its sweet smell cozies up around me. Waiting for some sign of activity I'm rewarded a few minutes later when I spot Brady begin to climb the same thick tree behind the giant rock that he was in earlier. The rock blocks any clear shot I have at him until he makes it onto a sturdy branch. I'm down to just a handful of bullets, so I carefully set my sights on him and then pepper him square in the back just as he reaches up for the next branch.

I must have surprised and really hurt him because he spins in response to the sting of my direct hits, loses his balance, and falls off the branch awkwardly. His midsection slams into a thick branch on the way down sending him head over heels and crashing to the ground. The loud thump of his landing sends me scrambling out of the bushes to check on him.

When I get to the other side of the large rock, Brady is splayed out on his back. He's not moving. I kneel down next to him and shake him. His eyes remain closed, his body motionless. Kat comes running down the path yelling, "Is he alright?"

"He may be hurt," I say, hoping I'm wrong.

"I didn't see it. I was hiding behind a tree up there, off the path. I heard some shots then heard someone fall," Kat says, spitting the words out.

Brady's face suddenly spreads into a large smile. He howls a wicked laugh and his body twists and contorts with the pleasure of having fooled us.

"Gotcha!" he squeals with delight.

"That was awesome! It looked just like I'd really killed you. Did you try to hit the branch on your fall?" I say.

"I wish. I've been waiting weeks to do this. I saw you hiding in that bush and figured this would be the perfect time. The branch isn't too high and you wouldn't be able to see me land from behind that rock. I was gonna hit my landing and pretend to be dead, but I didn't plan on hitting that branch on the way down like that, though. But it was perfect!"

For some reason I get into trouble for telling a few harmless stories, but Brady never seems to get into trouble for pulling crazy pranks - which he's a master at.

"Are you alright?" Kat finally thinks to ask.

"Yeah. It didn't really hurt that much. The landing was a little rough, though. I landed on the back of my neck." Brady rubs the back of his neck and Kat and I help pull him to his feet.

"Man, you scared me. I thought you were hurt real bad!" Kat exclaims.

"What do you want to do now. You guys want to keep playing?" Brady says.

"I'm good, I'm outta ammo, anyway. We should probably do our science homework now," I say.

"Where should we look?" Brady says.

"Let's walk up to the parking lot, there's all kinds of stuff up there," I say.

The parking lot is littered with all sorts of junk. It's why we came down here. It'll be easy to find something that'll impress Mrs. Glennon. Brady finds an old compass with the hands missing that he puts in his plastic bag. Kat decides on a crusty old cog that must have come from one of the machines they once stored in the shed.

I prowl the parking lot, dismissing an assortment of items before I settle on a translucent object of pale green glass. I lift it up for a closer look. It's heavy and about the size of a softball, but in the shape of a pyramid, like it's been cut off the tip-end of a glass crayon. Grimy with dirt, it appears to be from another place, one with a noble past and an unknown future.

I take it.

Working my way back to the entrance where Brady and Kat are waiting for me, I'm surprised to find, of all things, the same Halloween skeleton bucket that Brady had thrown back into the river a few days ago. I kick it towards the middle of the parking lot where it rolls up against a broken-down recliner chair.

What's the bucket doing up here? Who moved it here?

CHAPTER FOUR

Friday, September 5th

Just one more day. All I have to do is survive one more day and then I get my life back. My summer life that is. For a weekend anyway.

My morning routine is disrupted because I overslept this morning. I stayed up late after last night's airsoft war at the riverbank to write a short summary of my dad's bloody elbow story. Mr. Curtin said he'd give me partial credit for turning it in late. I'm not exactly off to a good start with his class. In the kitchen, I notice the absence of my dad's overpowering cologne. Don't ask me why it's so important for a plumber to smell nice, but my dad swears by the stuff. My mom is all decked out for work, dressed very professionally and businesslike. Her hair is trim and neat, tied in the back in a perfect knot.

"Oh, Dennis, your dad needs you to help him after school today. He's trying to finish up that job at Bruno's Restaurant and then he's gotta take Myles to hockey tonight. He said he'll swing by and pick you up at school. Can you text him and tell him where to meet you?"

"Sure. But I'm not in shop this week. I'll need to get changed after school. I'll let him know, though."

In some ways his school sounds appealing. One week he has all the typical classes, such as English, and math, and science, which he mostly tolerates; but the next week he's in shop, meaning he works on plumbing projects all day, which he loves. And he never has any homework, it isn't allowed. It strikes me as unfair that I, a seventh-grader, have an hour of homework everyday while he, a sophomore, has none.

"Where is Dad?" I say.

"He got an early start. Busy day for him, it's Friday, he has a lot to do. He asked me to remind you to take your cod liver oil. Both of you." She fixes her eyes on us like she's ready for a stare-down.

"Dad's not here? That mean I don't have to take it?" I say, fixing my own hopeful stare.

"You heard your dad. And I don't want to hear any bellyachin' from either one of you."

"Can I at least eat breakfast first? Without the taste of fish slop in my mouth," Dennis pleads.

"Me, too?" I say.

My mom's stare-down weakens. "That's fine. But don't forget. I gotta run. I'm showing a house this morning," she says, grabbing her car keys off the counter.

She starts for the door, then turns back. "And Myles, can you set the table when you get home after school? I may not be here when you get home. Set the table for six, Nanna and Pappy are eating dinner with us."

"Are they coming to my game too?"

"They might."

"I almost forgot, your dad got us tickets for the bobsled run while we're at Lake Placid."

"Really? That's awesome!" Dennis shouts.

"And your dad is looking into renting snowmobiles at some place near the hotel. You'll have to ask him about it when he gets home."

"Am I going snowmobiling?" I ask.

"That depends on you. Which reminds me, I emailed Mr. Curtin. I asked him to stay after school with you today. He's offered to help you with your writing assignment."

"What? It's Friday!"

"So, what does that mean?"

"I've been in school all week. I want to hang out with my friends. I'm not staying after."

"Yes, you are staying after, and if you don't - well, then you can just forget about that all-star game! Okay, I've gotta run. Love you both. And Dennis, don't forget to text your dad."

And that's that. Mom's gone. Good, cause I ain't taking that cod liver oil now if she paid me.

Being as my breakfast didn't include any fish oil, my day at school is thankfully uneventful. All my homework is complete, my twitching is remarkably mild by my standards, and I open my own locker on just the fifth try. It's days like today that I swear I can imagine what it would be like to be a normal, average, get-lost-in-the-crowd kid. And that's all I want to be.

I have to admit, I've always liked to read. A good story makes me believe that I can do anything. That anything is possible. Caldwell is a swell town, it really is. Most people would even say it's a great place to grow up. But from my view, I just don't see the point. Finding a dead body was the first thing to ever happen here - and even then, no one believes me. But I just know there's something happening somewhere. It just isn't here. Reading takes me where the action is, and that's where I want to be.

Now, writing is another matter. It's not that I don't try. I do, really. It's just that my brain is like a bunch of pieces to a jigsaw puzzle. Make that ten jigsaw puzzles. All mixed together. To put one puzzle together, I've gotta sort through the pieces to nine other puzzles. And therein lies the difficulty. My writing assignments often look like a glued-together jigsaw done all wrong.

Mr. Curtin's *dead man* story has gotten me thinking about the dead man we found. Who was he? What happened to him? What was *his* story? I have some ideas for the story I'm supposed to write, but it's like that jigsaw thing, I've got a bunch of pieces but no clear idea what to write about or where to start.

Hoping that my mom didn't email Mr. Curtin, I'm disappointed when I peek into his room and see him cleaning the whiteboard.

"Oh, hey, Myles, come in, your mom said you'd be staying after today."

I sit at the desk closest to the door. "You know that story you told us yesterday, the one about the old man and the radiator? Was that a true story?"

Mr. Curtin sits at the desk next to me and puts his glasses on. "It's not very often that someone walks in and finds something like that - but it really did happen. A sad story, but true. Why? What's up?"

Aware that no one believes me about finding a body in a bag, and lacking any proof, thanks to the dead man's disappearance, I scrounge up the courage to try my story on Mr. Curtin. Someone with even stranger stories than me. I make a point of leaving out the part about taking a ring off the man's finger.

"Did this really happen? Or are you making this up for your writing assignment?" Mr. Curtin asks.

"I'm not making it up. Of course, my parents and no one else believes me. But we really did find a dead man in a bag. And he was a real person. I'm certain of it. I think anyway. I just don't understand what happened to him - why the police didn't find the body."

"It must not have been a real person then. Or a really dead person. It must've been a kid or someone pranking you guys. No big deal."

"But it was a real dead person. I know it was," I say.

"Okay, if you say so. I believe you. You really should leave this to the police, though. It's their job to figure these things out."

"But the police aren't doing anything,"

Mr. Curtin removes his glasses. He pauses. "Well, then it may actually be a good thing that you kids found this dead person."

"What do you mean?" I say.

"If the body had been left there and the police recovered it, it would be one thing. This would be their responsibility. But there's something peculiar about a dead body disappearing like that, and so quickly. You kids probably weren't supposed to find it. No one was supposed to find it. But you did, anyway. You may be that man's only hope of learning what happened to him. What really happened."

At least one person seems to believe me.

"Brady tells me you're a pretty good storyteller - is that so?"

"I'm alright, I guess. I like to tell stories, but it doesn't seem to help my writing, they only get me into trouble."

"Still, being able to tell a story is a start, and shows a real talent. We just need to channel that into your writing."

"That's the whole point. I stink at writing, I always have."

"I believe you're capable of writing a very good story. If you enjoy telling stories, then you have it in you to be a writer. You just have to believe in yourself. In the meantime, I'll believe in you, for you. What do you think? Do you think you can do this?"

"I guess so."

"I guess so too. In fact I know so."

Mr. Curtin has me believing that maybe I can write a great story, but those old self-doubts are still clouding my thoughts.

"The fun and joy of writing, is using our imagination to create something beyond the experience of our own lives. Writers are storytellers. Just think of yourself as one. When we become storytellers, stories have a way of finding us. Stories need to be told, indeed sometimes they beg to be told, that's why they come looking for us. All one has to do is keep one's eyes and ears open to make sure his story finds him. I think, Mr. Walsh, your story has found you."

Friday night is pizza night at the Walsh's, and the only pizza we eat is cheese pizza. There's nothing more awkward than being a guest at a friend's house and they order pizza with toppings like tuna fish and chick peas, or buffalo chicken and asparagus. If I want tuna fish I'll eat a sandwich, and I like my buffalo chicken right off the grill, not on my pizza.

"Keep your fingers crossed, the clients liked one of the houses I showed them this morning," Mom says. She's a real-estate agent who helps people either buy a new house, or sell their old one.

"That's good," Pappy says, his eyes smiling behind the thick lenses of his dark-rimmed glasses.

"How about you, Myles, how was your first week of school?" Nanna says.

Assessing the first week of school I can count a few successes among the more stressful moments. Either way, it was a week of progress, although I'm well aware that next week could bring almost anything.

"It was alright," I reply.

"He had a bit of a tough day yesterday, but he got through it. He has the same team of teachers Dennis had, except there's a new English teacher. What's his name again, Myles? He sounds interesting. He told Myles a story the other day about his grandfather being able to take his eye out," Mom says.

"Come again?" Pappy remarks.

I have to explain. "It wasn't a real eye. It was a glass eye."

"Geez, not too many people with those," Pappy says.

"He told you this story?" Nanna says.

"Yeah," I reply.

"And he said it was true?" Nanna says in a voice that's as pleasant as a cat coughing up a hairball.

"He said it was."

Nanna grunts, then turns her attention to Dennis. "How's school for you Dennis? Do you like it?"

"It's good. This is the first week so we haven't started our shop weeks yet. That starts next week."

"You still doing the plumbing program over there?" Pappy says.

"Yep."

"Well, good. You'll be working with your dad some day. You'll be able to keep the business going. Good money in plumbing. Your dad's done alright for himself."

"Dennis has already been working with me," my dad says.

"I helped Dad today actually," Dennis says.

"How do you like it?" Pappy says.

"I love it. It's fun and I'm learning a lot."

"It's good to get a taste of what hard work is. I always said that no one ever drowned in sweat. What'd you work on today?"

"We installed a new water heater at Bruno's Restaurant, down in the basement. And you know what I saw down there? A cat. Almost scared the crap out of me."

"What do they got a cat for?" Nanna says. "Is that legal? Does the health inspector know?"

"Cats are still the best thing out there for getting rid of mice. Nothing works better," Dad says.

"Maybe, but it smelled like cat piss down there. And that's not anything I want to smell in a restaurant," Dennis says.

Nanna laughs, getting everyone's attention.

"What's so funny, Mom?" my mom asks with a curious look on her face.

"You just reminded me of something. I was thinking how much some things have changed since I was young. For example, if you had a hole in your shoes, which would often happen living in the city and walking everywhere like we did, you wouldn't just throw your shoes away and buy new ones like people do today. We'd bring the shoes to a shoemaker and he'd put new soles on them while you waited in a tiny booth. That reminds me of a cat we used to have."

"A cat?" I say.

"Yes, a cat. I had just started a new job working for a law firm in a beautiful, brand new building downtown. I worked in the library as a librarian. Anyway, I had a pair of shoes that had a hole in them and I had put a piece of cardboard in them," Nanna says, chuckling and smiling.

"Sometimes people didn't have the money to bring them to the shoemaker. Maybe your dad's check was small that week, or your parents had bills to pay that week."

"You actually put cardboard in your shoes?"

"Yes, cardboard. You'd just put a piece of cardboard in the shoes so you wouldn't be walking on the pavement, and you'd bring them to the shoemaker when you had the money. That's what people did back then," Nanna says with a soft laugh.

"Well, this one time, right after I started a new job working at this beautiful new building, our cat had peed in my shoes!"

Nanna bursts with laughter that rumbles out like faraway thunder. Her head leans back and a broad smile sweeps across her face as she relives an old embarrassment. My mom, enjoying Nanna's story, tries to hide a giggle that I've never heard before.

"That darn cat! She liked to pee in shoes. If you happened to leave your shoes out by mistake she would pee in them. She had ruined so many of my shoes that I had to go out and buy a new pair for work. Well, guess what? She peed in those! And you're right Dennis, cat piss sure does smell bad. I was so upset, but there was nothing I could do. When I got to work in this brand new building, other people could tell that something didn't smell right. People around my desk would ask each other, "'Do you smell that odor?'" Naturally, I replied that I didn't smell anything.

"Finally, someone called the maintenance department to have them check it out and see what was causing the bad smell. Two guys came and brought a ladder with them. They looked everywhere. Crawled around on the floor, looked under desks and chairs. They opened vents and ceiling tiles and inspected the walls and windows trying to figure out the source of the bad smell. The people I worked with were trying to help, too. Of course, I knew the bad smell was my cat-peed-in-shoes. I was so embarrassed.

And so mad. My brand new shoes! I could have killed that cat!" My mom laughs, and Nanna's face glows as she reflects on a cherished memory.

Nanna's story gets me thinking about cod liver oil. I flicker with a pair of shoulder shrugs. I feel anxious. I begin reliving the nightmare of my near twitch-meltdown in the middle of Mr. Curtin's classroom yesterday. I can just feel the embarrassment of the whole thing spill over me.

Nanna smiles and pats my hand. It sinks in that she too once had to deal with an embarrassing situation and that she managed to live through it without dying. My anxiety slides away, not much, but enough.

After dinner I talk Kat into meeting me at the riverbank. Her mom left for work so she welcomes the chance to get out of the house. We have just enough time to sneak over before our game. I'm no risk-taker like Brady, but that skeleton skull has been bothering me. The riverbank has been our private hangout for the past few years, and in all that time we've never seen anyone else there - not even a lonely fisherman. But some-one's been down there - someone who leaves dead bodies behind. And a Halloween bucket doesn't just walk itself from the river up to the parking lot. If it isn't right where I kicked it yesterday, then I know that someone else has been visiting our hangout spot with the purpose of playing games with us. And that creeps me out. But I need to know.

We ride our bikes around the Keep Out sign and down the gravel road into the parking lot. When I kicked the skeleton bucket yesterday, it had rolled up near an old recliner chair in the middle of the parking lot. I see the chair but no skull. However, I notice that the TV, an old-fashioned box TV with the screen smashed in, is facing the chair - as if someone were at home watching television in their family room. That's not good.

Someone's been moving things around.

I scan the parking lot to make sure we're alone. We move through the debris and as the front of the TV comes into view that's where I find the skeleton skull. It's been placed inside the TV, like one of those floating heads in a magician's trick box - the kind that makes people's bodies disappear.

A large black crow swoops down and perches itself on top of the TV. Its leathery wings flitter and its sharp claws scrape the battered box which set off a barrage of twitches. Kat decides she isn't sticking around and takes off in a sprint. The crow's dark eyes hold my gaze for a moment before I, too, race to my bike.

When I make the turn onto Weston Drive, my tires skid off the gravel sending me out into the busy road. I nearly collide with a truck that roars by me. It's booming rattle can be heard as it speeds away, leaving a trail of dark smoke that clouds up in my eyes and nose and sends my neck into a shuddering spasm.

It's a white box truck with bold letters in a simple black font that reads: Royal Ltd. Casket Company. It occurs to me that just a few more inches and I would have been a customer.

CHAPTER FIVE

Monday, September 8th

We haven't been back to the river since Friday when Kat and I found things rearranged. The thought of walking into the woods and down the narrow path towards our hangout fills me with fear. Images of being chased by a kid-stealing lunatic hiding along the path, has woken me in the middle of the past several nights. I miss the seclusion of our river spot, but don't dare chance my life to visit it. Not for awhile anyway. Instead we find ourselves biking around the neighborhood and occasionally stopping at the water tower around the corner from my street. It's become our replacement hangout.

The tower is painted the color of a sky blue that looks out of place in the neighborhood. Its shape is that of several drums stacked on top of each other, reaching maybe seven stories high with the top slightly domed. Along one side is a small shed that's enclosed by a chain link fence. A small ladder is attached to the tower and runs up its entire length to the top.

"How much water do you suppose is in this thing?" Brady says.

"I don't know, maybe a million gallons," Kat replies.

"Well, it's enough water for everyone on this side of Caldwell," I remark.

"It could be empty, you ever think about that?" Brady says.

"I doubt it's empty. If it was, no one would have water. Nothing coming out of the faucet. No water for a shower. Someone would have called the Water Department and they'd be here right now filling it," I say.

"Well, that's just it. When have you ever seen anyone filling this thing?" Brady exclaims. He has a point. All the years I've lived here I've never seen a worker at the tower.

"Maybe the last time someone filled this thing was ten years ago. And let's just say it needs to be filled every ten years, so it may be practically empty now. Maybe tomorrow when you go to take a shower there'll be no water, then what?"

"Then they come and fill it...duh," says Kat.

"You have any idea how long it would take to fill this thing? We have an in-ground pool and it takes us almost two days to fill our pool. And our pool is like a small puddle compared to the size of this thing."

"Luckily it's not our job to worry about it," I say.

"We all use the water, why can't we check and make sure it's not empty?" Brady says.

"And how are you gonna to do that?"

I hate having conversations about stupid things. Sometimes this is Brady's specialty.

"What do you think that ladder is for?" He points to the tiny ladder attached to the tower's side.

"Not for you."

At this point Brady starts climbing the fence which stands about eight feet high. Once he reaches the top of the fence he swings one leg over and then as he straddles the top he gives Kat and I a triumphant smile. He climbs down the other side of the fence a few steps and then jumps to the ground.

"Brady, you shouldn't be in there. You'll get us in trouble," I protest, aware of my mom's warning about stunts. Brady ignores me, of course, and begins to climb the ladder.

After he's climbed a few steps, Kat yells "Brady, what are you doing?"

Brady just keeps climbing, ignoring Kat and moves upwards with more and more confidence. Step by step, he keeps going, undaunted. I look up and watch nervously, twitching a series of jerky shrugs and crunches as he moves higher and higher. He climbs nearly to the top, probably six stories high, higher than any tree he's ever climbed. He seems small and vulnerable just hanging there. I look over at Kat, her face is stricken with panic. She screams at Brady again, her voice trembles.

Brady climbs a few more steps, then suddenly, as if sensing Kat's concern, he stops. I can't shake the thought of him losing his grip or footing and plunging all the way down. Now I'm spooked as I imagine Brady free-falling off the tower to a certain death. I glance at Kat and she seems relieved that Brady's at least stopped his progress. But I fear that the worst is not over.

"Hey, you guys should check out this view, it's awesome," he says, in a voice that sounds small and distant. "I can see all the way over to Winn Street from up here."

Brady's casualness tingles my nerves, and I shudder with a rapid flurry of shoulder twitches. My feet can't sit still, my heart races, until I too yell up to my daredevil friend, "Come on down, you're making me nervous."

"What are you guys so nervous about, I'm fine."

"Brady, please, come down!" Kat begs.

"I'm gonna take a picture for you guys," Brady shouts down toward us.

He digs into his pocket with his left hand, while the bony fingers of his right hand hang onto the ladder. Once he has his phone out he he twirls it to get the viewfinder into position, but it slips out of his hand. Brady reacts by reaching out with his left hand to grab the phone. His left leg hangs off the ladder causing him to lose his balance, then he loses his footing altogether. His right foot comes off the ladder and both legs swing around in the air. Only those five bony fingers are left gripping the thin metal rung of the ladder, keeping him from falling six stories.

"Geez!" I scream. I squeeze my eyes tight.

I don't want to see it.

Kat screams. A thunderous screech that feels like a thousand sharp needles being sent into every nerve in my body. I force myself to look up again, praying I don't see an empty spot where Brady was. But he's there, back securely on the ladder.

"Are you alright?" I yell up to Brady, who's clearly shaken by what almost happened.

"I'm alright. Boy, that was close. Can you guys find my phone. It should be around there someplace in those leaves." He points with his head, keeping both hands and both feet on the ladder this time. Kat is bent over trying to compose herself. She's trembling so hard I'm worried she might get sick.

"Sure. I'll get it. Just be careful coming down, will you."

"You guys should climb up here next. It's easy," Brady says in an offhand sort of way, regaining his composure. A true daredevil. Better him than me. Of those who are deathly afraid of heights, I am one.

Finally, Brady begins his descent, coming down more carefully than he had gone up. When he is a mere ten feet off the ground I can feel the stress and tightness of my muscles soften. My twitching subsides into gentle spasms.

"I don't know why you guys got so scared. I nearly made it. I was fine and I could have climbed all the way to the top, no sweat. It's easier than climbing a tree."

"That's awful high Brady, you almost fell for crying out loud," Kat says, her voice edged with irritation.

"Let's hope we don't run out of water," Brady says, his normal swagger returning.

Seeing that this has been enough excitement for one day, I say, "What do you say we go back to my house?"

"Sure neither of one of you guys want to climb the tower next?" Brady asks.

"Not if my life depended on it," I answer.

"You know, you almost killed yourself back there," Kat says.

"What do you mean?" Brady responds.

"If you'd fallen off, you would have died. That's what I mean. It's a long way down, you know."

"Yeah, but I didn't. Did I?"

"Why do you always have to do crazy things?" Kat says.

"I don't know, it's fun."

"You never think anything bad is gonna happen do you?" I say.

"It never has. Has it?"

"I bet that dead man didn't think anything bad was gonna happen to him and look where he wound up," I say.

"Well, actually, we're not really sure where he wound up, are we?" Brady says.

"We know he's dead, that's for sure," I say.

"What do you think happens to you when you die?" Kat asks.

"I don't know. You go to heaven, I guess," I say.

"But how do you know if you do or not? Have you ever met anyone who's been there?" Brady says.

"No. But I've heard about people who have these after-death experiences. Like they die, but they're still alive at the same time. You know," Kat says.

"Maybe that's what happened to that dead guy. Maybe he was dead, but then came alive again and that's why the police didn't find him. He probably got up and went home," Brady says.

"And what, he walked away with his plastic bag, too? I seriously doubt it," I say.

"Well, I haven't got him in my pocket, that's for sure."

"And where's he live anyway?" Kat asks.

"Hey, kids! Can you guys do me a big favor?" a man shouts in a congenial tone, interrupting our discussion of heaven and earth. The unknown voice calls from above. We all look skyward and see a man with a thick mustache and beard wearing a white helmet. He's standing in a bucket the size of an average garbage barrel attached to a scissor-like contraption that extends up to the top of the telephone pole.

We each stop and peer up at the man in the bucket.

"See that house?" He points with an outstretched arm at the house across the street from us.

It's an older, shabby house that sticks out in a neighborhood of clean homes with bright green lawns and coal-black driveways. This home is of two colors, royal blue on the bottom and chocolate brown on top. A large porch with thick white columns frames the front of the house.

The lawn looks as if it hasn't been mowed for weeks, and it's covered with dull, brown leaves. The driveway is a speckled gray with chunks of it torn loose where it meets the road. I notice that the front door is wide open. Its blackness inside beckons us.

"Yeah, that house, the blue and brown one. I'm installing cable service and I need your help. Can one of you go inside and check something for me, so I don't have to get down from here? Can one of you kids do that?"

Brady answers without hesitation, "Sure."

I glance at Kat, but the blank look on her face tells me she's unsure of what to do. So I say to Brady, "I don't know about this."

Brady is about to say something when the man's voice booms out of the sky again. "Thanks. There's no one in the house, no one lives in it. Not yet anyway. A new family is moving in, in a few days. I need to get this done today."

Brady whispers to me, "Sounds cool. Myles, your dad's a plumber and you know how helpful it is to have an extra set of hands sometimes, right?" Although what he says sounds reasonable, I dislike the words in his mouth.

"Brady, were not just gonna walk into a strange house."

He smirks at me and yells up to the cable man, "What do you need us to do?"

"There's a cable box on the floor in that front room, the one to the right when you go in. When you hear me call, just let me know if it lights up. You should see a blinking red light when I give the signal. That's it. Thanks."

"See. No big deal. We're helping someone. This'll be our good deed for the day," Brady says.

My shoulders sag in surrender as a rib crunch rattles through me. Seems easy enough, but there's something unsettling about all this. The bones of the old house lean and sway in an unnatural way. I don't like going into a strange house, even an empty one. Especially an empty one.

Brady says, "C'mon, let's check it out." We leave our bikes at the end of the short walkway that leads to the front steps of the porch, then we walk up the steps and enter through the open door.

"It's the first room on the right. Just give me a minute while I set the connection," yells the man from his safe perch.

Sure enough, a small black box lays on the floor in the bare room. I can't recall ever having been in a house with nothing in it. There's not a single piece of furniture. No curtains on the windows, no pictures on the walls, and no books in an empty bookcase. It's as if the house has been stripped of any sign of life. A dead and abandoned relic, like the old storage shed at the river, which we never go in.

Brady wanders towards the staircase and says, "Let's go check out the upstairs."

It's moments like this that I wonder why I'm friends with Brady. He's always looking to do things I'd never do myself. He senses my hesitation and gives me that look that says, 'You're not going to pull this baby stuff are you'?

"The guy says he needed our help and that we should stay in the room with the cable box."

"No he didn't," Brady says sarcastically. "Look, the house is empty and Kat will keep a lookout down here, c'mon."

Against my better judgment, I give in. "Alright, but let's make this quick."

Brady leads the way. The first step creaks and echoes in the empty house.

"Where are you guys going?" Kat says.

"We're just gonna see what's upstairs, we'll be right back."

Kat nods then turns to look out the window to make sure the cable guy is still in his bucket. Brady darts upstairs, and I follow figuring it won't cost me anything. At the top of the stairs is an L-shaped landing bordered by two bedrooms and a bathroom. I stay close behind Brady as we investigate each room. The rooms are empty like the ones downstairs, and I'm beginning to feel bored by the whole thing when the cable guy interrupts the silence with a shout to ask if the red light is blinking on the box.

We can hear Kat's voice ring through the empty house that nothing is lit up or blinking.

"What's up here?" whispers Brady, opening a door where small wooden steps lead up a narrow stairway to the attic.

"Probably just another boring room like all the rest," I say, trying to convince Brady to end our tour right here before we find any trouble I'm not looking for.

Truth is though, there's something about the narrowness of those stairs and the inability to see what's at the top that makes me think that we just might find another unwanted surprise in the attic. I know it's a bad idea to climb these steps because I hammer off a couple of roaring shoulder shrugs that does little to relax my tension. My apprehension grows with each shaky step up the stairs. My only consolation is that Brady is in front, so if there is anything up there he'll be the one to deal with it first, not me.

When we reach the top it's more of the same, but the rooms are laid out differently. There's a large room to the left that we check out first. It too, like the rest of the house, is completely empty, nothing to see. We now move about more naturally as the suspense is gone. The room to the right we enter next. Nothing in this room either, but there is a small door in the middle of the wall at the end, perhaps no more than my shoulder height. Brady opens the door and crouches down to enter what is another room. I have to hunch over considerably to pass through the door myself. I stand next to Brady.

Both of us are surprised to see that this room is not empty.

It contains two items, both placed at the far end of the room. Under the room's only window is a large wooden chest with black leather straps and a large gold buckle in the front. It looks like one of those old treasure chests you see in pirate movies, and this one is big enough to hide a ship full of treasure.

Or a body.

A dead one.

Next to the chest is a rocking chair with a blue floral seat cushion. The rocking chair is placed at an angle as if it's guarding over the wooden chest and whatever contents might lie within it. Brady and I look at each other. It is indeed a strange and peculiar scene we have happened upon.

My heart nearly bursts. Out of the corner of my eye I would swear on my mother's grave that something has moved. I stiffen all over. I practically stop breathing and with all the effort I can muster I turn my view towards the rocking chair.

It begins to rock back and forth. I glance at the chest to see that it is still closed shut.

For the moment it is.

To run would be the most sensible thing to do...but who has sensible thoughts at a time like this? Before I go screaming out of here I inspect the room, looking for a logical explanation.

I stare hard at that lone, decrepit window.

It's sealed tight as a drum.

I inspect the ceiling, hoping for a ceiling fan that might be there and has been carelessly left on.

There is no ceiling fan.

I bounce on the wooden floorboard under my right foot wishing this might be the cause for the rocking of the chair.

It does not budge.

The chair keeps rocking.

Sheer terror crawls up into my throat. There's neither a reason nor a logical explanation for why a chair would just spontaneously begin rocking.

And keep rocking.

Every muscle in my body feels like it's trying to strangle me. I'm too terrified to twitch, blink, or breathe. I glance at the chest, back to the chair, then once more at the chest.

Is it beginning to open?

I'm not waiting to find out and neither is Brady. We hurtle down the narrow attic steps two at time then down the second floor steps three at a time like prisoners on a jailbreak. We yell GET OUT OF HERE!! to Kat as we pass by the family room and make our exit from the ghost house.

It's déjà vu all over again. We are pedaling for our lives once more. The cable guy hollers after us, as we have not given him the help he had so kindly asked of us.

To most kids, most of the time, the world is a place of discovery and wonder. Everyday is a chance to experience a new adventure. But then there are times when the world makes kids feel powerless, scared, and confused. This is one of those times.

Why are all these strange things happening?

We're racing our bikes towards my house when we spot another bike rider coming in our direction. We slow down and slide closer to the side of the road. The heat of the afternoon presses down on us. The quietness of the street calms my nerves. An unexpected breeze pushes past us.

We wait for the approaching rider, who we now see is an older, brown-skinned man. His face is wrinkled and serious, but his presence is non-threatening. He's dressed oddly wearing a tattered blue suit coat that is too big for him over a ratty-looking t-shirt. His bike tires squeal with pleasure and wire-frame baskets that hang on either side of the rear tires rattle with joy. I notice that each basket contains brown paper bags stuffed full of newspapers.

We nod courteously, but he doesn't look our way or respond. He glides by as if he were an apparition.

"That was random. I've never seen that guy before," Brady says.

"Neither have I. What's his story? What's he doing in this neighborhood?" I say.

"Why did you guys run out of the house like that, anyway?" Kat says.

"You're not going to believe it, but we saw a ghost in the attic," I say.

"Where's Dad and Dennis?" I ask, as I enter the kitchen where Mom is cooking dinner. Brady and Kat each grab a seat on the stools at the counter.

"Dad had to go to the plumbing store to get some supplies for a job he's starting tomorrow and Dennis went with him."

Brady looks my way, a grin climbs up onto his face. "Hey, do you want to tell your mom about the ghost we saw?" I glare at Brady. Apparently he's forgotten about the no more monkey-business thing.

Mom, who's in the midst of cooking meat in a frying pan, looks at me with a sideways glance. She turns the meat over causing it to sizzle. Grease sprays out, showering the stove in an oily mess. I expect our latest adventure will land me in a frying pan of grease. She looks at me waiting to hear another of my crazy stories, none of which she ever seems to believe.

She wipes her hands with a dish towel that's draped over her shoulder, then says, "A ghost? Now you're seeing ghosts? Really?"

I gulp a mouthful of air before beginning my story. One I hadn't planned on telling. "We saw a ghost in an attic," I say. My voice frayed with nerves that are greased raw.

"What attic?" My mom says with disbelief in her eyes and impatience on her lips.

I consider making up a harmless story, one that won't get me in trouble. But liars need good memories and I don't always have one. Even though telling the truth may be a bad idea, I go ahead with it just the same.

"We were riding our bikes over on Mountain Avenue and some cable guy asked us to help him. We had to check to see if the cable was working at this house. The house was empty, Mom."

"So you just went into an empty house by yourself?"

"No, I was with Brady and Kat." I can tell my mom doesn't approve, but what's done is done, plus I didn't die, nor did we find another dead body.

"Do you know how dangerous that is? What were you thinking?"

"Mom, just let me tell the story, okay?"

"I didn't think it was a good idea either Auntie Anne," blurts Kat.

"Yeah, well you went into the house too," Brady says.

"Only because you guys made me."

"We did not!" Brady shouts.

"If you guys don't mind, I'm trying to tell a story," I say, interrupting their spat.

"Go ahead, but I sometimes wonder what goes on in that funhouse mirror of a head of yours, Myles."

I tell my mom about the house and the haunted attic. Of our discovery of the treasure chest and an empty rocking chair that rocked.

"Where was this house?" she asks.

Kat jumps in, "It's that ugly house on Mountain Avenue, the one that's two different colors. It's two or three houses in from Beaver Brook Road."

"I think I know which house you mean," my mom says with more excitement than I was expecting. "It's blue on the bottom and brown on the top, right? It's been for sale. Someone must have bought the house. That explains why the cable company was there."

Thinking this would be a good time to make an acceptable excuse for why we were wandering around in an empty house, I say, "It was the guy from the cable company that asked us to do him a favor. He was working up in this bucket and we were just riding by when he needed help. All we had to do was see if a light was flashing on a black box in a room right near the front door. No big deal. Aren't you always telling me, Mom, that we should help people? Especially when they ask for it?"

"Yes," she replies warily, "but you have to use good judgment about these things. You don't know who this guy is. Right? Have you forgotten *stranger danger*?"

"Alright, I got it," I exclaim.

"And what were you doing in the attic if you were supposed to be checking the cable in the front room?" she asks, suspicious that we were up to no good. Monkey-business.

"It's my fault Mrs. Walsh. It was my idea to look around. I'd never been in an empty house like that before. I just wanted to check it out, that's all. I asked Myles to go with me. You know, just in case," Brady says, doing his best to cover for me.

"Well you're lucky all you saw was a ghost. I think I remember the attic though, it was really big but had low ceilings, is that right?"

"Yeah, it did, and it had all these small rooms. Almost like little dungeons or jail cells," I say.

"Anyway," she continues, "did you know that house was my very first sale when I became a real estate agent? We took the commission I earned and used it to help start your dad's business."

"You've been in that house before?" I say.

"Sure, several times. It's my job as an agent to know the houses I represent inside and out. It was an old house, even older now I suppose, with three bedrooms and two baths. Wood floors throughout if I recall, and the garage is a good size barn in the back of the house. Wow! That brings back memories."

"Do you remember if the house had any ghosts, Mrs. Walsh?"

"Ghosts? No, no ghosts. And I doubt you guys saw a ghost either. You may think you did, but there is no such thing as ghosts. But I remember that the sellers were a nice professional couple. They were older and were from another country, I forget where, but that's why they were selling the house, they were moving back to the country they came from."

"You may not believe in ghosts, but I do. I saw that rocking chair move for no reason, except maybe because it didn't want us looking inside that chest," I say.

"What if that dead man was in the chest? Maybe that's where he is." Brady seems convinced of this and he's got me thinking too.

Mom rolls her eyes. Kat chirps in, "I'm glad I didn't go up there. How could anyone live in that house now?"

Brady then says exactly what I'm thinking, "Just think, the chest is still there. Probably no one knows it's been left behind. When the new people move in they'll see the chest and open it. I bet you they find a dead body in it."

"Brady, you've been hanging around Myles too long," my mom says.

"At least then you and the police and everyone else would believe us," I say.

"You should call the police Auntie Anne," Kat says.

Mom shakes her head and rolls her eyes, again. "Dead bodies and ghosts. What are guys doing, celebrating Halloween early this year? And I am certainly not calling the police, we've already sent them on one wild goose chase. We are not sending them on another. You kids have stirred up enough monkey-business already. Remember what I said, Myles. You're on thin ice. You hear me?"

CHAPTER SIX

Tuesday, September 9th

Kat doesn't like school so it's no surprise that her grades are poor. I don't know what her issue is, but she and school go together as well as pizza and tuna fish. Brady is as smart as a whip. He just breezes through everything. It all comes easy to him. Having him around to occasionally help with homework is my ace-in-the-hole. Homework that would have taken me ninety minutes by myself, takes the three of us working together half the time, meaning the rest of the afternoon is ours. We decide to walk over to Brady's house to play street hockey. He has the perfect setup for it. His dad splurged on two nice nets, and his driveway is lined with a retaining wall on one side, just like a rink with boards, so we don't have to chase the ball everywhere. Plus, Brady loves to play net and has a set of top-of-the-line goalie equipment with all the works: goalie pads, chest protector, blocker, glove, and mask.

Brady lives in a neighborhood on the other side of the McFarland Middle School. On bike it's only about ten minutes to his house, but on foot it's twenty-five which gives us time to talk.

"So, how do you guys think that guy was killed," Brady says.

"I think he tried suffocating himself in the bag. He must have blacked out, but then after we found him, he woke up and took off," Kat says.

"Maybe. But how did he tie the knot from inside the bag? The way the knot was tied, someone did that from outside the bag," Brady says.

"Maybe he had someone help him. I don't know," Kat says.

"I still think he was killed and dumped there," Brady says.

"Yeah, but then why put him in a clear plastic bag? Why not put him in one of those green or black plastic bags? That's what I would do," I say.

"You'd never kill anyone, Myles," Kat says good-naturedly.

"Maybe the person ran out of garbage bags and that's all he had," Brady says.

"But then if someone killed him why would that person go back and move him?" Kat says.

"Because we found him? And we weren't supposed to?" I say.

"Then who was supposed to find him? And why would you want someone to find the person you just killed?" Kat says. We're all frustrated with this. There are many more questions than answers.

"Well, one thing's for certain," Brady says.

"What's that?" I ask.

"We'll probably never find out."

"I don't know. It would be neat if we could figure it out." I think of the ring I have, the dead man's ring, and wonder whether I should get it back to him. Somehow. We just have to find out who he was. We could do it if we worked together. Brady's not afraid of anything. And even though Kat doesn't do so hot in school, she's still good at figuring things out. We know more than the police do, they're not even trying. We at least saw the man. We know what he looks like. We have a description.

"You know, your mom said the people who used to live in that house, where you and Brady saw the ghost, were from another country," Kat says.

"Yeah, she did," I reply, my hope renewed.

"Well, the dead guy we found looked like he was from India. That's another country. Maybe he used to live in that house," Kat says.

"Maybe," I say.

"You should ask your mom, she might be able to look it up. Maybe she could find out their names," Kat says.

"I don't know. My mom is ticked off about this whole thing. You heard her yesterday, I'm on thin ice. If I cause her just the least bit of trouble

I won't be able to go to Lake Placid. No tournament - no all-star game - no St. Michael's. She's in no mood for me pestering her with a whole lot of questions."

"You don't have to ask a bunch of questions, just one," Kat quips.

"It's not that simple," I say.

"Well, how else are we gonna find out who he was?" Brady says.

"He's right, Myles. It's just one question. Your parents aren't gonna tell you that you can't go to Lake Placid because of one harmless question," Kat says.

I've been thinking about those brown feet. They may have been bony and wrinkled, but they looked strong enough to walk all the way to India, leaving a thousand miles of footprints behind. Instead, their stillness under the heavy plastic was their final resting place. This image is a reminder to me that I somehow feel responsible for the man. He needed my help. And I ran away.

"Alright. I'll think of a way to ask her and let you know."

When we turn onto Brady's street we come upon a most astonishing sight. It's perhaps the biggest and strangest Christmas tree any of us have ever seen. The branches of a large, sprawling oak in front of the Hopper's house are brightly decorated with Brady's bicycle, disassembled into twenty or so pieces, each an odd and shiny ornament. Jake even used Brady's goalie equipment which hangs from the lower branches. Disbelief and disgust spreads across my face. I know Brady is angry and embarrassed. Jake, for once, has managed to outdo himself. It is a malicious masterpiece that he stands and admires with his entourage, a throng of wrestling buddies. They're all smiles and snickers.

The confrontation begins.

Jake, being much larger, throws his younger brother to the ground. He pounces on Brady before he can get to his feet. Brady gives up when Jake gets him into a vicious headlock. It takes no more than ten seconds. I feel sorry for Brady and before I realize what I'm doing I yell at Jake to get off of my friend. Jake lifts his head and looks at me for a long surprised moment like he's forgotten who I am. My eyes flutter and my shoulders twist into an uneasy shrug. My twitching makes me feel even more awkward than I already did, before I summoned the courage, or stupidity, to confront Jake myself.

At first Jake doesn't know what to say. A meaty vein that runs the length of his muscled neck pulses angrily. Then his eyes come to life. They glimmer in his reddening face. "What's wrong SPAZ! You nervous about something? You afraid of getting your butt kicked too?"

Brady squirms pathetically, but Jake just tightens his headlock grip on his brother's head. He finally let's Brady loose when Kat yells at him. Jake takes a few steps towards me. I struggle to control my twitching.

Jake is all business.

I'm ready to give him what I got.

Then he decides he's getting the last word.

"Wait a second." He flops onto his back and just lays there for a few moments.

"What am I?" he shouts towards his friends who are gathered nearby. Of course, none of the lug heads can guess what he's doing.

"I'm a dead guy!" Jake laughs at his own joke. His friends, slow to get the joke, laugh too. "Hey, Brady, am I dead or alive? Or don't you even know the difference!"

"Knock it off Jake," I snarl at him. He may have it easy tossing Brady around, but I'm just as big as he is, and he knows it. I'll give him a dustup he won't forget.

Jake takes his time getting up. Grass falls off his crumpled shirt. He takes a few steps in my direction, then stops and turns around. "Guess what I'm doing now?"

He doesn't know when to quit. No wonder he drives Brady nuts.

"I'm walking away, because that's what dead people do. They just walk away and disappear."

Brady goes after his brother again. Jake gives him a hard shove sending Brady sprawling on his back. The whole gang laughs. But Brady isn't done yet, he darts after Jake once more. I reach out and bearhug Brady before he gets to Jake, saving him from even more embarrassment.

"You better put that bike back together Jake!" Kat yells. It's no use. Jake's not listening. He and the goon squad turn and head towards the deck at the back of the house.

Kat and I walk with Brady into the house. He runs into the bathroom and slams the door. It sucks getting whipped by your own brother. Especially in front of your friends and your brother's friends. Dennis and I have had our battles. All brothers do. But compared to Brady and Jake, what we do is kid stuff. I remember when I was younger I was mad at him and doing my best to annoy him. I don't even remember what it was about. He ignored my taunts for as long as he could, but when he decided he'd had enough he started after me. I ran as fast as possible to the safety of the house and locked the back door on him. I mushed my face up against the glass and made faces at him, thinking there was nothing he could do. But he just up and slammed his fist right through the glass into my face. The suddenness of it knocked me off my feet and left a small cut under my eye. Ever since then I try to remind myself that Dennis has a limit, and it's not in my best interest to push him over it.

Mrs. Hopper comes into the kitchen and sees Kat and me standing there. "Where's Brady? Who slammed the door?"

Kat looks my way, but before either of us can answer Brady comes out of the bathroom, his eyes are red and swollen.

"Brady, what happened?"

"Nothing," he snaps.

"C'mon, something happened, what was it?"

It's Kat who breaks the silence. "Jake took Brady's bike apart and put all the pieces in the big tree in front of the house. Then he and Brady got in a fight."

"Oh no," Mrs. Hopper cries. Her expression reveals her frustration which then turns to defeat.

"I'll let your dad know when he gets home. He's not going to be happy when he finds out about this."

"Dad never does anything," Brady wails, his hurt and anger flooding out.

"That's not true."

"Yes it is and you know it, Mom. Jake does whatever he wants because you and Dad never do anything. That's my bike, the one Grampa and Nana bought me for my birthday. I use it all the time. Now what am I supposed to do?"

"Don't worry, Jake will be putting the bike back together piece by piece. I don't care how long it takes him."

She sounds like she means it, but Brady isn't buying it. "Yeah, right. You're always making excuses for him. He gets away with murder!"

My mom got her realtor's license and began selling real estate shortly after she and my dad were married. She thought it would be a good way to make some extra money and still be home to raise a family. Back then my dad worked for a big plumbing company. Most of the time things were busy and he worked a lot of hours and made good money. But other times business was slow and the money would be tight. He always wanted to be his own boss, so eventually he struck out on his own. Since he started the business he's grown it so that he has three trucks and five other plumbers working for him. The trucks are lettered with, *Walsh & Sons Plumbing*. I guess he expected I'd be a plumber too. Oh well, at least he has Dennis.

"Anything good in the paper?" my mom says.

"Not really. I was just checking the scores."

Truth is I'm still scouring the paper every day just in case there's a story about the dead man. But there's been no mention of him in the obituary or anywhere else.

"All your homework is done?"

"Yeah, Brady and Kat came over after school and we did it together."

"That's good. You guys should do your homework together more often."

Time to switch gears here and get to the question I need to ask. "Why did Dad start his own business?"

"Oh, you know your dad. He isn't really cut out to work for anyone."

"I never knew Dad started his business because you sold a house."

"We'd been planning to start a family, but your dad didn't want to do that until he got the business off the ground. I'd sold a few condos, but nothing with a big enough commission to get the business going. I really needed to sell a house, and that house over on Mountain Avenue was just the miracle we needed."

"Why was it a miracle?"

"The real estate market was very slow at the time, not many houses were selling. But I had a young couple I was working with who had flown in from Texas. The husband was being transferred to this area and they desperately wanted to find a nice family home here in Caldwell. The wife was pregnant and they wanted to be in a new home before the baby arrived."

"And they bought the house?"

"Well, not at first. They were here for just two short days, and we couldn't find anything in their price range that suited them. They were ready to give up. Then just a few hours before they were gonna get on a plane and fly back to Texas a new listing came up."

"What's a listing?"

"It's what they call a house that's being offered for sale. The house that you and Brady were in was owned by a foreign couple. The story was that one of their relatives back home had become very ill, and they needed to return home as soon as possible. They needed to sell the house quickly. I brought my Texas couple over right away and they loved it. They bought the house, and Walsh & Sons Plumbing was born."

"I ride my bike past that house all the time. I never knew it had anything to do with Dad's business, though."

"Well, it does, and now you know."

"Who were the owners? What were their names?"

"Why do you want to know?" My mom must suspect that I'm trolling for information. Which I am, of course.

"Just because," I reply, twitching an eye-flutter.

"It wouldn't have anything to do with this dead man thing that's got you all stirred up, would it?"

"I didn't make it up Mom. I don't why you keep saying that."

"I'm sorry Myles, but dead bodies don't just vanish. What else am I supposed to think?"

"Well you could believe me."

"I'm sorry, we've already discussed this."

"I know, but telling me I can't play in the tournament at Lake Placid unless I get all A's and B's is unfair. The St. Michael's coach is gonna be there! Brady and Kat saw the same dead body I did, but their parents aren't punishing them. They're going to Lake Placid even if they get D's and F's."

"Your dad and I are very upset about what you kids did. It's not right to get the police involved in something because you've decided it would be a fun Halloween prank. This isn't the first time you've done this, Myles. You have to learn that you can't just make up stories, especially ones that get other people involved your schemes."

"Mom, I'm telling you, I'm not making this up. I don't know why the police didn't find the body, but ask Brady if you want to, we saw a dead body, I'm telling you." A rib crunch howls through my frustration.

"Well, suit yourself. Remember, until we get to the bottom of this, if you so much as think about pulling another stunt like this, there'll be no

Lake Placid for you. You understand? Let's hope, for your sake, we don't find anymore dead people, okay?"

"Fine," I say, surrendering. Finding one dead body is one more than anyone needs to find in a lifetime.

Regrouping, I try again. "I'm just trying to figure out what happened, that's all," giving her my best helpless puppy look. I even throw in a few big, rumbly rib crunches to make her feel sorry for me. She looks away and considers my request. Silence sits between us. I'm close to winning her over, but I need to push a little more.

"You said the people who used to live in that house were from another country, right? Do you remember what country they were from? Was it India?"

"That was about twenty years ago, Myles. I don't remember. Like I told you already, they don't even live in this country anymore. Plus, I'm sure they have nothing to do with the person you claim to have found."

"Please, Mom. Can't you just tell me what their names were?"

"What are you planning on doing, Myles? I don't want you poking around in other people's business. You're in enough trouble as it is. If I catch you stirring up any more trouble whatsoever, you can forget not only Lake Placid, but the rest of your hockey season, too."

"Well, no one believes me, what am I supposed to do?"

Aggravated and out of patience she replies, "I have no idea what their names were, it was a long time ago, before computers. I'm sure I've lost or thrown out any paperwork I may have had on it. Sorry, Myles."

"Well, is there a way to find out?"

"Myles, that's enough."

Agitated to the point of surrender, I walk away. Question after question spins around in my head. My neck and shoulders twitch like they're running from a fire.

I take the ring out and inspect it. It's dark silver, thick and bulky, with an intricate and ancient design that gives the impression that it's very important in some unknown way. At the center of the ring is an upright rectangle shaped like a door. On either side of the door are three circles, which are intertwined with three strands that resemble rope. I feel its weight in my hand. I imagine it holds some secret message from the past. But what?

I'm gonna find out.

Twitching like a madman I want nothing more than relief, but none comes. I make a hasty retreat from the kitchen where death, deadlines, and anxiety are like an unlucky spill waiting to happen.

"Where are you going?" my mom asks as I stride towards the door.

"The library."

My dad wears a claddagh ring that my mother gave him before they were married. I once asked my dad what the big deal was with them, and he told me that it tells a story. Claddagh rings are given from one person to another as a way to express their love and devotion. On the ring, a pair of hands holds a heart that is topped off with a crown. The ring's design means, "I give you my love in my hands, and crown it with my loyalty." The heart symbolizes one's love; the hands symbolize friendship; and the crown symbolizes loyalty.

Somehow, I know the dead man's ring means something, too. I need to find out.

My chance for the St. Michael's coach to see me play in Lake Placid may depend on it.

Being as I haven't told either Brady or Kat about the ring, I don't invite them onto an errand I have to take care of myself. I told my mom I had to pick out a book for a book report in Mr. Curtin's class. Which is true, though sometimes my truth has a curve to it. I have a few weeks before I need to pick one out and show it to him. Nevertheless, my situation requires a sense of urgency. I could try searching online but spending too much time on the computer can over stimulate my anxiety.

The library sits at the heart of Caldwell. Its walls of cozy red bricks are topped with a painted green dome. A stone walkway leads to the entrance - large wooden doors cut from an old maple tree. Inside, books tightly packed into shelves, each as colorful as a box of crayons, are flooded with sunlight that pours in from several majestic windows.

A twitch that began as a howl weakens into a whisper. The irritation I felt earlier dissolves as the need to twitch leaves me. Before me, stretches endless rows of books. A carnival of choices - each one more enchanting than the other. For our book report we can choose any book, just so long as it's fiction and at least one-hundred pages. The book I bring up to the counter is by Ray Bradbury, *Something Wicked This Way Comes*.

The librarian that stands before me is a young guy with long blonde hair, and a busy collection of small earrings in both ears. A tattoo on his left bicep peaks out from under his rolled-up long sleeve shirt. On both hands are a hodgepodge of large rings. Each a different size and shape with its own design. I steal a quick look to see if one of them is similar to the ring I have in my pocket. But nothing seems to match.

He smiles and asks if I need help with anything else. Because he isn't the kind of librarian I expected, it seems easy enough to ask him about rings. He places both hands on the counter and leans up on his toes.

"Are you looking for any particular ring or just anything in general about rings?"

I'm tempted to show him the ring I have, but I don't want anyone to know I have it. If my mom ever found out, my hockey season would be over.

"My grandfather has an old ring, a really unusual one, with a unique design to it. He bought it at a yard sale because he thought it might be valuable. Seems to think the design means something, like a claddagh ring does, but he doesn't know what it might be."

"If you have the ring, or a picture of it, I'll take a look at it for you."

"My grandfather has it. I just thought I'd surprise him with the story behind it." I describe the ring, the dead man's ring, to the librarian.

"Sounds like a neat ring. Can't say I've ever seen anything like that before. Do you know if there are any inscriptions on it?"

"What do you mean by 'inscriptions'?"

"Lettering or writing that may be inscribed or kind of written into the ring somewhere. Usually it's inside the ring. Here, I'll show you." He takes off one of his rings, a plain silver band that's very thick, like a finger handcuff of some sort. He turns it over so I can read what it says inside: *be free.*

"See? That's an inscription. Your grandfather's ring, does it have an inscription?"

"I don't know." I hadn't thought to look inside the ring, but now I'm anxious to see if there's an inscription, or not.

"Alright, you can find out later. Follow me, I'll show you where we have some books that might help."

He takes me to a section where books extend from the floor to well above my head. He hands me one that's the size of both my English and math textbooks combined. I hurriedly skim through a few pages. "Wow! There must be a picture of every ring ever made in this book."

"You said it. Happy hunting, kid."

The plan was to check out a simple, average-looking book on rings and take it home, where in the privacy of my room I could take my time going through it. There's no way I'm going to be able to hide this beast from my mom. One look at this thing and I'll have to explain why I'm suddenly so interested in the history of rings.

My mom went to pick up a few groceries and said she'd meet me here in about thirty minutes. That gives me only fifteen minutes to look through a million pictures. I take the book and sit at a table and begin skimming its pages. When my eyes get blurry and all the rings start looking alike, I realize that this is hopeless. I put the book back where I got it from and go wait outside for my mom. I reach into my pocket and scoop out the ring. I don't see any inscription written inside it. Of course not. Why is it that nothing is ever easy?

Despite my apprehensions I get online and start searching images of old rings. After an hour of torturing myself into a twitch frenzy, I decide to take a break when I hear my mom calling from the kitchen.

"This is all I could find." She hands me a small thank you card that smells like it's from the past. I take the card and open it up, hopeful there's something in here that can help me. The card reads:

> Dear Mrs. Walsh,
>
> Please accept our deepest gratitude for helping us sell our home, a home we loved for many years and will forever miss. Your kindness and professionalism enabled us to return home to care for a relative who has gratefully recovered his good health once more because of our speedy return and your timely support.
>
> Love,
>
> Sanjana & Amar

"They're from India!" I exclaim. "No last names?"

"That's all I could find. It was in a box where I keep mementos and special things. I must have thrown the envelope away. Make sure I get that back. By the way, I also did some math and figured out that either one of these people would be in their late seventies or close to eighty years old by now - if they're even still alive. That's much older than the man you described seeing last week. These people may be from India, but there's absolutely no chance that Amar is the person you claim to have found, Myles."

Resuming my search online turns up nothing. I must have looked at images of about ten-thousand rings. Not one of them resembles my ring. Or rather, the dead man's ring. The solution I had hoped for seems beyond my reach. But, learning that the people who used to live in that ghost house were from India gives me an idea. I use my phone to take a few pictures of the ring from different angles, trying to show as much of it as I can.

Maybe Jogesh, or his parents, will know what the ring is. But then the fear that they'll *know* what it is, and *know* that it doesn't belong to me, and will question where I got it from overcomes me. Instead I text a description to Jogesh. I hope that will be enough to get the answer I need.

CHAPTER SEVEN

Wednesday, September 10th

I'm a good kid. Really, I am. But, as I once heard my nanna say, desperate times call for desperate measures. That's why I got up ten minutes early this morning. My dad wants to live forever and he seems to believe that the best way to do that is to eat only the healthiest foods all the time. In addition to his shot glass of vitamins, a typical breakfast includes a sturdy bowl of oatmeal, a tall glass of orange juice, and a fat glass of prune juice. Finally, he washes it all down with a hefty ladle full of cod liver oil.

However, this morning when he's done and places his empty bowl, glasses, and ladle in the sink he finds another white ladle coated with cod liver oil.

I'm busy enjoying a bowl of cereal when my dad says, "Whose ladle is this? Is this yours, Myles?"

"Yeah, that's mine."

His lips curl into a frown. His eyes twitch with suspicion.

"Oh yeah? Let me smell your breath. It's not like you to take your cod liver oil without complaining about it."

I sit up and let my dad take a whiff. He leans in and sniffs. Satisfied, he nods his head and goes about the rest of his morning. As soon as he's out of view I rush over to the sink, wet the washcloth and wipe off the cod liver oil that I had smeared on my lips earlier. No fish breath today!

Mr. Curtin picks up my torn and tattered homework off the floor and comments, "Is this your graphic organizer Mr. Walsh? This thing looks like an ancient document from Colonial times. How long have you had this thing, about 300 years?"

It's the graphic organizer for my story, which he reads. "Your outline's a little thin - it needs more specific details. Remember, good writing is in the details. But overall, it looks like you have the bones of a good story here." I rub the heel of my hand on my pocket, comforted by the presence of the stolen talisman.

Ideas and words come easier than they have before. Still, the same doubts and fears linger. The pressure of earning a 'B' in English, with Lake Placid hanging in the balance, has me feeling more anxious than usual. The squeaking of my desk alerts me that I'm twitching and probably have been for a few minutes without realizing it. Brittney, a straight 'A' student who doesn't have to worry about 'C's', looks away when I glance over at her. She's probably annoyed that my twitching has been such a distraction.

"How many of you tell stories? Raise your hand if you do," Mr. Curtin says.

A scatter of hands go up, including mine.

"Good. I see that some of you like to *tell* stories. How many of you like to *listen* to a good story, but you'd rather someone else be telling it?" A majority of hands go up this time, including Kat's and Brady's.

"It's important that we *all* tell stories. Hopefully, after we've read this next story you'll understand why. I need everyone to open their Literature textbooks to page 119. We're going to read an Indian folktale. It's called *Untold Stories*."

Mr. Curtin begins reading:

"'A Gond peasant kept a farmhand who worked for him in the fields. One day they went together to a distant village to visit the Gond's son and his wife. On the way they stopped at a little hut by the roadside. After they had eaten their supper, the farmhand said, "Tell me a story." But the Gond was tired and went to sleep. His servant lay awake. He knew that his master had four stories, which he was too lazy to tell.

When the Gond was fast asleep, the stories came out of his belly, sat on his body, and began to talk to each other. They were angry. "This Gond," they said "knows us very well from childhood, but he will never tell anybody about us. Why should we go on living uselessly in his belly? Let's kill him and go to live with someone else." The farmhand pretended to be asleep, but he listened carefully to everything they said.

The first story said, "When the Gond reaches his son's house and sits down to eat his supper, I'll turn his first mouthful of food into sharp needles, and when he swallows them they'll kill him."

The second story said, "If he escapes that, I'll become a great tree by the roadside. I'll fall on him as he passes by and kill him that way."

The third story said, "If that doesn't work, I'll be a snake and run up his leg and bite him."

The fourth said, "If that doesn't work, I'll bring a great wave of water as he is crossing the river and wash him away." The next morning the Gond and his servant reached his son's house. His son and daughter-in-law welcomed him and prepared food and set it before him. But as the Gond raised his first mouthful to his lips, his servant knocked it out of his hand, saying, "There's an insect in the food." When they looked, they saw that all the rice had turned into needles.

The next day the Gond and his servant set out on their return journey. There was a great tree leaning across the road, and the servant said, "Let's run past the tree." As they ran past it, the tree fell with a mighty crash, and they just escaped. A little later, they saw a snake by the road, and the servant quickly killed it with his stick. After that they came to the river and as they were crossing, a great wave came rushing down, but the servant dragged the Gond to safety.

They sat down on the bank to rest, and the Gond said, "You have saved my life four times. You know something I don't. How did you know what was going to happen?" The farmhand said, "If I tell you I'll turn into a stone."

The Gond said, "How can a man turn into a stone? Come on, tell me." So the servant said, "Very well, I'll tell you. But when I turn into a stone, take your daughter-in-law's child and throw it against me, and I'll become a man again."

So the servant told his story and was turned into a stone, but the Gond left him there and went home. After some time, his daughter-in-law heard about it, and she went all by herself and threw her child against the stone, and the servant came to life again.'"

Mr. Curtin paces back and forth, then stops. He looks out at the class, silent, serious. Sandy, a girl whose hair color matches her name breaks the silence, "That's a weird story. She had to throw a baby against a stone. That would kill the baby."

"Did it kill the baby?" Mr. Curtin answers.

Nick, another kid who plays hockey, but for a team called the Riverhawks, replies, "No. When the man threw the baby against the rock it turned the man back into himself again."

"So, what does the story mean, that we're supposed to throw babies against rocks? That's awful," Sandy says.

"Let's talk about what the folktale means. Why do you suppose this story was told? Why has it survived for hundreds of years, being passed down from one generation to another, and today seventh graders in Caldwell read it in English class?" Mr. Curtin resumes his pacing.

"To teach us to throw babies against rocks!" Sandy shouts.

"No. I think we all know that we shouldn't throw babies against rocks - unless we're pretty sure that by doing so we'll be turning someone from stone back into their human form. Then it's probably okay," Mr. Curtin says. "Stories have the power to change lives. Stories make us human. The point is that stories can change form depending on the person telling the story. No two stories are exactly alike, even when they are alike. There's an art to telling a story. So, what does this story teach us?"

The whole class waits for Mr. Curtin's answer. This is one of those times when it pays to sit nice and quiet at your desk - typically an impossible task for most seventh graders, but especially for me, Mr. Twitch. At the moment, however, I'm as still as everyone else. Mr. Curtin has obviously had practice with staring contests and quiet contests, because he's neither moving nor talking.

Thankfully, Nick comes to the rescue again, "That we should tell stories?" He says it like there's no way that's the right answer. It's too simple. Even I could have guessed that, but I don't like to look stupid. My twitching already does that for me.

"Nick, that's correct," says Mr. Curtin.

Huh? That's the moral of the story - to tell stories?

"Why is it so important that we tell stories anyway? Ms. Labbee, do you want to take a crack at that?"

Kat, who is slumped at her desk, startled by the question, sits up.

"Because people like them?"

"That's one reason, sure. Stories entertain us. Why else do we tell stories?"

A few weeks from now Mr. Curtin won't be able to shut us up, but at the moment, no one is willing to volunteer a guess. "C'mon guys, we've already learned all this." Ahhh, a much needed clue. Suddenly hands are up and answers are snapping, crackling, and popping.

"It's how we learn things."

"To pass on traditions."

"To find out about our family history."

The class gives Mr. Curtin another half-dozen reasons when he's finally heard enough.

"Alright good. I'm glad everyone remembers why we tell stories. But what would happen if we didn't tell stories, that's what this folktale is about.

Mr. Walsh, what does this folktale tell us might happen, or probably will happen, if we don't tell our stories?"

I squirm like a bag of jelly beans under the spotlight of twenty other faces looking at me, waiting for an answer. Mr. Curtin senses my situation and buys me some time. "Think about it. If we have stories to tell, and we know that we need to tell stories, but we don't tell them, what happens?"

I search for a response, but it doesn't come to me. But Mr. Curtin provides another valuable clue. "What happened to the Gond because he was too lazy to tell his stories?"

I croak out my answer in a near mumble, "He died."

"Correct Mr. Walsh. His untold stories changed form and killed him. So the moral is, if we have stories to tell, then it is extremely important that we tell them. Stories cry out to be told, to be passed on, and so kept alive."

Sandy blurts out, "You mean Mr. Curtin that if we don't tell stories that we're going to die?"

"Not literally, but you never know. How many of you have ever watched or read the news, or read something online about some person who is accidentally hit and killed by a bus, or dies in some other freak-ish way?"

What does that have to do with anything?

"Well, I'll bet that if you were to investigate the real reason for that person's death, it wouldn't be that they weren't paying attention and some-how stepped in front of a bus. I think you may discover that the person was pushed. Pushed out into the road in front of the bus and SLAM! Was killed by his or her untold stories."

"Are you serious Mr. Curtin? Are you saying I may be killed by a bus just because I don't tell my stories?" Patriots-boy says, challenging Mr. Curtin.

"All I'm saying, all the folktale is saying, is be extra careful the next time you're waiting to cross the street and a bus is coming. If there's anyone near you and you have an untold story, then it may be a real good idea to tell it to that person. Quickly. Before it's too late. Remember, if you have stories to tell, then you must tell them. Stories keep us alive, in more ways than one. Believe me."

Brady looks my way. A smile leaks across his face.

The smile of a snake-charmer.

The look on his face tells me everything I need to know.

I can't believe I'm doing this.

We leave the bikes hidden in the scraggly remains of a battered tree. It appears to have been the victim of a storm that gasped its last breath along the New England coast last month.

"Brady, stop."

"What?" he answers annoyed.

"This is crazy."

"Didn't you hear what Mr. Curtin said?"

"Do you believe everything he says?"

"Stories need to be told. First we find a dead guy. Then he disappears. Then we find a ghost rocking a chair. I'm telling you there's a story here that needs to be told."

"You better be right."

My twitching is non-stop, has been since Brady talked me and Kat into coming back to this ghost house. It's already dark, although a nearly full moon shines brightly through the darkening clouds that cluster around it.

The house is dark and menacing. Its creepy appearance invites any and all thrill-seekers to enter. So it can swallow them alive. Kat is in back watching for anyone that might come through the back entrance. Brady and I slink up the driveway and around to the front of the house like burglars on the prowl. Darting across the lawn, we hesitate before climbing the front steps as quietly as we can. The deal is that I don't have to go into the house. I just need to stay on the front porch and keep an eye out for anything.

Brady is convinced that he can pick the lock on the front door to get into the house. Although, I've seen him pick the lock on Jake's bedroom door, I'm betting the house that he can't pick this lock. But Brady has the outlook of a hopeless optimist for whom no sensible reasoning can defeat. Try as I might to persuade him otherwise, he's convinced that our missing dead man is in the chest in the attic. And when we find him, everyone will finally believe us.

I crouch down below the porch railing, out of view if a car should drive by. Brady tip-toes to the front door and tests the knob. Expecting it to be locked, he's delighted when the knob rotates and the door opens. Damn. Why's the door unlocked? I suppose we're really gonna do this. I try to calm myself while putting out the fire in my shoulders. This is no time for my twitching to be acting up.

"I told you this would be easy. It's not even locked," Brady whispers.

My hope was that after a few minutes of trying to pick the lock Brady would realize he was no match for it, and we could go home, safe and sound, no harm done.

No misadventures.

No ghosts.

No dead people.

So when Brady slips into the house and closes the door behind him, I suddenly feel alone. However, I'm startled a few seconds later when the door opens and Brady sticks his head out.

"Darn it! I forgot to bring a flashlight, did you bring one?"

"No" I answer. "Don't the lights work?"

"I don't know, but we can't turn any lights on."

The thought that maybe now Brady will chicken out and we can go home is abandoned when he once again closes the door and is swallowed up into the darkness.

My arms, shoulders, and neck burst in violent spasms causing my feet to scrape noisily on the wooden boards of the porch floor.

Minutes pass by and everything seems quiet and ordinary. I begin to relax and think of my mom standing here on this same porch twenty years ago, shaking hands with the sellers, congratulating them on their sale and wishing them luck as they move back home.

I look up to the sky that is now inky-black on account of a large mass of clouds that have blotted the moon, making it disappear. The darkening of the night makes me feel more secure, making it harder for anyone to see me. I feel almost invisible. A soft breeze has the smell of a rain shower coming. My twitching has calmed considerably, enough to risk looking over my shoulder into the blackness of the window.

I see something.

All my senses sizzle to life at once.

Just on the other side of the murky window is a ghostly light shining directly into my eyes, blinding me. I put my hand up to block the glare. A cold recognition passes through me. It's a flashlight.

Someone is inside the house.

And they're just a few short feet away. I clench down hard on an overpowering urge to scream. I hold it down tight as I follow the light as it heads upstairs.

My thoughts skitter in a hundred different directions. But one thought screams to me - Brady is in danger! My mind races thinking of what to do. I kneel down and feel my phone jab into my leg. There's the answer.

As fast as I'm able, I speed dial the most important text message I've ever sent.

- sum 1 is in the house

When the reply text buzzes my phone I nearly jump out of my shoes.

- i know

Minutes feel like eternity. The house is strangely quiet, making me even more fearful.

Then the ghostly light reappears. It heads in the direction of the front door. A few agonizing seconds pass and I stiffen when I hear the door knob turning. The door creaks open.

I want to cry but I'm too numb and rigid to produce any tears. The shadowy shape of a man steps out onto the porch. He turns and closes the door shut behind him. Reaching into his pocket he takes out a key, then looks out towards the road to see if anyone is watching. He stands just a few feet from me. I wrap every muscle I have as tightly into myself as I can. I wish to cease to exist, to be enclosed by the sheltering porch as if I were a chair, a swing, a welcome mat. I'd pulverize myself into dust if I could. Anything not to be found. I close my eyes and squeeze down on a breath that tries to escape.

I hear the man's footsteps descend the porch stairs then plod down the short walkway. I open one eye just enough to peek through the porch railings and see the man move like a wisp of fog towards the road. He vanishes into the blackness of the night. Then a car door opens. The headlights from the car can barely be seen from behind a large bush where it's parked. The unknown man drives away as silently as he had appeared earlier. Best I can tell, the car itself is unremarkable, just an average dark-colored car.

Brady appears a few minutes later. The treasure chest was locked meaning that only the ghost knows what's inside. Or the shadow man. I slip my hand into my pocket and feel the talisman. I roll it around between my fingers, wondering if it's the object of the shadow man's pursuit. I wonder whether it's worth all this.

The smell of freshly fallen rain permeates my senses, but not a drop of rain has fallen.

CHAPTER EIGHT

Sunday, September 14th

The Hoppers' house is on Porter Road, a cul-de-sac street clustered with seven new homes, each one a stately mini-mansion with impeccably manicured lawns, long windy driveways and in-ground pools. I like Brady's house, especially when Jake isn't there. The best part is the family room. With a 100-inch flat screen TV, surround-sound speakers all over the room, and comfortable leather couches set-up in a U-shape, it's the ultimate media room. There isn't a bad seat in the house, and Mrs. Hopper keeps the pantry well-stocked with everyone's favorite snacks.

We're watching football which means Brady and I are on our phones tracking our fantasy league players. The Patriots are leading the Jets 21-7 at halftime, thanks to Tom Brady who has thrown three touchdown passes. I wish school was as easy as fantasy football. I won last year's fantasy season championship and used the cash prize to buy a sweet Bauer Supreme hockey stick.

"What are you guys doing on those phones?" Mr. Hopper says. He seems annoyed with us, but of course, he's busy with his laptop. Brady says he practically lives on the thing. When he gets home from work he parks himself on the sofa and spends the whole night on it doing more work. He's a vice president at some bank where he spends all his time thinking of ways to make as much money as he can.

"Just checking out some scores and stats for our fantasy team," Brady says, getting updates from other games around the league.

"It's halftime. Why don't you guys go out and throw the football around?" Mr. Hopper says to Brady.

"I'm good."

"When I was your age and it was halftime, we'd race outside to play some football. Watching football would get us fired up to play football."

"Managing my fantasy teams gets me fired up to watch football," Brady replies.

Mr. Hopper grunts and then occupies himself with work again.

Mrs. Hopper walks in and slumps into the sofa next to her husband. "Honey, did Jake tell you what happened at football practice the other day?"

"Hmm?" Mr. Hopper is still engrossed with his laptop, so Mrs. Hopper taps him on the knee to get his attention.

"What'd you say?" Mr. Hopper says, popping his head up like he's underwater coming up for air.

"I said, did Jake tell you what happened at football the other day?"

"No. What happened?" He seems only half interested, then puts his head back into his laptop.

"Apparently a couple of kids jumped on the golf cart they keep at the field and were racing the thing around and broke it. Jake said he heard that they lost control and rolled the thing onto its side. Fortunately no one was hurt, but can you imagine the nerve of those kids?"

Mr. Hopper looks up again, this time with a smile on his face. Mrs. Hopper is surprised by his reaction and adds, "Isn't that awful?" Just to make sure neither Brady nor I get any ideas about stealing a golf cart.

"I don't know, they're at an age when they're gonna find ways to have fun."

"Yeah, but damaging a golf cart? Do you know how expensive those things are?"

"Did they get in trouble?" Brady asks.

"They may be kicked off the team. They should be," Mrs. Hopper says.

"It's one thing to do something crazy, it's another thing to do something stupid. I did some crazy things in my day, but I can't say I ever did anything stupid like those kids did."

"What'd you do that was crazy, Dad?" Brady asks.

"I remember when I played football, we had some fun once," Mr. Hopper says, closing his laptop, a smile stretches across his face.

"What'd you do?"

"Me and a bunch of buddies, let me see, it was Jimmy, Brian, George, and Paul. We would weightlift at the high school all summer to get ready for football season. Right outside the weight room there was a big shiny fire extinguisher. It was just sitting there. It wasn't locked up or behind a glass panel or anything. Just sitting there. We figured, no one ever uses the thing, we may as well use it for something," he says with a devilish twinkle in his eyes.

"What did you do"? Brady asks.

"Well we took it. We didn't really do anything with it at first, but then one night, early, maybe six o'clock, I get a phone call from Jimmy - "'what are doing?'" - "'nothing, why?'" - "'we'll be over in fifteen minutes, be ready'" - "'sounds good.'" Fifteen minutes later Jimmy pulls into the driveway in his Firebird. Brian is in the front seat and I climb in next to Paul and George in the backseat, and what do you know, the bright, shiny extinguisher is in the backseat, too." Mr Hopper giggles.

"Now, back then running was just becoming a big thing. All kinds of people took up running and they'd run everywhere - back roads, main roads, every neighborhood in town. We'd drive around for awhile until we found someone running by themselves. Older ladies, say, about my mom's age at the time, were perfect. What we'd do was slow down and pass by, then pull over ahead of them. As the runner got closer we'd roll the windows down and signal them over. People are so friendly. They'd come over and lean in thinking we were lost and needed directions. That's when we'd hose them down with the extinguisher!"

"Honey! I can't believe you'd do that," Mrs. Hopper squeals. Brady and I laugh.

"The extinguisher was a big tank. We figured, under pressure it held about twenty gallons of water and we'd drench people with the entire twenty gallons in about ten seconds. They'd be soaked from head to toe. Of course they'd duck or try to hide, but there was nowhere to hide. They'd be on a sidewalk with no cover."

"Dad, that's awesome! I never knew that you'd done anything crazy," Brady shouts, beaming a big smile that he can't contain.

"You are so bad. I thought you were a nice guy," Mrs. Hopper shrieks, although I can tell that she's just as impressed as Brady and me.

"I was a nice guy, still am, I think, but I had friends who liked to mix it up and were very creative. This was before videos games, so we had to find ways to make our own fun. After a while we figured out that the best way to hose people down was to cruise parking lots where there were phone booths. With smart phones nowadays you don't see pay phones anymore. But they used to be in every parking lot. People would be gabbing away on the phone, and of course they'd never close the door. Once we turned on the water there was nowhere to go, they'd be trapped in the phone booth and we'd really soak'em good. We'd drive off real quick making our getaway."

I can't picture Mr. Hopper, who has the personality of a cardboard box, stealing a fire extinguisher to soak unsuspecting victims. Makes me wonder who you can trust if someone as boring as Mr. Hopper has a wild and crazy side.

"Luckily one of the guys, I forget who, maybe Paul, was a pretty good science student and knew how to refill the tank and pressurize it, so we could keep reusing it. See why science and school are so important? You need to know these things. I've always wondered what those people told their husbands or wives or kids when they walked in the door and they were soaking wet. We had so much fun extinguishing all summer long. Or, almost all summer."

"What happened to the fire extinguisher? Do you still have it?" Brady says. I can just see him cooking up plans to find our own victims.

"No, unfortunately our summer of fun did finally come to an end."

"Yeah, you guys finally came to your senses and returned the extinguisher that you had wrongly stolen. What would you do if a bunch of troublemakers did that to me and I came home soaking wet?" says Mrs. Hopper.

"Mom, I'd laugh so hard if that happened to you!" Brady shouts.

"Well, no one got hurt. But there was this one perfect summer night when we were out looking for the perfect victim. There wasn't a cloud in the sky, a beautiful late summer night, but we couldn't find any runners or any phone booth users. We were cruising the Mall parking lot with no luck, but then Paul spotted someone and had an idea." Mr. Hopper pauses and smiles.

"There was a little old lady putting groceries into the back seat of her car. We parked in the same row, about 3-4 cars over. She couldn't see us, but we could see her. Paul aimed the nozzle of the extinguisher out the window and up in the air so that the water sprayed up and then down like a rainbow. A rainbow of water right on the little old lady's head. It was so funny. She kept looking up trying to figure out why it was raining on such a beautiful night."

"Dave, I can't believe you would do that to an old lady. That's terrible!"

"I know. We tried to talk Paul out of it, but he thought it would be funny - and it was."

"Dad, that's awesome! The lady must have been freaking out. What did she do?"

"She scrambled like crazy to get all the groceries into the car. Back then grocery bags were made of brown paper and when they got wet they would just fall apart. She was bending down to pick up groceries that had fallen out, trying desperately to get everything into the car before they were ruined and she was soaked. Although I felt bad for her, I have to say it was funny," Mr. Hopper says, giggling.

"But unknown to us, there were two people in the car next to the old lady, and as it was such a perfect night the person on the passenger side had the window rolled down and his arm was resting out of it. Some of the rain we were making landed on the man's arm and unlike the old lady, he was able to figure out what was going on. Before we realized it, he was standing next to Jimmy flashing a police badge. The game was over and so was our summer of extinguishing."

The Pats win easily, and thanks to Tom Brady, my fantasy team loaded up huge points. Seeing 60 Minutes come on TV is my cue that it's time to get going.

"Myles, it looks like it's beginning to rain. Do you want me to drive you home?" Mrs. Hopper says. I think of accepting her offer, but don't want to trouble her, and besides it's just a ten minute bike ride home, a little rain isn't going to kill me.

Biking home gives me the chance to be alone. It's quiet times like this that I'm able to relax the most. A misty September rain rustles up the sweet smell of autumn leaves as I stroll through the empty neighborhood. A few larger drops begin to spatter randomly on my back. The rain washes down all over the roofs, patio sets, hockey nets, and skateboards of Caldwell. Before I reach the end of Brady's cul-de-sac my Bulldogs hockey jacket is soaked, though I don't mind.

I'm pedaling at a leisurely pace when I turn left onto Janet Road and become aware that a car, further down the road, is moving towards me from behind. Figuring it's someone heading to Weston Drive, the main road that leads into the town center, I casually maintain my pace. The rain falls harder and the wind rises. Soon after I make a right onto School Street, which cuts over to my street, I notice the headlights of the car swerve onto

School Street, too. The rain, coming down hard and steady, glistens in the car's headlights.

I pedal a little faster, my tires sloshing on the wet pavement. The car also speeds up and the engine roars as it gains on me. That's not good. A pang of anxiety that began as a small moment spins into a large whirlpool of panic. I tremble with a rain soaked shiver. Thoughts of the dead man and his killer swim in my head. I pedal as fast as I can.

When I reach the corner of Ruthellen Road I cut a sharp right and speed downhill towards home which is getting closer, but not close enough. Bright headlights and squealing tires echo through the desolate streets. It takes all the courage I have to glance over my shoulder at my pursuer who takes the same turn. What I see next nearly unhinges me with fright. Under the glow of a corner light post is a dark-colored car. Just like the one I saw at the ghost house. The car's motor revs up as it speeds closer and closer. Exhausted and numb, when the car pulls up alongside me, a desire to surrender the chase overwhelms me.

Just as I'm about to give up I realize that I'm near the water tower. A sense of safety bolts through me. I abruptly skid off the road and ditch the bike. The car keeps going. I run into the woods through a cluster of trees and hide behind the largest one I can find. The same fence that Brady climbed a few days ago is just a short distance away. I'm still shaking, but at least now I'm hopeful that perhaps I've lost my pursuer. I'm wishing he won't be determined enough to chase me into the dark woods on a rainy night. I fight to control my emotions and catch my breath. The smell of rotting leaves and dead moldy wood creeps up my neck. I can't tell if I'm shivering from the chilly rain or twitching myself into a frenzy.

Peering around the trunk of the tree, I see the car turn around and then stop in front of the tower, its headlights beaming towards School Street. It sits motionless. I pray it will begin moving again and drive away, but instead I hear a car door open and then close. A dark shadow passes in front of the headlights, projecting an eerie figure silhouetted against the glare of bright lights. The shadowy figure sees my abandoned bike, inspects it for a moment, then heads towards me. I nearly collapse under the strain of nightmarish visions that pulse through me. If this person killed the dead man, he'll have no problem killing me.

I imagine my parents reading tomorrow evening's Caldwell Chronicle about their son who was found dead in the woods near the neighborhood water tower. They'll wonder who did it and why I was here. I wish I was anywhere else but here. I feel sick with regret.

The man gropes his way into the woods. His footsteps are slow and clumsy. The tree that I'm using for cover is too thin to hide me completely. I look around, none others appear suitable for my large frame. I close my eyes. Think Myles. Think. Should I run deeper into the woods? Warm lights glow in the homes across the street. Would anyone hear me scream? The further I run into the woods, the further away my screams would become. I wish I could be made invisible by the woods as if I were a twig, a pinecone, an acorn. I struggle to gather myself. An instinct to survive tells me to move in the direction of the fence. But I worry that making a dash for it will only speed up the violence that's planned for me. The man moves deeper into the woods. I make a dash for it.

I begin climbing the chain-link fence but between my twitching and shattered nerves I rattle the fence so loudly I'm certain I'll be killed at any moment. When I reach the top I don't waste the time to climb down - in a panic I jump the eight feet and land with a thump. I wedge myself into a sitting position in the tight space between the tower wall and the storage shed. My eyes search for hope. A faceless shape stands on the other side of the fence. The blackness of the watery night conceals me in my cramped hiding place. He says something in my direction that the heavy rain drowns away. I can't understand what he says. I say nothing in return and close my eyes. He moves closer as if he can smell my fear. My feet push hard into the back of the shed to smother a jerky spasm of twitches that scream to be freed.

After a few agonizing seconds of silence I force my eyes open and look into the darkness. The faceless man is not there. I exhale a deep, relieving breath. He's gone. I get on my feet and shimmy out from behind the shed. I can see the car's headlights shining away from me through the trees that separate the tower from the street. Then I hear the sound of a car door opening, I'm delighted at the possibility that my escape is close at hand. I relax and breathe a long, deep breath. My reprieve is interrupted when I notice a light flickering and dancing towards me.

He is returning.

This time he has a flashlight.

Desperate to scream, my voice is throttled by a suffocating fear. I fight back tears and nausea. The strobing light reflects the rain cascading in sheets. Trapped inside the fenced area, I confront the reality that I'm left with just one option now.

I don't like ladders.

I don't like heights.

But I figure it's my only chance.

I feel for the ladder and nervously climb a few steps. My legs are wobbly and my footing unsure. My courage, if I had any to begin with, evaporates like mist in the dark moon of my nightmare. Soaked like a wet pig, I climb. One shaky rung at a time.

The rain beats down without a care whether I live or die.

I'm frantically trying to reach the top when the light reaches the base of the tower below me. It floods the fenced area searching for me. With every shaky reach for the next rung on the ladder I pray it will be the last, that my hellish climb will finally be over, that the top of the tower will mean the end of my nightmare.

I don't even bother to try and muffle my twitching, but focus instead on making each grip and step mistake-free. The light circles around the perimeter of the fenced area. I'm soaked to the bone. My Bulldogs jacket sags with the weight of a dead man's grip. It's still not enough to stifle my twitching.

If I don't win this race I could be dead come dawn.

I reach for the next rung and momentarily wave at the empty air, my balance wobbles, then my hand finds the ladder again, this time close to my chest.

I have reached the top.

The ladder bends with the shape of the domed top. I pull myself past the edge of the tower wall when I see the menacing beam from the flashlight spread out on the side of the tower just below me.

The light continues to search the ladder where I just was. I'm now practically lying on my stomach on the ladder as it tracks its way to the very top of the dome, almost certainly leading to where there is a small door that opens into the tower itself. I hope that I'm safely out of view from the probing flashlight, and stay where I am, the angle too great from below to see me up here.

The muscles in my arms and shoulders and legs which had ached during my arduous climb, pulse with relief as I lay on my chest catching my breath. I concentrate on keeping my shaky feet steady on the ladder.

This would not be a good time to slip.

I cannot see the car itself, just the glow of its headlights and the steady rain that spray through the light. Several more minutes pass and then a car door closes and the car drives away, its surrender heard in the whine of the tires as they splash on the wet pavement. I follow the car, searching for some clue or reason why I have been forced into this dangerous predicament. As the car passes a street light further up the road I notice that it's a dark-colored car.

The elation of my escape is tempered with the realization that my wretched journey is only half completed. I must now make it down the side of the tower. My descent is a nerve-wracking adventure, but one that's already won in my mind, as I have already accomplished the more difficult task of climbing to the top. In a pelting rain no less. Brady and Kat won't believe me when I tell them.

When I walk into the kitchen my mom is making my lunch for tomorrow. She gasps when she sees me soaking wet from head-to-toe, like one of Mr. Hopper's extinguishing victims. I feel like some putrid fish-boy that the sea has vomited up.

"What the heck happened to you? How come you're so wet?"

"It started pouring on the way home."

"You should have called. Dad would have given you a ride."

"Mrs. Hopper said she'd give me a ride, but I told her I was alright. It was only sprinkling. I didn't know it was gonna pour."

"Myles, you have to learn that it's okay to ask for help if you need it."

Lesson learned. Next time I will.

Once I'm showered and changed into dry clothes I send a text to Brady and Kat. I let them know that the dark-colored car and the mystery man have reappeared once again. This time chasing me through the neighborhood and up to the top of the water tower.

Brady: u the man
Me: thx
Kat: why was he following u
Me: don't know
Kat: he wants something
Brady: hes looking for the body 2?
Me: maybe
Kat: u should tell ur parents

Me: no way

Kat: should we tell the police?

Brady: no way

Me: hes following us though

Kat: this is scary

Brady: police wont help - they dont believe us

Kat: what r we gonna do

Me: find out who that dead man was

CHAPTER NINE

Monday, September 15th

To help offset the cost of going to Lake Placid, each person on the hockey team has been given a stack of raffle tickets to sell. When my dad gave me mine he added, "Let's hope these get put to good use and you get to play." I hope so too. In fact I'm counting on it. Not wanting to encounter the dark-colored car and its mystery driver alone, we decide to work together to sell our raffle tickets.

Brady comes winging down my driveway with his Bulldogs hockey jersey flapping in the breeze. Mr. Hopper made Jake put Brady's bike back together again. It may have taken Jake only thirty minutes to take apart, but it took him all weekend to reassemble. In one motion, Brady skids the bike sideways and jumps off, nailing the landing. Everything is a performance with Brady.

"I thought it would be cool if we all wore our Bulldogs jerseys. You know, we'll probably sell more raffle tickets if people see us in our hockey uniforms."

"That's a good idea, I'll go get mine." I run into the garage to get my hockey bag off the shelf. A few years ago my dad built this huge wooden shelf thing he calls a *bag caddy*. It has a shelf for his hockey bag, even though the only time he plays is once a year in the *Never Was, Never Has Been Tournament*, Dennis's bag even though he doesn't play anymore, and mine. When I pull mine off the shelf it feels much heavier than it usually does, like something is in it that shouldn't be.

I waver with several fidgety twitches as I unzip the bag, afraid of what I might find. If not a body, then maybe an arm, or a head. Though I don't see any body parts, I do find several pairs of socks and about a half-dozen sweaty t-shirts that my mom's been looking for. I have to dig through about twenty mostly-full water bottles to find my jerseys at the bottom. That explains why the bag is so heavy. I toss the bottles in the recycle bin and throw my home jersey on. Right away I wonder if this is a good idea. After all, I was wearing my Bulldogs jacket last night when I was chased up the side of the water tower. The logo, a bulldog biting a hockey stick in half, is like a bullseye on my chest. Over here! I'm the kid you're looking for! I throw it on, anyway.

"Your shirt's all wrinkled. What'd you do, put the thing in a blender?" Brady says.

"And it smells like roadkill," Kat says.

"What? Who cares. At least people will know we're real hockey players, they'll be able to smell it."

"Suit yourself. I guess it's better than smelling like fish," Brady teases.

"Funny."

"Where should we start?" Brady says.

"I have to get my shirt, so why don't we start with my building," Kat says.

Aunt Betty is vacuuming the living room. She stops the vacuum and smiles at us. "What are you guys doing here? Hey Brady, it's good to see you."

"Hi, Mrs. Labbee," Brady greets my aunt. I think Brady feels uncomfortable around my aunt because of some of the stories that Kat tells us about the fights she and her mom have. But every time we see Aunt Betty she's always friendly.

"My gosh, Myles, you must be a foot taller than me. You get bigger every time I see you."

I force an uneasy smile. Being taller than some adults makes me feel awkward, like I've done something I'm not supposed to. Kat doesn't even bother to say hello to her mom. She just hurries to her bedroom looking for her hockey shirt.

"So what are you kids up to? Look at you guys all decked out with your hockey shirts on. Are you hungry? I can make sandwiches if you want."

"No thanks. We we're just stopping by for Kat's jersey," I say.

"We're gonna sell these raffle tickets to people in the building," Brady says, holding his pile of tickets like it's a wad of cash.

"Oh, that's right, you guys are going to Lake Placid this season. Should be fun."

"It'll be awesome. Coach says every team gets to play at least one game in the 1980 rink."

This means nothing to my Aunt Betty so Brady explains, "It's where the US beat the Russians in the most famous hockey game ever. They even made a movie about the game."

"Well you kids sure are lucky you get to do things like that."

"Do you want to buy a raffle ticket Mrs. Labbee?" Brady says.

"Thanks, but I'm sure I'll be buying some of Kat's tickets."

"Yeah, but her tickets won't win any of the prizes - but, mine will," Brady says.

"Oh yeah, what are some of the prizes?"

"First prize is four tickets to a Bruins - Canadiens game. Plus there are autographed sticks by some of the Bruins players and a signed jersey by Patrice Bergeron."

"Sounds good, you should have an easy time getting people to buy your chance tickets, plenty of Bruins fans around here and they'll love seeing you guys wearing your spiffy Bulldogs jerseys."

Kat strides into the room wearing her jersey and looks like she's ready to keep going right out the door until Aunt Betty stops her. "Hey, what's the rush? I haven't seen you since you got home from school."

Kat stops and draws in a deep sigh before replying, "We just came here to get my shirt, not to visit, Mom."

"Don't forget, you got homework you have to do." Aunt Betty, sensing Kat's impatience, turns from Kat and glances at Brady and me. "The boys were just telling me about the raffle tickets and all the prizes. Did I ever tell you kids the story about the time I sold a raffle ticket to the President?"

"You sold a raffle ticket to President Obama? I didn't know that," I say.

"No, not President Obama, President Reagan. This happened when I was a little girl."

"The President of the United States? How'd you do that?" Brady says.

"Our school was having a fundraiser for something. It may have been to build new science labs or something like that, I forget. I'd go out and canvass the neighborhood everyday after school. By the end of that week I'd sold maybe $50 worth of raffle tickets, that was a lot of money back then. Well, the next week was April vacation and I spent the whole $50 on movies and food and some pretty jewelry that I liked. When we returned to school, everyone had to turn in any unsold tickets, plus the raffle tickets they did sell with the money. Of course, I didn't have the money, I'd spent it all."

"Oh my gosh, mom," Kat says. "I can't believe you'd do that!"

"What'd you do?" I say.

"I turned in the unsold tickets, that was no problem. Then I turned in fifty ticket stubs, but as I had spent the cash, I had filled the stubs out with President Reagan's name on them and the address for the White House. I explained to my teacher that the President doesn't carry any cash with him and he promised he'd send a check."

"No one believed you, I hope," Kat says.

"My teacher, one of the nuns, Sister Elaine, asked me if it were true that I had sold raffle tickets to the President and reminded me about how lying is a terrible sin. I told her that it was true. She asked me how it had come to be that I had sold these tickets to the President. I told her that my family had been visiting relatives in Quebec City in Canada during April vacation. And my Uncle Doug was the Chief of Police and had arranged for us to briefly meet with President Reagan while he was there for a summit with Brian Mulroney, who was the Prime Minister of Canada."

"Geez, mom, we don't have any relatives in Canada, do we?" Kat says.

"Not that I know of, but I'd seen the news on TV about the summit meeting. I don't know what possessed me to lie like that, but I did. I suppose...."

"But aren't you always saying how wrong it is to lie?"

"I know, but I was young, perhaps fifth or sixth grade. We never had much extra money to do things, and all my friends would invite me to the movies and we'd go to the mall afterwards. I wanted to have the same fun they were having. So I used the raffle money."

"Did you get in trouble?" Kat says.

"I sure did. Once my parents found out what I'd done they had to pay the school the $50 themselves. They made me work to earn that money back. I did the dishes, scrubbed the floors, dusted, folded laundry - you name it, I did it all - for six months. Kids don't always know how harmful a lie or a practical joke can be. For me it was a painful lesson. But one I'll never forget."

Much to my annoyance and despair, Aunt Betty looks at Brady and me like we've made off with her fifty bucks ourselves. I shiver with a twitch that escapes like a shoplifter sneaking out of a store.

Kat's condo complex is a gold mine and not just because we sell a bunch of raffle tickets, but also because I learn some new things. Although most people aren't home when we ring the bell, the times that someone has come to the door they're usually friendly and generous. Or old and lonely.

Kat's neighbor, Mrs. Hennessey is delighted to see three kids at her door all wearing hockey jerseys. After she feeds us big bowls of ice cream we learn that her son played hockey when he was younger. Back then kids played hockey with no helmets and no mouthpieces. Also, instead of using plexiglass to go around the top of the boards, they used chain link fence. The only time I ever see chain link fence is at the zoo to keep the animals in their cages. The way she describes old-time hockey it must have been like survival-of-the-fittest. Of course she's a Bruins fan so she buys five raffle tickets from each of us.

Another lady, Mrs. Rivera, is ecstatic to see us and gets us hanging a bunch of old black and white photographs in dusty frames for her. She insists that the church has sent us to help her, even though we tell her that we're not from any church but are hockey players. Instead of ice cream, she thanks us with a series of prayers that makes Brady and I giggle. We spend twenty minutes hanging pictures of the woman's long dead relatives while she tells Kat all about her arthritis. At least she buys three tickets for our time and trouble.

We get two no-answers in a row and are having no luck with number three when the first door we rang finally opens. The man is wearing a shirt that looks like one of those paper napkins at a Thanksgiving table. He doesn't seem too happy to see three hockey players standing in the hallway, but he invites us in, anyway. Huge wrap-around sunglasses hide his eyes and practically cover his whole face. His head is small and wrinkled like a dried-up prune. Stiff gray hair that's combed-over covers his bald head. He's stumped over and shuffles to the center of the room with the coordination of a three-legged dog. He falls into a big recliner chair and when he does, it pushes his shirt up, exposing a plastic bag underneath. One that has something brown inside it. I notice it, but don't say anything. But Brady does.

"Hey mister, you got something stuck under your shirt."

"It's not stuck. So what do you kids want?"

"We're selling raffle tickets. Our hockey team," Kat points to her Bulldogs shirt, "is going to Lake Placid for a big tournament. Do you want to buy some tickets?"

"Is that bag supposed to be there?" Brady asks.

"When are you going to Lake Placid?" the man says, ignoring Brady.

"Thanksgiving weekend," Kat replies.

"What's that bag for?" Brady asks.

The man sighs. "It's a colostomy bag. You ever seen one of these before?"

"No. What's it for?"

The man lifts up his shirt and pulls the bag out some, so we can see it better. It's nearly full with what looks like chocolate cake batter.

"You see this brown stuff?" We all look at the contents of the large bag and a tube that seems to disappear into his midsection. "Take a guess what it is."

I consider what it might be, but nothing comes to me.

"Looks like it's one of those nutrition sports shakes, or something," Brady says, uncertain of his answer.

The man shakes with a deep laugh, making the brown sports drink swish around in the bag. "Well, no, it's not a sports shake or anything else you'd want to drink, that's for sure."

"Well, then what is it?" Brady asks.

"It's my poop."

A curious smile sneaks across my face. Brady and Kat beam, incredulous that anyone would walk around with their poop in a bag.

"Really!?" Brady says. "What's it doing in that bag? How'd it get in there?"

"I had colon surgery last year, so that means I can't go to the bathroom like I used to, like you kids do. Now when I have a bowel movement it goes from my large intestine, right into this bag. That's what the tube is for. What do you think? You want one, too?"

"Naw, that's alright, I kinda like going to the bathroom the old-fashioned way," Brady says.

"I've heard of those," Kat says. "My mom's a nurse and she takes care of people who have these things."

"Where's your mom work?"

"Clinton Medical Center."

"That's where I had my surgery. What's her name?"

"Betty Labbee."

"Oh yeah, I know your mom. I was in the hospital for a few days, and she took care of me for part of my stay. She's very nice. You guys live in this building, right?"

"Yeah, downstairs."

"What do you when the bag is full," Brady says, pointing to the bag.

"Oh geez, what'd you know, it's full. Well, then it's time to empty it. You kids want to help?"

So we help Mr. Marcantonio, learning in the process how to empty poop from a colostomy bag. Besides not wanting to be a plumber and cleaning other people's toilets, the other thing I'll add to the list is being a nurse. Mr. Marcantonio is so grateful for our help that he buys five tickets from each of us and tells us that if he wins any of the raffle prizes he'll give them to us.

At this point we've each sold thirteen tickets, not a bad start. Being as we're on a roll we decide to keep going and work the building in the back and down the hill, Building F. It's Brady's idea to start on the lower level. The building is much older than Kat's. It reminds me of the boarded-up shed by the river, but without the boards. We follow Brady down a flight of stairs into a coffin-narrow corridor that reeks of burning oil.

My shoulders strain with a twitch that warns of more trouble to come. Kat and I trudge behind Brady to the last door on the left. The concrete floor is littered with newspaper shreds, broken fragments of an old beer bottle, and an assortment of dead insects. A small, brass nameplate on the door reads: Property Manager. A few more twitches rumble through me, a reminder, as if I needed any, that this dark, enclosed space is making me very uncomfortable.

Kat fidgets nervously next to me before voicing her own concerns, "This place is creepy. Why don't we go upstairs? Or better yet, leave. We've already sold a bunch of tickets."

Enjoying the creepiness of all this, Brady replies, "No way. This is cool. The property manager owns all these buildings - he must be rich. I bet he buys a bunch of tickets, you'll see."

Sucking down a deep breath I try to smooth the rough edges of my anxiety. Brady raps the door with his bony knuckles. The sound of feet scuttles from behind the door. A moment later the deadbolt springs loose, snapping loudly. The door creaks open revealing a man with a scowl scratched into a face marked with deep craters. A face only a mother could love.

"What are you kids doing here?" he growls in a smoker's voice.

I begin to form the shape of an answer, but it's Brady who replies, "We're selling raffle tickets...sir," his voice shaky.

"Who gave you permission to disturb people in this building?" the man says, his cabbage-face unable to hide his displeasure. None of us respond. He leans toward us, his face just inches from ours. Deep creases stretch out like a spider web over his face. The smell of cigarette smoke seeps into my nostrils causing me to cough. My shoulders twitch. A sloppy twitch, like a runny egg.

"Huh?" he says, through teeth that are as dirty and grimy as an oil rag.

"We're just trying to raise money for our hockey team," Kat stammers.

"Her mom," Brady points to Kat, "lives in 'A' Building."

The man reaches into his shirt pocket, removes a cigarette from a pack, lights it, and blows the smoke in our faces.

"She does? What's your name? What's the unit number?"

The smoke sets off a sequence of twitches strung together, one after the other, that bedevil me.

"What's wrong with you kid? Can't you relax? Why do you have to be like that?"

I manage to gasp out, "Like what?" My shoulder clicks like I'm a giant Pez dispenser.

"Like that...that's what I'm talking about. What's the matter with you kid?"

Now I'm twitching away like I've been possessed by a spirit, an odd one at that...how embarrassing.

It occurs to me that if I can't get my twitching under control I'll soon download a whole program of twitches, one miserable twitch at a time. Slipping towards an anxiety attack, I look for an escape route and begin replaying last night's ESPN Top Ten Highlights in my head.

Brady comes to my defense. "He has a condition. It's not his fault."

"Ahh, I see," the man says, though he clearly doesn't.

Then suddenly he seems perplexed, like he has some untold message to deliver.

"You boys live around here, too?"

"Sort of. Over behind McFarland," Brady says.

"You the same kids I see snooping around over by that parking lot?"

This unexpected pronouncement stuns all three of us. My mouth goes dry. That same fear from the night of the tower thickens in my throat.

"You know you kids shouldn't be messing around over there, don't ya?" He points at us with a hand whose five fingers are crooked and twisted like corkscrews.

I nearly collapse under a barrage of shrugs and crunches. My eyes, fluttering in a spasm, water up. The man studies me closely like he's gonna draw my portrait. Tobacco stains are dried across his teeth. His black, cavernous nostrils flare open as he takes another drag on his cigarette. The stain-colored smoke hangs in the air like a foul mood. Then his face changes from one of intimidation to one of recognition.

"I've been looking for you kids. Wait right here." He turns and steps back into his office to retrieve an object from the corner of his desk.

A flashlight.

Its familiarity screams at me like a howl from beyond the grave.

I don't to wait to find out what happens next. I bolt down the hallway as fast as I can. The sound of Brady's and Kat's footsteps racing behind let me know they didn't wait either.

"Great idea, Brady. You almost got us killed!" I shout, annoyed that I was talked into another of Brady's misguided misadventures.

"What are you talking about? What'd you run away like that for?"

"That guy was really scary, Brady. We shouldn't have gone down there," Kat says.

"You guys don't understand. Last night when someone followed me home from your house," I poke my finger into Brady's chest, "the person was driving a dark-colored car. The same kind we saw at the ghost house the other night."

"What does that have to do with this guy? Do you know what kind of car he drives?" Brady says pointing back towards F building.

"No, but last night when I climbed the water tower, the guy went back to his car and got a flashlight. A big one. Did you guys see what was on his desk?"

Brady and Kat shake their heads.

"A flashlight. A big one. The same kind the man had last night."

Brady's and Kat's eyes grow wide as they take it all in. They turn and look back at the building and the door we just made our hasty retreat from.

"I think the guy who's been following us may be that guy in there," I screech with what my dad calls an Irish whisper.

"Are you sure?" Kat says.

"I don't know, but what I am sure of is that he owns a huge flashlight and he knows we hang out down at the river. And he doesn't like it."

Not taking any chances we race back to Kat's place, our raffle-selling adventure coming to an end.

Having a routine helps with my anxiety. It doesn't have to be a rigid, minute-by-minute routine, but as long as I know what to expect I can prepare for it. The three of us have been friends for so long that we know what to expect from each other. That's why the riverbank is so awesome. Was, anyway. I could hang out there all day without stressing about something crazy happening. Lately though, we've had to scrounge up fun in other ways. And it's been fun. Mostly. But all these crazy, unpredictable things have wreaked havoc with my anxiety.

One of our most important routines is dinner. Mom cooks a hot meal almost every night of the week. We'll order pizza or Chinese once in awhile, but during the week Mom makes a point to cook. Tonight it's one of my favorites, stuffed peppers.

"How's school going?" Dad says.

"It's alright."

"You keeping up with homework?"

My chest tightens. "Yeah, so far. They give us a lot of homework, though."

"You think you have a lot now, wait til' eighth grade," Dennis says.

"Easy for you to say, you don't even have homework."

Dennis is about to say something but Mom gives him that look. "You're doing fine, Myles. Just keep track of what you have to do in your agenda book and make sure you bring home everything you need. And then everyday after school, just get it done. When you keep up with it, it's no big deal. You're doing great so far, honey."

"Yeah, but, it takes such a long time. Plus I have writing assignments and book reports. Plus the homework. It's too much."

"You'll survive. Just remember what Mrs. Thompson and Mr. Curtin said, once you've been working on something for more than thirty minutes, just stop. If that happens, I'll write a note. So don't worry about it."

"You never told me I could do that!" Dennis shrieks.

It's Dad's turn to give Dennis the look. Changing the subject he says to me, "What'd you learn today?"

I have to think about what I did in school today, which is something I try to avoid once my homework is done. Dad digs into another bite of his stuffed pepper as he waits for my answer. Finally, remembering the stinky breath of that cabbage-face man, I think of something, "In health class, we learned that people shouldn't smoke, it's really bad for you."

"Well, that's worth learning."

"If people know that smoking causes cancer and kills them, plus it smells and tastes so bad, why do they do it?"

"I don't know. I've lived a lot of life and I gotta tell you that along the way you learn a lot, you figure some things out; but even after more than forty-five years I still haven't figured out why anyone would smoke. That, Myles, I don't have answer for."

Changing the subject, Mom says, "Have you kids still been going down to the riverbank?"

I fidget before responding, "Nah, not really."

"Why not, I thought you kids loved hanging out down there?"

I look away from my mom. I glance at Dad, who looks at me, waiting for an answer.

"We do, it's just that we've been busy, since school started, plus, you know..."

Mom smirks at me. "Well, you kids haven't been around much, what do you do all afternoon? Where have you been spending your time?"

My back heats up like someone is ironing my shirt while I'm still wearing it. Despite this, I try to answer as casually as I can, "We've been hanging out by the water tower."

"Since when do you hang out at the water tower?" Dad says.

I don't answer, but Mom does, "It wouldn't have anything to do with that whole dead body business, would it?"

"I just don't feel like going down there, to the riverbank, that's all."

"Can't say I'd be too enthusiastic about hangin' down there myself if I'd found a dead person," Dennis blurts.

"There's nothing to be afraid of. There was no dead person, okay?" Mom says.

"What's to do at the water tower?" Dad says.

I shift in my seat, "Nothing, really. It's just nearby and a place to hang out without anyone bothering us."

"I hope you guys aren't doing anything stupid over there," Dad says, pointing his fork at me.

"Such as what?" Mom says.

Dennis's eyes twist into a grin.

Dad cuts into his food and takes an angry bite. "Like climbing the water tower."

I can't prevent a very noticeable eye-flutter, a double one at that, followed by a powerful rib crunch that causes my chair to scrape on the floor.

"Myles! You're not climbing that water tower are you? You know how dangerous that is? You could kill yourself if you ever fell off the thing!" Mom howls as Dad glares at me.

No way I'm gonna tell them about last night. That's just the monkey business that'll end my hockey season. "No." But I say it so uncertainly, and my parents stare at me so coldly, that I feel the need to say something. Quick. "Brady climbed up the ladder a little ways. Not a big deal."

"Oh my god!" Mom wails, her fork drops on her plate with a loud ping. Dad shakes his head and gives me that look. The kind that doesn't need words.

"He's a good climber. We climb trees down at the riverbank all the time. Nothing happened, he didn't go that high."

"I'm letting his mom know. And Aunt Betty, too. No more water tower for you guys. You hear me."

I can only hope that Brady hasn't told his mom about my dangerous but necessary climb up the tower. Kat hardly talks to her mom, so I don't have to worry about her.

After dinner I send a text to Brady warning him about tonight's dinner conversation. He doesn't get in trouble, but he's been told that the water tower is off-limits too. Now what'll we do?

I grab my book, *Something Wicked This Way Comes*, and slump into bed to read. Reading is the one thing that usually relaxes me when I'm as agitated as I am right now. But dinner got my twitching all fired up. Reading is impossible at the moment. I reach into my pocket and take out the ring which reminds me that I haven't heard from Jogesh since I sent him that text. It's time to check in with him.

Me: what did ur mom say bout ring?
Jogesh: she duznt know - sorry

Jogesh's reply is disappointing. My chance to learn the meaning of the ring and find out what happened to that dead man is slipping away. So is my opportunity to prove myself to the St. Michael's coach. I'm also dimly aware that the cabbage-face man may be the person who chased me up the water tower.

Is he after the ring?

A minor moment of worry enlarges into an hour of panic.

Is he after me?

CHAPTER TEN

Tuesday, September 16th

I forgot to check the newspaper last night, so when I see it on the kitchen counter I scan the headlines for any news about the discovery of a dead body. Coming up empty with that, I next try the weekly police log.

Having read these for the past week or so, I'm amazed at what some people are crazy enough to do. From time to time I'll show my dad videos that Brady sends me. Weird hockey shirts aren't the only things he's good at finding online. He has a knack for scouring the far corners of the internet for videos of people doing things I would never dream of doing myself. Mostly because I make it a point not to hurt myself.

Like one guy who tried jumping off of a building into the back of a moving pickup truck, except he missed and landed butt-first on the pavement. Another kid lays on his skateboard, and bare-chested goes screaming a thousand miles-an-hour down some street. It looks pretty neat until he hits a crack in the road and goes flying off his board and scrapes along the pavement for about twenty yards. All the skin tears right off of him. He was left looking like a slimy turkey. My dad just shakes his head and says something like, "I often worry that someday the world may run out of oil, or it may run out of clean water, but when I go to bed at night I sleep well knowing that the one thing the world will never run out of is stupid people."

I suppose he's right. Today's log doesn't disappoint: a bus driver reported seeing a male place something in a sewer using tongs. A woman reported a $3,000 gold ring missing while getting coffee at a donut shop. An 86-year old woman fought off a knife-wielding robber at a convenience store. A house was egged on Clover Hill Drive. There are maybe a dozen calls for Animal Control about dogs barking or wandering without a leash, plus a half dozen reports of suspicious vehicles, but no details are provided.

The last item is a caller who reported a dark-colored car acting suspiciously on Winn Street. That's near here. But, there are no details and unfortunately, no stories about dead bodies.

Smelling my dad's cologne from upstairs reminds me that I haven't smeared the cod liver oil on my lips yet. My plan has been working and much to my relief the whole fish incident from last week has been mostly forgotten by everyone at school.

My locker is still a hassle to open, but I've managed to keep up with homework. Except for that first assignment from Mr. Curtin, I haven't forgotten anything else. I should feel good about myself and school, but if history has taught me anything, it's that school is never easy for me - especially when it seems like it is. That's why my neck and shoulders tighten into an uncomfortable twitch when Mr. Curtin announces that we'll begin reading a book together as a class, *Where the Red Fern Grows*.

The picture of a sad-looking dog on the cover does little to excite me. But I like to read, so I'll get through it. Knowing how much Kat hates to read I look over to see her reaction. The first thing she does when we start a new book is flip to the end so she knows what her prison sentence is. She buries her head into her chest when she realizes 225 pages of pure drudgery have been hung around her neck like a hangman's noose.

"This is an awesome book and you kids are going to love it," Mr. Curtin gushes.

"Pleeeeaase! Why do teachers say things like that when they only read the book themselves because they're paid to?" Kat says, not one bit shy about voicing her displeasure.

Mr. Curtin laughs.

"What's the book about?" Jogesh says.

"It's about a country boy, Billy Colman, about the same age as you kids. The story is about his adventures growing up in the Ozark Mountains."

"Sounds boring," Kat says.

Mr. Curtin shakes his head, smiles and laughs again.

"Nowadays, you kids need permission to go *outside*; when I was a kid we needed permission to go *inside* the house. We'd be kicked out of the house early in the morning so our moms could clean. Later in the afternoon when I'd be hot, tired, and hungry I'd come home to find all the doors locked. I remember banging on the family room window where my mom would be watching soap operas while she was cleaning. I'd yell through the window: "'mom, I'm hungry and thirsty, can I come in and get something to eat and drink?'" - "'if you're thirsty go get water from the hose around front'" - "'mom please, can I come in?'" - "'no, go away, I'm cleaning, go play somewhere'" - "'but, mom, I'm hungry'" - "'I'll let you know when it's time for dinner.'" It's true. We needed permission to get into the house. What you kids need to do is get off the video games - they turn your brains to mush."

A couple of boys snicker.

"I mean it. If you feel some drippy, oatmealy stuff coming out of your ears - that's your brain turning to mush. Things sure have changed. Nothing boring about being a kid and being outside all day."

I wonder if Billy Colman lives near a river. I wonder if he finds things in plastic bags.

"Where are the Ozarks?" Brady says.

"The Ozarks are in the midwest, covering most of Oklahoma, Arkansas, and Missouri. It's probably the finest hunting country in the whole world. And did you know that Mr. Curtin once spent two glorious weeks in the Ozarks when he was fourteen years old?"

Is there anything this guy hasn't done?

"This is a true story. When I wasn't reading Hemingway, Fitzgerald, or Steinbeck, I loved reading *Baseball Digest*. In the back of the magazine were dozens of ads, many of them for baseball camps all over the country. One that caught my interest was the *Mickey Owen Baseball School* in Missouri. I saved my tip money from my paper route for an entire year to pay for the camp and a round-trip bus ticket to get me there and back."

"How much did it cost, Mr. Curtin?" Patriots-boy says, wearing a long-sleeve tie-dyed shirt with a Patriots logo across his chest.

"If I remember, it was about $350 for a two-week camp. It was another $200 for the bus ticket. That was a lot of money back then. The challenge I had was my younger brother. We shared a room and I often left my tip money on top of my bureau. You can't imagine how many times I'd see Scott around the house pigging out on candy, ice cream, soda, he always seemed to be eating some kind of thingamajig food that my mom would never buy us herself. I'd ask him, "'where'd you get that from?'" He'd just say, "'I got it, that's all.'" And I'd say, "'where'd you get the money?'" He'd answer, "'I have my own money.'" I'd tell him, "'Yeah, and I was born last night. You've been taking my money.'" Naturally, he'd deny it, but I'd recount my money and sure enough some of it would always be missing."

"Yeah, my brother sneaks into my room too and takes my things all the time," Mario, a Bulldog teammate, says.

"Then you know what I'm talking about. I had one of those brothers too, and his name was Scott. That's why I started putting all my tip money, nickels, dimes, quarters, and the occasional dollar bill into these long tube socks that were popular back then. The room I shared with Scott had a walk-in closet and inside the closet were stairs that led up to the attic. One of the steps was loose. I could actually remove it. Inside the step it was hollow - and that's where I hid my socks full of money."

"Did Scott ever find the money?"

"Nope. I'm sure he snooped around looking for it, but he never found it. As the tube socks filled up, I mailed a letter to the camp requesting a brochure and an application. I remember flipping through that glossy brochure with those beautiful color pictures of the camp, all the baseball fields, the cabins, batting cages, and the mess hall - it was baseball heaven. I'd imagine myself there, on those perfect green fields, playing baseball from sunup to sundown. When I showed my parents the brochure and told them that I wanted to go that coming summer, they asked me how much it was. "About $500" I told them. They just shook their heads and told me they couldn't afford it. I told them, "'I have the money, I've been saving.'" Of course, they didn't believe me. I mean how many kids do you know have $500 in cash hidden away, you know what I'm talking about? I ran upstairs, opened the hollow step, and lugged about five huge tube socks bulging with coins and bills downstairs, and dumped them onto the kitchen table. My parents couldn't believe it, and neither could Scott. I went to that baseball camp and had the best two weeks of my life.

"At one time or another we all want something badly. Badly, enough that we'll do whatever it takes to get it. I want you to interview a parent, or preferably, a grandparent. Have them share with you a time when they were younger, perhaps your age, and they worked hard to save their money for something important to them. Make a short video of their story and how you might use the lesson of their story in your own life. This is due on Friday."

Now it's my turn to feel like a noose has been hung around my neck - another assignment!

As I'm unlocking my bike from the rack, the door swings open, crashing the brick wall behind it. It's Jogesh.

His round face breaks into a smile when he sees me. "Hey, Myles."

"What's up Jogesh."

"Nothing, really. You going home?" He pauses and waits for my reply.

"Yeah." I can't tell what he's after, but suspect he wants to come over and hang out. Recalling that he lives at Cedar Gardens, I ask him what he knows about the property manager, but he's never met him before.

Jogesh begins unlocking his bike then turns and says, "I almost forgot. When I showed my mom the text you sent me about the ring," my eyes widen, hoping for good news, "she didn't know anything, but my dad said he'd look into it. He wanted to know if you could send him a picture of it."

It's discomforting to be carrying around something that someone wants real badly. And that person may be a killer. Plus, that something is something I took. I don't intend to keep the ring. I'll give it back. Maybe. I just want to know what it's for, what the meaning is behind it.

I hesitate, considering my options and how best to answer this. I don't want anyone knowing that I actually *have* the ring. Sending a picture would be an admission that I not only have the ring, but that I also *stole* it. From a dead guy. Who according to my mom, the police, and everyone else, doesn't exist.

"Yeah, I'll have to see. I'll have to ask my grandfather, next time I see him if I can take a picture of it."

"Okay, I'll see ya." Jogesh jumps on his bike and pedals away, leaving me alone and unsure what to do about this ring in my possession.

Mom isn't happy when I tell her about Mr. Curtin's assignment. Being an organization freak she hates waiting until the last minute to do anything. Reminding her that the video project isn't due until Friday does nothing to calm her. Luckily, Grammy is at home and happy to help. Mom throws me into the car and we speed off for Grammy's house.

"You can't wait until the last minute to tell me about these things, Myles. It's not all about you, you know. Now I have to drop what I'm doing and bring you over there and then go get you later. I'm too busy for this!"

"I didn't wait until the last minute. I just got the assignment today at school. If I'd waited to tell you Thursday night, that would be waiting until the last minute."

"How long is this gonna take?"

"I don't know. Shouldn't take long, maybe an hour."

Mom's rattling on about everything she has to get done before dinner. Much of what she says I ignore, distracted as I am thinking about what to do with the ring. Did the person who killed the dead man come back to get the ring? Would they kill me for it?

Grammy is pulling the meat off the bones of a boiled chicken when I sit at her kitchen table. She places the shreds of meat into a large bowl that includes carrots and onions. She's making chicken and rice with gravy - one of my favorites.

"So what's this project thing you have to do?"

"We're supposed to interview a grandparent about a time when they worked hard and saved their money for something they wanted really bad."

I get my phone out and start videoing Grammy's response.

"What's with the phone? Why you pointing it at me?"

"It's a camera phone, but it can take video, too."

"There's a video camera in your phone?"

"Yeah, I have to video the interview for my assignment."

"That so. Boy, the gadgets you kids have these days."

"It's no big deal, Grammy. So, what was it you saved up for when you were younger?"

"Well, lots of things. My folks didn't have much money to be buying things for us, such as your fancy camera phone. If there was something you wanted, you had to find ways to work for it. Then you'd have to save your money. Nothing was given to us, that's for sure."

"And what'd you save your money for that you really wanted?"

"When I was about your age I wanted a really nice camera, too. Not one of those dime-store Brownie cameras, although those things weren't cheap. No, what I wanted was a real good camera, like something a real photographer would use."

"What'd you want a camera for?"

"My best friend, Joanne, had invited me to join her family on vacation one summer. They always went someplace nice, and this particular summer they'd rented a place on Cape Cod for two weeks. I wanted the camera to take pictures while I was there."

"How much was the camera?"

"It was about a hundred dollars. May not sound like a lot, but it was. Plus I'd need film, and I'd have to pay to have the film processed, and I wanted to buy a nice photo album to display all the pictures. For me, two weeks on the Cape was like heaven, the trip of a lifetime. I wanted to make sure I had my own money to really enjoy it."

"What'd you do to save the money?"

"I got a job working as an aide at a nursing home. I made-over the bed sheets, changed bedpans and diapers, helped feed people who couldn't feed themselves, and read to the patients. Or I'd just talk to them. That's what I did mostly, just talk to them."

"You changed diapers?"

Grammy laughs. "Some people, when they get older, can't control their bowels, so they wear diapers. And just like babies, they need to be changed."

"Guess what, Grammy? I learned how to change a colostomy bag yesterday. That's sort of like changing a diaper, but not as gross. I guess."

"You did? Well, good for you. It may be a bit messy, but who else is gonna do it? You get used to it after a while."

"Did you like working there?"

"I did. It was nice being around people that appreciate what you do for them. I made many good friends while I worked there and learned so much. That's where I learned how to sign."

"How to what?"

"Sign, you know, like sign language."

"You know how to do sign language? I didn't know that. Can you say something in sign language now?"

"Sure. Let me think. It's been a while, I have to remember. Okay, how about this." Grammy moves her hands and arms mechanically, hesitating once in awhile, trying to remember something she hasn't done in a long time.

"What did you just say?"

"What I signed was a question I just asked you."

"And what was that?"

"What is it that *you* want more than anything in the whole world?"

The car ride to hockey takes about twenty minutes. I always sit in the front seat and Kat sits in the back, usually listening to music on her iPod. Tonight she's in a world of her own, with both earbuds firmly planted in her ears, her head nodding to an invisible beat. My dad lowers the radio. It's time for another chat.

"How's school going?"

Grammy's sign language question got me thinking about Lake Placid, and hopefully, someday, playing hockey at St. Michael's Prep. The thought that just one mistake, a momentary lapse in judgment, like going along with one of Brady's crazy ideas, or even just one 'C' in school, has had me sizzling and crackling a marathon series of shoulder shrugs and rib crunches all afternoon.

"Alright, I guess."

"You guess? Is there anything giving you trouble"

"No. Not really. Well, everything. Well, not everything."

Dad waits while my stomach boils with the right thoughts and words to express my fears and frustrations with school.

"I got this writing assignment in Mr. Curtin's class, and I'm not sure if I'm doing it right. Probably doesn't matter anyway, I stink at writing and it'll probably get a bad grade, like always."

"I'm afraid I'm the wrong person to ask for help with writing. Why don't you stay after and ask Mr. Curtin to help you with it?"

"I did. He helped a little. But I'm still the one who has to write it, and I'll just mess it all up."

"You'll be fine, don't worry about it, I'm sure it doesn't have to be perfect. It's okay to make mistakes, you know. You don't want to make the same mistakes over and over again, but making mistakes is how we learn."

"That's easy for you to say."

"What, you think I don't make mistakes?"

"Doesn't seem like it."

"Everyone makes mistakes. You may not remember this, but we used to have a tree over on the side of the house that was leaning towards the deck. Your mom wanted it cut down. She was afraid that one big storm and the tree would smash onto the deck and ruin it. But, I didn't want to spend the money to hire someone to cut it down. Against your mom's objections, on a Saturday morning, on your birthday actually, I decided to cut it down myself.

"It was all going fine. I was making my cut so the tree would fall towards the woods, not the deck. But when I made the final cut, it started falling towards the house, which I hadn't expected. It just barely missed the house, and the deck, but it caught the electrical wire that runs from the telephone pole on the street to the side of the house. It ripped the main electrical line right off the house, meaning we now had no power, thanks to me.

"As if that wasn't bad enough, Mom had just taken a shower, her hair was soaking wet, and she was just beginning to blow-dry her hair. And your birthday cake, an ice cream cake, no less, was melting because the freezer had no power. You see, we had all these people coming over for your party.

Your mom can't dry her hair, the ice cream cake is melting, all the food in the refrigerator is getting warm, and we have no lights. Nothing. Boy, was your mom mad at me. And boy, did I feel like an idiot. I'd messed up big time. But, I learned from that mistake. From now on when we need a tree cut down, I call a professional."

"Wow! I'm surprised Mom didn't kill you!"

"Oh, she wanted to, believe me. But, hey, we all make mistakes. That's how we learn. In fact, one of my favorite quotes is: make errors of commission, not omission."

"What does that mean?"

"It means first, that it's okay to make mistakes. Unfortunately, many kids today are taught that it's wrong to make mistakes, but it isn't. Second, that when you make mistakes, and you're gonna make them, let the mistake be that you tried something and it didn't work, rather than, the mistake you made is you should have done something, but you did nothing. You see, if you try something and it doesn't work, you can learn from that... what worked well...what didn't work so well. We learn from mistakes.

"But if you should have done something, but instead, did nothing, then there's really nothing to learn from that. So, don't be afraid to try things, to take some chances, it's okay to make mistakes as long as we learn from them."

As my dad's voice rings its truth in my ears, a secret sits in my pocket making itself known.

"That's why you should get Mr. Curtin to help you with that writing assignment. Your mom and I are serious about you getting a good report card - all A's and B's - you hear?"

The ring squirms like an unkept promise.

CHAPTER ELEVEN

Wednesday, September 17th

Knee hockey is a passion that brings out my inner Patrick Kane. On a rainy afternoon we have a fast-paced 3 on 3 game going in our family room. However, the game ends when Mario's mom comes by to pick him up along with two other Bulldog teammates. We're resting on the family room floor, rehashing some of the spectacular saves Brady made when my mom asks us to go get a hand-mixer from Kat's apartment.

The apartment is a two-bedroom unit on the ground floor. A narrow kitchen, lined on both sides with counters, cabinets, and appliances, is immediately to the right of the front door. Stepping into the kitchen, the first thing I notice is a fist-sized blob of peanut butter sitting on top of the counter.

I'm surprised to see it there. "What the heck!" I shout.

Brady and Kat squeeze into the kitchen with me. We look up to see that besides the mound on the counter, peanut butter has also been splattered all over the cabinets. It looks as if someone opened a full jar, dug out five fingers full of the stuff and then just sprayed it all over the place.

Kat is stunned. Brady is speechless. I'm spooked. Someone has been here and done this. Either that or we're dealing with another ghost, one that has an issue with peanut butter.

"Who did this?" Brady says. "Did you do this Kat?"

"No! I haven't been home since I left for school this morning."

"Did your mom do this?" I say, hoping for a plausible explanation. One that doesn't include ghosts.

"Myles, seriously. Do you think my mom would randomly throw peanut butter all over the kitchen and just leave it?"

"I suppose not."

"Well, someone did this," Brady says.

"Or something," Kat says, her voice trembling.

"Maybe a mouse got into the peanut butter and made the mess," I say.

"I don't think so. Do you see the jar anywhere? And how do you explain the peanut butter on the ceiling?" Kat says, pointing above us where more brown splotches of peanut butter are spattered in a linear pattern, as if someone with peanut butter running in their veins, was shot. I've seen enough TV shows to know that what we're looking at is a grisly crime scene. But one with brown peanut butter instead of red blood.

The only thing missing is the victim.

No one is saying the obvious. Too afraid of the possibility.

Without warning, Brady begins taking pictures of the evidence with his phone. The camera's flash illuminates the clumps of sticky mess and the splattering drops that seem to have exploded all over the kitchen.

"This time I'm taking pictures. I should have done that the last time," Brady says. "This time everyone'll have to believe us."

Not taking any chances, I do the same. Kat too. Bright flashes of light record the remnants of the ghostly prank. Satisfied we've taken all the pictures we can, we slither out of the kitchen to search the rest of the apartment for any other evidence.

At the apartment's center is a sizable living room with a sliding glass door that leads out to a small pond overrun with geese. Brady steps into the room looking for the presence of an intruder, ghostly or otherwise. He tries to open the slider but it doesn't budge. "It's locked."

"Was the front door locked when we got here?" I ask Kat.

"Yeah. I needed the key to open it."

Off the living room is a short hallway that leads to the bathroom and two bedrooms, one on each side. We follow Brady into Aunt Betty's room.

Her room has a slider that also leads out to the pond. He checks the slider. That too is locked.

We cross the hall into Kat's room. Her room has the only window in the apartment. Brady checks the window. Once more another point of entry is shut tight. Back out in the hallway, I look at the bathroom door. I'm surprised to see that the light is on. The door is slightly ajar. As if someone went in to use it, but didn't close the door behind them. The muscles in my shoulders skid into my neck in rapid shrugs and flinches. Brady shoves me with his elbow. "Can you just calm down and relax for once?" When someone hears the expression 'calm and relaxed' I'm not someone you think of.

"If you haven't noticed, the light's on in the bathroom," I whisper.

"Yeah, so? I'm not afraid of ghosts like you yellowbellies" he replies.

"Only my opinion, but you'd be smart to be afraid of them," I answer.

Brady, once more ignoring the dangers, is clearly in denial about the risks, like a five year old surrounded by clothes and toys and declaring that his room is clean. None of us can know what's on the other side of that door. But that doesn't stop Brady from kicking the door open.

The bathroom is empty. But, Brady isn't satisfied. He steps into the bathroom and swings the shower curtain open to make sure there's no one there. Much to our relief, the shower contains nothing but several bottles of shampoo, a grungy bar of soap, and an assortment of other shower items. Relaxation eases into my shoulders and everything is back in place again. Then my phone vibrates. The text is from my mom: where r u?

We race back to my house in a misty rain. As we had once before, we barrel into my kitchen with bizarre news of another ghost encounter. My mom is sitting at the kitchen table getting work done on her laptop. She listens to our description of what we found at Kat's house. Her expression is one of disbelief and waning patience with what seems to be another of our made-up antics.

Showing her the pictures we took does nothing to convince her. Her eyes watch me like something smothering, suffocating, and suspicious. That thin ice I'm on is getting thinner by the minute. I remain silent as I consider the events of the past week. The sound of the door opening means my dad and Dennis are home from work. My mom trudges over to greet them, carrying with her the weight of dead people and ghosts, and gives my dad a kiss.

"What's going on here? Why's everyone look so tense?" Dad asks.

"You're here just in time, honey. Myles was just telling me about another ghost sighting."

"Another one?"

"This time over at Kat's house," Mom says, smirking.

"A little early for ghost sightings, wouldn't you say, Myles?"

"I know it sounds crazy, Mr. Walsh, but it's true." Brady's fingers supply the evidence, which he shows my dad.

"Where's the ghost? I don't see any ghost in these pictures. I just see a kitchen that needs to be cleaned," Dad says, smiling at his own joke.

"We didn't *see* the ghost, Mr. Walsh. But we saw what he did. Look. See all that brown stuff on the cabinets and ceiling? That's peanut butter! And the ghost did that!"

My dad chuckles. Not the reaction Brady was hoping for.

"Mr. Walsh! It's true," Brady says, irritated with my dad's lack of belief. Now he knows how I feel.

"Why would a ghost wipe peanut butter all over a kitchen?" Dad says.

"Maybe it thinks one of us has a peanut allergy and is trying to kill us," I say.

"A peanut-allergy-killing ghost! Now I've heard it all. Myles, your stories used to be so good. They were always off-the-wall, but lately they've obtained the wonderful Irish gift for fantasy," Mom says.

"This is serious Mom. I think there's a ghost following us."

"There's no ghost and even if there were, it wouldn't be killing anyone with peanut butter. None of you are allergic to nuts," Mom says.

"Well, none of the kids are, but I used to be," Dad says.

"You were allergic to nuts? I didn't know that," I say.

"I was. In fact, I almost died because of it. A long time ago when I was on a school field trip in Washington, D.C."

"Really? What happened?" I say.

"I was in the eighth grade and our school went to Washington for a field trip. It was the last day and we were having lunch in the food court at the National Air & Space Museum. Hundreds of kids from all over the country were there on field trips, too. I had a reaction called anaphylaxis, which can be life-threatening. I didn't personally eat any foods with peanuts in them, but the people around me must have. I was affected either by cross-contact, or someone who was eating a peanut product who touched me or the table where I was eating."

My dad pauses to take a deep breath before continuing his story.

"I was having trouble breathing. It felt like someone had placed a rope around my neck and they were squeezing it real tight. I began to panic. I couldn't see my teacher anywhere. She always carried an epi-pen just in case of an emergency. And this was an emergency and sure enough she was nowhere to be seen."

"What did you do?" I say.

"Fortunately for me, a guy was standing nearby and noticed me struggling to breathe. He had an epi-pen that he administered right away. He saved my life. They called an ambulance which took me to the hospital to make sure everything was okay. Grampy and Grammy had to drive all the way down to D.C. to bring me home. It was a close call, though. Too close."

"I never knew that. Did you ever find out who the man was?" I ask.

"Not really. It all happened so fast."

"You're kidding. You never found out who saved your life?" Kat says.

"The only thing I found out later was that he was a teacher. But no one thought to ask him his name or where he was from. He was just one of those people who was in the right place at the right time. He saved my life then disappeared. A simple case of serendipity, I suppose," Dad says, using a word I'm neither familiar with or know the meaning of.

"I've never heard that story before," I say.

"I'm not allergic to peanuts anymore. Luckily, I outgrew it. But I've never forgotten that person, at least what he looked like anyway. So, no I don't believe in ghosts, but I do believe in heroes."

Aunt Betty made the mess. She was using the blender to make a diet shake when it practically exploded, spraying peanut butter everywhere. Then the property manager called to complain that us kids have no business peddling raffling tickets to people - there's a policy against soliciting at Cedar Gardens. He also told my aunt that he'd better not see us over at the old public works parking lot anymore. That there's a Keep Out sign there for a reason. Aunt Betty had to get ready for work, but she couldn't get cabbage-face off the phone. Running late, she left the mess just as it was. She forgot about it until Kat sent her some pictures at work of what we found. So much for my theory of a peanut-allergy-killing ghost. The reward for my story is once more finding myself in hot water. Water that I've stupidly boiled myself.

My other reward is having to help Kat clean up the mess. The stress of the day's events has scraped away the glue that holds me together. I feel like pieces of me are coming undone and that their shape has changed and won't fit back together again. The warmth of the afternoon has faded away and the chill of a wet evening tingles my arms. I pick up my bike and hop on, eager to get home as soon as I can. Cars zip by on Weston Drive making me wait to cross the busy road. I glance down the street to the gravel drive where we found the dead guy. A car pulls out from the parking lot entrance where the storage shed is. Light rain glistens in its headlights. It crunches over the loose gravel of the driveway and stops. My shoulders burst into a twitch that rattles my bones.

What's a car doing in there? I've been standing here for almost five minutes and I haven't noticed anyone pull in there. Even if someone drove in there by accident they'd turn around and come right back out realizing their mistake. The car was in there for a reason. They may have dumped something in there. Either that or they're looking for something.

Or someone.

There's a break in the traffic and the car pulls out. It makes a left turn and heads toward me. I don't waste anytime and head up the hill for a place to hide. Pushing my bike slows me down. I dump it. Then scurry behind some small shrubs that circle the Cedar Gardens sign. I crouch down and use the large sign for cover. Hoping the car will pass in just a few seconds, I'm surprised when it instead slows down. It's right signal light flashes and it pulls into Kat's apartment complex.

The dark-colored car.

I flatten onto my stomach to avoid being seen. My chest tightens, and breaths come in short bursts. I'm wet and cold laying in the rain-soaked grass. From beneath the sign, all I can see are the car's tires. It slows to a crawl as it seems to consider which direction to go. I peek around the corner of the sign to see who the driver is. To see if it's the man with the stained teeth and smoky breath. The car's windows are as dark as the night. Its driver concealed in the darkness.

He takes a right towards Kat's building.

Unsure of what the man's intentions are, whether he's heading back to his office, or if he's driving around looking for me, I can't decide whether to run for it once he drives out of view, or not.

So, I do nothing.

As each second goes by I curse myself for hesitating. Why do I always have to be so afraid of everything? Why can't I be like Brady? He isn't afraid of anything. The car stops and idles near the entrance to Kat's building. After a few moments, it backs into a parking space facing Kat's front door. The engine goes silent. Expecting the driver to get out, I'm surprised when several minutes pass by and no one exits the car. That's not good.

Silence.

He waits.

I wait.

Thirty minutes later I'm soaked and freezing. And running out of options. My mom sends me a text asking what's taking me so long. I let her know that I'll be home soon. I hope, anyway. I need to do something. Reaching the point of desperation, I decide to make a run for it.

I slither away from my wet but safe spot, leaving my bike behind. Then I slither down the shallow embankment towards the edge of the road. Tires squeal behind me. Waiting until the traffic slows I dart out between two cars, just making it across the street. I look over my shoulder. The car is moving towards the exit. At first the busy traffic prevents the car from following me, but soon enough, it too, makes it across the street.

The race is on.

I dash in behind someone's house and run in the direction of home cutting through people's backyards. The darkness of the night gives me the cover I need to reach my house. I stagger to the back corner, gasping for air. Knowing my mom will be suspicious if I use the back door, I try to catch my breath before walking in the front door. I wait. A few moments later the car appears, driving slowly, like a cat on the prowl. I give the car's trunk a good look and wonder if I'd be in there right now if I hadn't acted sooner. Or run faster.

CHAPTER TWELVE

Thursday, September 18th

I texted Kat when I got home last night that I'd left my bike over at her place. Lucky for me, it was right where I left it. I wish I could say the same for the dead man we found. My Aunt Betty was kind enough to drive my bike over in return for her hand mixer. Glad to have my bike back, I lock it up then hear Jogesh clatter up to the rack. His chubby face fills his safety helmet to its limits. The strap pulled tight under his chin makes him look like he has two of them. He smiles and greets me with a friendly hello.

I'm uncertain how to ask Jogesh about the ring, again. I hate to pester anyone, least of all someone I hardly know. After another encounter with the mystery driver of the dark-colored car, I'm well aware of the seriousness of my situation. Recent events have me more anxious than ever to learn the ring's truth. And right now Jogesh's dad is my best hope of learning anything about the object I snatched from the dead man.

"Your dad find out anything about that ring?"

"He thinks he may know what the ring is for. He's just not certain that what you have is the real thing. He was hoping you could send him a picture. He'd like to see what the ring looks like. Did you ask your grandfather, yet?"

I hesitate before answering. "I don't see him all the time. But maybe the next time I do I'll take a picture and send it to you."

It's disappointing that the description I texted to Jogesh hasn't been more helpful to Mr. Dhruv. I don't have the luxury of being careless with this. I've got to decide how willing I am to play with fire. The last thing I need is to have this thing blow up in my face. What if Mr. Dhruv told my parents about the ring? That would be just the thing to keep me from playing in Lake Placid.

I've settled into a comfortable routine at school. I can tell because I'm mostly twitching when I'm at my locker or walking in the hallway between classes. I don't seem to be attracting anyone's attention, and that's just the way I want it. The beautifulness of the ordinary - that's what I strive for.

In English class Mr. Curtin hands back a grammar quiz we took yesterday. I'm crushed to see that I scored a '72.' I can just feel my chances of getting a 'B' slipping away.

At least he gives us time to work on our writing assignment. I'm glad because it gives me a chance to sort through all the things that have happened since our strange discovery. I take out my graphic organizer and look at my list of the unusual things that have happened. I add a few new ones that have occurred in the last few days, then try and make sense of it.

Every story has a beginning, a middle, and an end. Having lived through some of the details on my organizer, it's easy enough to figure out the beginning and most of the middle. The only part I'm not sure about is how my story ends. A feverish twitch trembles through my shoulders and into my chest. I look around to see if anyone notices. Everyone is busy writing their own stories. A part of me wishes I could write their stories - made up and harmless.

Mr. Curtin ambles over beside my desk. He peers over my shoulder and reads what I've written so far. "Myles, I think you have, so far, the most interesting story I've seen. Your intro is very good, makes me want to read more - good job!"

"Thanks." My chest swells into a grin and my anxiety slides off me like rain on a roof. This is the first time a teacher has ever complimented me on my writing before. For me, writing has been something to be avoided, like going to church. But this story is different. Unlike before, the pieces are coming together. It's helping me figure some things out. I just hope I'm around to finish it.

"I'm serious, your writing shows a real talent for storytelling - that's a gift, you know. I told you."

After lunch I chase down Brady and Kat to tell them more about the appearance of the dark car at the riverbank, how it parked right outside Kat's door, then once more, chased me through the neighborhood.

"What do you think, Myles?" Brady says.

"I don't know what to think. I don't exactly have much experience with finding dead bodies and trying to hide from killers. Do you?"

"You sure someone's been following you? This isn't another one of your stories, is it Myles? After all, he only seems to be following you," Kat says.

"No! I'm telling you, someone has definitely followed and chased me - it's no story."

"What are we gonna do, then?" Brady asks.

"I think we should call the police and let them know," Kat says.

"No way. My mom already warned me about sending the police on any more goose chases. My goose is cooked as it is. Besides, do you think the police are really gonna take me seriously when I tell them that a dark colored car, one that I don't know who's driving, by the way, at least not for sure, has been cruising around the neighborhood looking for me? C'mon, I'll be in even bigger trouble than I am now."

"We need to do something. This isn't funny anymore," Kat says.

I feel the ring's weight in my pocket and its burden on my shoulders.

A ring snatcher - that's what I am.

Have I done something crazy? Or, have I done something stupid?

When school ends I meet Brady and Kat in the hallway outside Mr. Curtin's class. We walk in together as if we're in trouble for some unnamed offense. Mr. Curtin looks up from his desk and seems surprised to see all three of us.

"What's up? What do you guys need?"

I take the lead. "Can we talk to you about something?"

"Sure. What is it?"

"You know how I told you we found a dead body?"

"Yeah, did you kids find out what happened with that?"

"Not yet. But ever since we found that man, all these weird things have been happening." I twitch. An irksome twitch like an untied shoelace.

"What kind of weird things?"

I fill Mr. Curtin in on the odd things that have frightened and worried us for the past two weeks. A silence settles around us when I finish rambling.

He leans back in his chair and places his hands behind his head. His forehead crinkles into a patchwork of creases. "What did your parents say when you told them all this?"

"Our parents don't believe us, and if we go to them with more stuff that they think we're making up, we'll be in even bigger trouble," Brady says.

"My mom's told me that if even one more little thing happens I won't be able to play the rest of my hockey season. Unless I get all A's and B's, I can't play in Lake Placid for my tournament! We need to find out who that dead man was and what happened to him. We need your help Mr. Curtin!" The words spill out, tinged with desperation

"Let me think...it sounds to me like you guys may have a couple of clues about who that poor man may have been. It isn't much, but it's more than nothing. It sounds like all these things have happened right in your neighborhood, more or less. I'd start there. Ask around, see if anyone else might have information about that family that used to live in the house where you say you saw a ghost. You never know where it may lead."

I exchange glances with Brady and Kat. Our minds arrive at the same thought.

"Of course, in the meantime, I'd keep your eyes open. Both of them. And your ears too. Be aware of who and what's around you. And if you see that car again, promise me that you'll tell your parents and the police?"

"We promise. Thanks, Mr. Curtin," I say.

"By the way, Myles, that object you brought in for science, where did you get that from?"

"Over in the parking lot by the riverbank. Why?"

"Do you know what it is?"

"No idea. What is it?"

"Mrs. Glennon didn't know either. She showed it to me thinking I might know. It's what's called a deck prism. They were used on old sailing ships, like that ship in Boston Harbor, *Old Ironsides*. The prism would reflect light down below deck where it was dark. It was safer than using candles which could start a fire - never a good thing on a ship. Deck prisms provided light so the captain could see while writing in his captain's journal. It's curious that you picked it out."

Brady and I wait outside while Kat runs in to get her hockey jersey. Within moments we hear shouting coming from inside. Aunt Betty is upset because she received an email from the school that Kat hasn't been turning in her homework assignments. She doesn't seem to learn that it's easier to just do the work, no matter how boring it is, than to deal with all the grief and fighting that happens when she doesn't do it. Brady and I trudge back to our bikes dejected that our plans for the afternoon are dashed.

"She won't be coming with us now, that's for sure," I grumble.

There's an unexpected lull in the screaming and I twist out a lazy shoulder shrug.

"It sounds like they stopped," Brady says, with a glimmer of hope.

"I'll send her a text."

- u coming

A few seconds later my phone buzzes with her response:

- giv me a few

I no sooner sit down on the front step when a grungy white pickup truck pulls in and parks in front of Kat's building. It looks like a pile of scrap metal. Several ladders are strapped to the top of the truck and the driver side door is caved in with a rusty dent. A man steps out and I immediately tense up. I look to see if it's the building manager with the corkscrew fingers.

It is.

Corkscrew fingers and all.

He doesn't notice us as he busies himself with unbuckling one of the ladders. When he finally gets the buckle loose he sees Brady and me sitting there like a couple of lumps on a log. He snarls at us, "Hey, you're the kids who ran out on me the other day!"

Brady and I take the cue and scamper away from his craggy face and crooked fingers. He shouts after us, but we ignore him and hightail it to my house.

"What's his story?" I say.

"You see his fingers?" Brady says, catching his breath.

"I don't know, man. But I don't trust him."

"I don't either, but if you noticed, Myles, that guy doesn't drive a dark-colored car. In fact, he doesn't even drive a car."

"Maybe he uses the truck for work and has a car that he drives home. I don't know. There's still something about the guy I don't like."

I text Kat, assuming she can still join us, to meet us at my house. I fish my jerseys out of my bag and give Brady my road jersey, keeping the home one for myself. Fifteen minutes later Kat shows up, but without her hockey shirt.

"You alright?" I ask.

"Yeah. Just the same old, same old. You know how it is."

"You sure it's alright to just cut out like this? Sounds like you had a big fight," I say.

"It's cool. She went to lay down. She's tired from working all day and I told her I'll do my homework later."

We leave our bikes where the walkway meets the road. The presence of the ghost house draws my attention. A kid's big wheel toy, a Nerf football, plastic lawnmower, and other items are scattered across the small front yard. The lawn has been mowed, and the driveway, although still in need of repair, has been swept and looks fresh and clean with a sporty family car parked in it. Curtains on the windows and a glimpse of furniture inside make it look lived in and cozy. A far cry from the menacing way it looked just a week and a half ago when Brady and a mystery man snuck around in its dark emptiness.

I get antsy when the neighbor on the left side of the ghost house isn't home. We ring the doorbell of the neighbor to the right twice with no response. Feeling agitated I release a flurry of twitches, but it does nothing to calm my frustration. I had high hopes that the clues we have might lead to something. But it sinks in that we're just kids; this is grownup stuff and we're dreaming if we think we can figure out who that dead guy was.

Plus, my mom said she'd kill me if she caught me poking around in other people's business. The operative word there being, caught. All three of us are headed back down the front steps to our bikes when we hear the doorknob rattle and the door squeak open.

"Can I help you kids?" It's the voice of an old man.

The man that greets us has stubby legs and the flat nose of a circus dwarf. His face resembles an old baseball glove that's been left out in the weather. A pair of friendly eyes flickers behind glasses overrun with eyebrows like a patch of chickweed.

"Hi!" Brady yells back. We shuffle back towards the kindly, old face standing on the porch. "We're selling raffle tickets to raise money for our hockey team. We're playing in a tournament in Lake Placid."

"I see that you two play hockey," the man says pointing to Brady and me. Nodding to Kat he asks, "Where's your hockey shirt?"

"I have one, but I forgot it at home," Kat replies, with a sheepish frown.

"She plays on our team," I say, letting the man know that we're legit.

"So you're one of them *girl* hockey players, is that right?"

"Yeah, I've been playing for seven years now."

"Is she any good?"

"She is. She's a real good skater," Brady says.

"Well in that case, come on in. I'll go get some money."

We step into the front entrance, a small foyer, with wood floors and big, thick moldings that serve as shelves. Small ceramic figurines of children engaged in a variety of childhood activities are displayed on the moldings. They appear to be Hummels. My nanna has a few herself, but this woman's collection is large and impressive.

"You kids wait here, I'll be right back." The man shuffles down the hallway and out of view into the kitchen. The sound of a game show blares from the family room on our left, although we can't see the television itself. The curtains are heavy, like winter blankets, and hang all the way to the floor. It's got the musty odor of a typical grandparents' house, one that usually induces me into a state of sleepiness. The same thing happens the moment I walk into a church. I can be running around the neighborhood with enough energy to burn for three people, but the minute I walk into a church, all I want to do is go to sleep.

The ghost house neighbor returns a minute later. He buys twenty dollars worth of raffle tickets, a real score for us, but not the main reason we trekked over here. It seems the chance to ask him the questions we came to for have passed us by when he begins to walk us out.

At the door, Brady halts and speaks up just in time, "Do you know if there are any kids our age that moved into that house?" He points in the direction of the ghost house.

"You mean next door? Nope. Just a little tike. A boy." He places his hands on the door waiting for our exit.

"That's too bad. We live a few streets over. It would've been nice if some kids our age had moved in." Brady's attempt to get the conversation going stalls and our chance is once again slipping away.

"My mom said she was the realtor that sold that house a long time ago," I blurt out, desperate to keep the door from closing on us.

"To these people?" The man gestures towards the ghost house.

"No. It was people from India that were living there. She helped sell the house for them."

"That was a long time ago, I forgot about those people," the man says, his shaggy eyebrows scrunching up like they're gonna sneeze.

"Do you remember what their names were?" I ask.

"What do you need to know that for?"

"It's just that my mom was talking about it a few days ago and she couldn't remember their names. I figured I'd ask, just in case you knew."

"I haven't thought about them for a long time. The people that just sold the house lived there for a few years and they had bought the house from a couple that were from out west, Texas I think. They're the ones that bought it from the Indian couple. I don't remember their last names though. Maybe my wife does."

The man yells in the direction of the family room trying to shout over the television, "Hey, honey, do you remember the names of the people that used to live next door?"

"What'd you say, Larry?" A woman's voice screeches.

The man walks to the family room entry and leans in. "Martha, turn the TV down for a second."

An annoying commercial that was blaring about cat litter is muted and a moment later the man's wife appears in the hallway. She's wearing a dress that reminds me of the shower curtain in my nanna's bathroom. She's taller than her husband and has spongy cheeks that crowd around her mouth.

"The kids here are asking if we remember the names of the people that lived next door, the ones from India. Do you remember?"

The old woman narrows her eyes and twists her lips trying to recall people she probably hasn't thought of in twenty years.

"They were nice people; he was a little odd, though, but nice. What were their names?" We all wait patiently. "I don't remember his name, but I think the wife's name was Sanjana. That's gonna drive me nuts now, that I can't remember his name."

"Do you know what their last names were? My mom found a thank you note from them and she has their first names, but she can't remember their last names, either."

"I can't say I remember their last name. Isn't that awful? They were neighbors of ours for many years and I can't even think of their last names. How about you, Larry, do you know their last name?"

"I have no idea. He was Amar, that I know. How about their son, what was his name?"

I look at Brady and Kat. I didn't know they had a son. My mom didn't say anything about that.

"They didn't have any kids. What son are you talking about?" the wife says.

"Yeah, they did. Don't you remember? He moved back to India, I think."

"Wait a second, they did have a young man that lived with them. He wasn't their son, though." It's the first thing the woman has said with any certainty.

"Well what was he then?"

Brady, Kat, and I watch in amusement as the two elderly people struggle to free memories from the cobwebs of their past.

"He was a relative. A nephew or something like that I think," the woman says.

"Was he a kid like us?" I ask.

"Oh no, he was much older, he was a young man. He was going to school here, college. I think he went to the university, or someplace like that. He was studying to become a teacher. Or a doctor. I forget."

"A doctor," the man interjects.

"How do you know, Larry," the woman says, dismayed that her husband remembers something that she doesn't.

"I just do, that's all," he says matter-of-factly.

"No. I think he was a teacher," she says, disagreeing with her husband.

"Do you know where he lives now," I ask.

"I think he went back to India," the man says.

"No!" the woman says scolding her husband and his poor memory. She herself struggles to recall facts dusted over with the rust of memories. "He moved away when he got a job. I forget where, though."

"We hardly saw him after that. It's gotta be twenty years or more since the last time we saw him."

"That's true. We haven't seen him in a long time. I don't recall that he came back to visit his aunt and uncle very much before they moved back to India."

"You wouldn't happen to remember his name at all, would you?" I ask, but not expecting an answer.

"Not a chance. We hardly even knew him," the man says. "He didn't really live there, he would just come to visit once in awhile, that's all."

"You're right Larry!" The woman seems pleased about this and says, "He lived at school, but he'd come to stay for the weekend once in awhile. That's the only time we'd see him. He was very nice, and very smart, too.

Gee, I haven't thought about him in years. I can't think of his name, in fact I don't know if we ever knew his name."

So much for that. It seemed promising for awhile. We still don't have a last name. I'd gladly trade the twenty dollars in raffle tickets for that information.

"Why do you kids want to know, anyway?" the old woman asks.

"My mom was just telling me the story about how the sale of that house helped my dad start his own business. But she couldn't remember the last names - it was driving her crazy. She'd like to send them a card. See how they're doing. That's all."

"What's the name of your dad's business?" the man asks.

"Walsh & Sons Plumbing."

"Sure. I see their trucks on the road once in awhile."

Even though they're nice enough to have given us their time, they aren't much help other than finding out that another person lived in that ghost house. Although, he hasn't been seen by anyone in more than twenty years. But, they do contribute twenty dollars towards our Lake Placid tournament, which is looking very iffy for me right now.

"It was nice chatting with you kids. I hope you have a good time in Lake Placid."

"Thanks, ma'am," I say, unable to hide my disappointment.

"If I remember the names of those people, I'll be sure to let you know. I promise."

I read the name written on the raffle stub: The Browns.

Brown feet.
A stolen ring.
Two ghost encounters.
A nameless relative.
Lake Placid.

I feel like I'm hanging on with my fingernails to the edge of a slippery slope.

CHAPTER THIRTEEN

Friday, September 19th

I know how the story starts, but I haven't figured out how it ends. Not yet, anyway. I've been using some of the details from recent events to fill in the gaps of my story. But the threat that future events could spiral into a muddy mess has me anxious that despite all the positive feedback from Mr. Curtin my writing assignment could still flop and not help me get the 'B' I desperately need.

I'm working on a scene in my story, when Brady walks over wearing another one-of-a-kind hockey shirt. The logo for this one is a frog holding a hockey stick, and it gives me an idea.

"Hey Brady. What do you think about going to the riverbank after school today?"

Brady looks at me like I've just asked him if he wants to play with the Boston Bruins.

"You serious?"

"Yeah. We haven't been there since.....well, since you know..."

"What do you want to go back there for?" Brady says, getting excited. "Look, it's fine with me, I'm all for it, but I'm surprised you'd want to, that's all."

"It's for the story I'm writing. I just need to see that spot where we found the guy in the weeds." Brady gives me a smug look. "To get some details for my story," I explain. He's not buying any of this. "Plus, I thought that while we're there we could look around a bit. Maybe we'll find something the police overlooked."

"How about Kat?"

"I'll ask her, but she got in big trouble after skipping out yesterday. I won't go by myself, that's why I need you to go."

Naturally, the opportunity for danger excites Brady. "After school it is."

At the end of class Mr. Curtin checks in with me. He picks it up my draft and reads it. His eyes dart from side to side and his lips move as he speed reads my draft. He places it down and taps my desk with his knuckles. "Looks good Mr. Walsh. You're making good progress." He bends down and whispers, "Speaking of progress, how's your own little investigation going?"

"Good. We interviewed the people that live next to that house we told you about, the one with the ghost."

"Were they able to help you at all?"

"Sort of. They didn't remember the names of the people who lived there, but they remembered that a nephew or a relative anyway, used to visit there once in awhile."

"That's something new that you didn't know before. Did they give you any other information? Like, what happened to the nephew?"

"They didn't know that either, but the woman, Mrs. Brown, thought he was going to college to be a teacher."

"Another clue. Sounds like you have made some progress. Good job."

"My mom was able to find out the first names of the people who used to own the house, the ones who moved back to India, but no one knows their last names."

Mr. Curtin bites his lower lip and creases his eyes. "If you could manage to get a last name then you could search online, and then there's no telling where that may lead."

That's all the hope and encouragement I need. After all, Lake Placid and my good name are riding on this.

My courage and enthusiasm sag when I walk in the door and see that Mom is home. That means no riverbank until homework is done. I text Brady letting him know that we have to delay our fact-finding excursion for about an hour.

While slogging my way through homework, I fall victim to a succession of twitches that tire me out completely. I begin having second thoughts about going to the riverbank. I'm kinda hoping that Brady will cancel. But a few minutes later he texts me that his dad will be home at four o'clock to take him to get a new hockey stick, but he can meet me after that. My resolve rebounds. This means I have to speed things up.

My twitches aren't anything I wanted, or asked for, or deserved. But they arrived one day anyhow, uninvited, like an annoying pop-up on a web page. Although I hate being the 'kid that twitches,' it has its advantages. A flurry of acrobatic twitches combined with a doomed expression gets my mom's sympathy and support. With her help, I figure it trims my homework time by at least thirty minutes.

The strangest thing about finding a dead body is how no one cares. I've woken up in the middle of the night terrified that the dead man is standing next to my bed. I have to fight off a panic attack every time I open something that's big enough to hide a person. Whenever I walk around a corner or enter a room I wonder who else might be there. Just the sight of a Ziploc bag makes my stomach feel like a dryer spinning around with two alley cats inside fighting it out. Images of the dead man and his stony face come to me in ways I can't predict. And as if I needed any other reminders that this is all real, a mysterious person driving a dark-colored car is looking for me.

And it probably isn't to buy raffle tickets.

While Brady and I bike down Weston Drive, people zip by on their way to buy groceries, or hurry to dance class, or to get a haircut. They don't have a care in the world. And yet, just days ago, a man was stuffed into a clear plastic bag and left off the side of the road like a pair of unwanted sneakers. No one is aware that a killer may be lurking right here in this neighborhood.

We leave our bikes at the edge of the gravel driveway. It feels like months since we were last here. I can smell the mudbank of the river. The tall weeds that line either side of the driveway skitter to a gusty breeze. Their frantic motion offers us a grim invitation to enter. I glance at Brady. His expression is caught between excitement and concern. I uncoil a pair of shoulder shrugs. We turn left with the bend of the driveway and leave the safety of the road and its passing cars.

The chirping of crickets and the small noises of the woods pierce the afternoon haze. The sun has hidden itself behind the trees, but it feels like it's getting hotter. We're met by the decaying Keep Out sign. Where it once was a minor annoyance that I ignored, I now stop and ponder its message.

"You sure about this?"

I nod my head, but I'm not sure about this.

"What kind of things do you need for your story, anyway?"

"Just stuff. Some details that describe the setting."

"Well, let's check it out."

Walking around the chain I feel like I'm sneaking into someone's backyard. My mother's voice warning me to stay out of other people's business wedges into my thoughts. Brady heads straight to the spot where we found the man in the bag. I follow close behind. My eyes twitch back and forth on the lookout for anything. The last thing I want to encounter is that cabbage face building manager.

"I think this is where the guy was. But it's hard to tell."

"I think this is it. You'd never know it, though."

The weeds and grass which had once been matted down by the weight of the dead body, now stand tall and as high as my waist. Brady ventures into the weeds, pushes them aside and kneels down. I walk in a few steps and kneel down beside him. I feel silly being here. There's nothing here and it looks as if there never was. It's like we're trying to find a ghost that doesn't exist. Brady sweeps his hands over the grass, inspecting the ground for anything that may have been left behind.

"See anything?"

"Nothing."

"There's nothing to find," I say, disappointed.

"There's gotta be."

"When we were here before there was that rice-ball thing, remember?"

"Yeah, but I threw it into the woods. Probably over there." Brady points in the direction where he had flung the wad of rice.

"I know, but there were other smaller clumps of rice around here too. I just showed you the biggest piece. I don't see any of that other rice."

"Maybe we're in the wrong spot."

"Let's look around some more," I say hopefully.

We scour the area that edges the woods and the path to the river-bank. We can't find a single grain of rice or anything else of interest.

"What do you think?" I say to Brady when we're satisfied we've covered every inch of ground.

"I think this confirms that someone came back here and moved the body. And they did a good job of cleaning up after themselves."

Neither of us can figure out why someone would go to the trouble of leaving a body here but then take it back. Unless.

"I was just thinking. Maybe someone else found the body after we did, but they decided to take it for some reason."

"Why would someone take a dead body? Besides, no one else ever comes in here, except us. Or that building manager guy, come to think of it."

"I don't know. We'll probably never know. The whole thing is just crazy."

Brady and I trudge back up the drive when something familiar catches my eye. The muscles in my neck twist into a knot. I grab Brady's arm, which he swings casually as he strides ahead of me. I motion my head in the direction of the old mangy couch sitting off a ways in the middle of the parking lot. The couch has been arranged with the recliner chair and TV to create the appearance of a spooky-looking family room. One inhabited by ghosts.

I see something.

A plastic bag.

The bag is tied into a knot as if twisted by the dead. That's not good. The bag and the knot hang off the couch's armrest. The back of the couch, with an orange and brown plaid design, faces towards us, concealing the remainder of the bag's contents.

Brady's eyes grow large. Mine twitch wildly.

"What the heck," Brady whispers.

At this point I don't know what would freak me out more, finding another dead body...or a live one. We look over the entire parking lot and its collection of forsaken items for any sign of movement, any sign of life. Our attention returns to the plastic bag when a gust of wind ripples it.

"What should we do?" I say.

"It's the dead man. Again."

"How do you know?"

"Are you serious? Get your head in the game will ya'. Of course it's the dead man. Someone brought him back here."

"Well, what should we do?"

Brady Hopper is not a kid who walks away from danger. He ignores me and walks in the direction of the couch. Once more I grab him. "We can stay here and call the police."

"I'm gonna do what I didn't do last time. I'm taking a picture." His eyes bear down on mine. "Plus, I want to see the thing one more time. C'mon, let's check it out." I gulp down a deep breath of air. There are those who fly and those who sink. Me - I walk on thin ice. Very thin ice.

We walk side by side, ready for anything. Every muscle in my body is constricted so tightly that I couldn't twitch if I wanted to. It's a struggle to breathe. Visions of the dead man's face crackle in my head. After a seemingly endless journey through a junk-strewn lot we're finally within view of the length of the bag, the identity of its contents still obscured by the back of the couch. Brady removes his phone and we look at each other one last time then take the final step.

What I see puzzles me.

It's not the dead man, least not the one we found before. It's someone, though, or rather, something. Brady is the first to put words to my own thoughts, "It's a stupid mannequin!"

It's an old department store mannequin. A man. A plastic corpse. It's bald and missing both arms. Its eyes, bright green, swimming in a circle of ultra white, appear to be smiling, mocking us, like the joke's on us. Its left shoulder bears a jagged hole where its arm once was. The plastic man lays motionless as if he's been the victim of foul play.

Flapping in the breeze is a note, stapled to the bag, hand-written in large black letters:

STAY AWAY!

"Where did this come from?" I say, unable to imagine that things could get any stranger than they have.

"Take a guess," Brady says, snapping pictures of the plastic corpse.

When I get back to my house I see Grampy's car in the driveway. My nanna and pappy live about thirty minutes away so we don't see them as often. But Grampy and Grammy live just a few miles away on the other side of Caldwell. They come over for dinner several times a month and afterwards they'll sit around and talk about where they've come from, and what they've seen, and the things they've done.

"How's hockey going, Myles?" Grampy says.

"It's good. I scored a goal last night and we won, so I think we're 2-1, now."

"Your dad tells me you're thinking about going to St. Michael's Prep. You looking to play hockey there?" Grampy asks.

"I hope so. They're the the best team in the state. I've been invited to play in an all-star game that all the prep coaches come and scout. The St. Michael's coach will be there - hopefully, I'm there."

"If you've been invited then why wouldn't you be there?"

"Yeah...well, Myles first has to show that he's ready to handle the responsibilities of going to St. Michael's. That means getting good grades. No more slouching off on schoolwork. And no more unnecessary visits from the police," my mom says.

"Don't worry, Myles can handle it. What's happening with that whole dead man thing, anyway?" Grampy says.

"Nothing, really." Although I'm tempted to show him the ring, I decide against it.

"Strange business I tell you. One minute there's a body there, the next minute it's gone. Thankfully nothing happened to any of you kids and the only thing you saw was a dead body. Not much harm he could've done," Grampy says, snickering.

"Of course, this is all assuming there was a dead body," Mom says. "Dead people don't just disappear. I called the police and they went down there right away and didn't find anything. You know how Myles likes to tell stories."

Grammy gives me a skeptical look and says, "What do you make of all this? Did you really find a dead body? You sure it was a real person you saw?"

"He was real. I'm certain of it."

"I hope this isn't some kind of game you kids are playing," Grammy says.

"I believe you Myles. You say you and your friends found a dead body, then you found a dead body. And that's that," Grampy says. "Sad business, though, I tell you. Hate to see anyone die, least of all the way this man did

- just left on the side of the road like no one cared about him. When someone dies, as time goes by, we lose little pieces of them. You know, things that we forget about them. Hopefully, this man remains in someone's thoughts. Afterall, he lived a nearly full life - his life means something."

Grammy rolls her eyes at Grampy who avoids further confrontation by digging into another slice of pizza. It's getting late, the room has darkened, so my dad gets up and turns on a light. My mom opens up another box of pizza which everyone takes from.

Grampy, who's smart enough to know when to stop pushing Grammy's buttons, changes the subject. "How do you like working with your dad, Dennis?"

"I love it."

"I remember when your dad was little, he wanted to come to work with me in the worst way. Would practically drive me crazy with it. Remember that Brian?" Grampy says to my dad.

"I do," Dad says, smiling.

"Your father had this little red fire truck that we bought him for his birthday one year. It cost $35. That was a lot of money back then, but it was something he really wanted and he'd been a good boy, so we bought it for him."

"I remember. I would jump in that fire truck and pedal as fast as I could to keep up with you as you drove off to work. I'd be yelling and crying, "slow down Dad, you're driving too fast, I can't keep up!" Then I'd go home and cry to Grammy that you didn't wait for me."

"Why'd you want to go to work with Grampy so badly?" Dennis says.

"I don't know. I guess I was kind of curious about what he did."

"Weren't you a salesman, Grampy?" I say.

"I was. For almost forty years."

My dad says, "Well, that's the thing. I used to ask Grammy what Grampy did for work. Other kids in the neighborhood had dads who were teachers, or electricians, things that were easy to understand for a little kid. But when Grammy would try to explain what Grampy did, that he was a salesman, it didn't make any sense to me. I didn't know what sales was or what it meant. I'd keep asking though, and I think Grammy got frustrated trying to think of a way to explain it so that I'd understand. So she finally just told me that Grampy made money. I took it literally. Meaning I really did believe that my dad *made money*, you know, like an artist, like Harry Picasso, or something." A wide smile spreads across his tired face.

"His name was Pablo dad, not Harry," I say.

"Oh my god!" Mom shouts.

"What is it?" Dennis says.

"I just remembered the last names of those people that used to own the house on Mountain Avenue."

My twitching re-emerges just as suddenly and forcefully as the memory of people long gone and long forgotten have come to my mom from nowhere.

"What people?" Dad says.

"What are their names?" I shout.

"While you were telling the story about your dad making money, I remembered the couple gave me a coin, a rupee I think, that's the money they use in India. They gave it to me as a souvenir. The man said that the rupee was given to him by his father when he left India to come to the United States." My mom rocks up onto her toes, her shoulders sag in relief, a wide smile creases her mouth.

"So...what's his last name?" I say. My twitching revs up like a fireworks display. Just get to the point Mom, please.

"I'd forgotten about that coin, it's probably packed away someplace," she says absentmindedly, the suspense killing me, "but anyway, their last name was Harakatha. At least, that's what I think it was."

"Hara...what?" I say.

"Harakatha. I'm not sure of the spelling, but I'll try. Give me a piece of paper and something to write with." Dennis races to the microwave where we keep note paper on top, then opens a drawer for a pen.

"I can't believe I remembered. That's been driving me nuts for days now."

The phone rings, distracting my mom as I wait for this valuable piece of information. Dad answers the phone and Mom hands me a slip of paper.

"I don't know why you need this, but remember what I said - don't be poking your nose into other people's business - you hear me mister?"

"Don't worry. Thanks, Mom!"

Grampy and Grammy look unsure of what this is all about.

"Who was on the phone, Brian?" Mom says.

"No one. They hung up after I said, hello."

Before the night is over the phone rings twice more. Both times the caller mysteriously hangs up without saying anything.

When my grandparents leave, I get online and start searching for anything on the internet for an Amar or Sanjana Harakatha. Typically a search for just about anything online returns thousands, if not millions of hits. Not this time, though. There mustn't be that many Sanjana or Amar Harakathas in the world. I get all of nine returns for an assortment of social media pages from what I guess is India. They're all written in an arabic script or language I don't recognize. None of the faces match the one I remember seeing inside the plastic bag. My shoulders sag in disappointment. I thought for sure the last name would turn up something.

But once more, a promising clue leads to nothing.

The last few nights I've been haunted by unsettling visions of booby-trapped closets and dwarf-sized clowns sneaking around the house at night unsettling my sleep. I wake with my bedsheets and blankets twisted in knots around me.

Something my Grampy said about losing the memories of someone when they die is lodged in my head like a small pebble in one's shoe. My frazzled nerves finally settle into a sleepy dream.....

I'm digging like my life depends on it, heaping big shovelfuls of dirt in every direction. The reason I'm digging is unknown to me, adding to my sense of aggravation. Digging without a sense of purpose I pace back and forth as the hole becomes larger and deeper. Even though my efforts seem helter-skelter, walls of smoothly shoveled dirt rise up higher and higher. I have been digging for hours with no end in sight. Or has it been minutes? I'm tired and confused. The pain of blisters slows my maddening activity. For the first time since I began, I stop to check my progress and discover that I'm standing shoulder high in a hole shaped like a long box. My attempt to scream is snuffed somewhere in my throat when I realize that I'm standing in a grave.

Perhaps my own.

Why am I doing this?

Instead of stopping, or trying to climb out, I keep shoveling. I want to stop, but someone, or some unknown thing is telling me to keep digging. Just when my hands feel as though they'll shred to pieces, the tip of my shovel strikes something stiff and wooden, its echo shudders an escape from the enclosed tomb. Relief and fear sweep over me. I get on my knees and use my blistered and bloodied hands to scrape the moist dirt away. A juicy worm slithers on top of a pile of dirt that grows with each handful I scoop. Then my heart stops. My back stiffens as if someone has just rammed an iron pipe right up my spine.

A scratchy plastic bag emerges from below the dirt.

A clear plastic bag whose contents are hidden in darkness. I feverishly scrape more dirt away. Raindrops splatter on the plastic bag. The dull sound they make on the plastic echo within the grave. The hairs on my neck feel the presence of another person. But I am no longer afraid and this confuses me.

My hands, browned to the bone with mud, search for a face.

I use the rainwater that has pooled in the creases of the bag to smooth the dirt away. I'm jolted upright when I see my Grampy inside the bag. My heart lurches. I rip open the bag to save Grampy, but it's too late. Tears spill out uncontrollably. I tear open the rest of the bag to free my grandfather from his ghoulish tomb and to give him what comfort I can. Enclosing my fingers into his, I'm shocked that his hand is still warm. And then confusion turns to curiosity when I feel the coldness of metal. A ring wobbles loosely on a bony finger. I beg to hear his familiar voice, but there is none.

It's just me and my Grampy.

I slide the ring off his finger and bring it close to my right eye to see what treasure I have unearthed. Before I'm able to inspect it, it's jarred loose when a grisly hand grabs me by the wrist.

Grampy's hand.

His grip is strong.

A death grip.

He struggles to lift his head. Strange, unfamiliar words are spoken in a peaceful voice that does not belong to him. The voice of another tongue struggles to tell me something about the ring.

'Everyone has a story.'

The unfamiliar voice and the peace it brings slides away as mysteriously as it arrived when I'm awoken by the barking of the neighbor's dog, barking as if someone is in the backyard.

CHAPTER FOURTEEN

Saturday, September 20th

In the morning I drag myself down to the kitchen. Last night was a rough one in the sleep department and what I need now is a sugary bowl of cream-of-wheat. My dad and I have this little battle going, ever since he got on his health kick after Grammy tried to wipe us all out.

In addition to his vitamins, cod liver oil, and prune juice, he swears by his oatmeal as a miracle food. As far as I'm concerned, oatmeal has the consistency of a mouthful of hocked-up spit. And cod liver oil? I'd rather drink my own you-know-what. The smell of prune juice makes my eyes water, and that's before you even take the lid off. On the other hand cream-of-wheat tastes great with a little milk and sugar. Plus it's loaded with iron, the kind that powers up one's red blood cells which gives a growing body strength and energy. Right now I'm in desperate need of both.

"You feeling alright, honey?" Mom asks when I make my sleepy entrance.

"I'm just tired."

"Why are you so tired? You better not be up late texting. If you are, we'll take the phone away."

"I wasn't texting."

"Probably that pain-in-the-neck dog next door. The darn thing was barking like crazy last night. Must have been two in the morning. Damn thing woke me up," Dad growls. I can tell he's grumpy because he hasn't shaved yet. My dad wakes up early every morning for work and even though he works most Saturdays, he likes to sleep in a little later than normal.

"I forgot to tell you, Brian, we had another one of those hang-ups this morning. Someone keeps calling here and then hanging up," Mom says.

"What's the number?" Dad says.

"It must be a cell phone, it just comes up as anonymous."

"Are your friends calling here and hanging up, Myles?" Dad says.

"No." Dad's expression tells me he doesn't believe me. "If my friends want to talk to me they text me or call my cell. I don't think they even know the house number."

"You have a girlfriend we don't know about then?" Dad says, but he seems more annoyed than humored by this.

"No!"

"Well, I don't know why someone would call here and then just hang up. It started last night," Mom says.

A cold chill sweeps over me as a thought creeps into the back of my head. The person calling here is looking for me. That means if it's the same man who chased me home from the Hoppers and to the top of the water tower..... he knows where I live. An unsettling feeling surges through me. The reality that this whole dead man thing isn't a game jolts me like a frigid wind.

With my heart racing I excuse myself and hurry to my bedroom. I close the door and retrieve the ring from the top drawer of my desk. This is what he's after. I want to believe it's just a family memento, like Mom's thank you card from the Harakathas. Something cherished that a person holds onto, a physical reminder of a favorite memory. But not something a person would kill for.

The ring must be returned, though.

And I've got to figure out how to do that without being killed for it the way the dead man was. Then last night's dream sears into my head. The intricacy and beauty of its design captivates me. Grampy's words echo softly, weakening my resolve.

Everyone has a story.

I just need another day or so to sort things out. The substance of a plan begins to form in my head. I won't leave the house today. We'll be leaving for my hockey game in a few hours and then I'll get Mom to let me sleep over Brady's house. I'll stay at Brady's all day tomorrow watching football and this time I'll let Mrs. Hopper drive me home. Monday, I'll be back in school where I should be safe. Mom and Dad will be at work, Dennis at school. This buys me time.

I check the daily police blog on my phone. As usual, there's nothing about the dead man. I try one more time searching the internet for an Amar or Sanjana Harakatha. I even try different spellings, thinking my mom may have gotten their names mixed up. But, same as before, my search leads nowhere. Feeling I've reached a dead end and worried that Lake Placid is slipping away, I dig into my pocket and roll the mysterious talisman onto my desk. I take a few pictures, then decide on one that shows all the important features with enough detail to satisfy Mr. Dhruv.

I send it.

As much as I see Aunt Betty, heck, she lives less than half a mile from us, and Kat and I go to school together, there's a lot more I don't know about her than I do. Sometimes it seems that even though she's there in the room, she's really off somewhere else. I've always chalked it up to Uncle Doug having disappeared a long time ago. That can't have been easy on her. But then again, she never talks about it.

Our dead man, I think of him as ours, because no one else has seen him, and no one believes us, either, is like Uncle Doug. He exists. He's out there somewhere, but no one talks about him. So I'm surprised when Aunt Betty, of all people, brings him up when we're all sitting around the kitchen table eating a big breakfast served up by my dad.

"Myles, do the kids at school ever ask you about that....person... you found?"

"Not really. They did at first, but not anymore."

"Boy, what a strange thing to stumble upon. Of all the things you might find, that's got to be the last thing I'd ever expect. A broken bicycle, or an old computer that doesn't work anymore, but a person, a human being. My gosh - that poor man. And not even that old. As my grandmother used to say, old age is a grace denied many."

I don't know what else to say other than to agree, "I know."

"It was awful, mom. You should have seen the man's bare feet inside the bag. They were all wrinkled and gross looking. It was creepy," Kat says.

"I don't know how you kids aren't having nightmares about it," Aunt Betty says.

"I doubt what they claim to have seen was a real person. But you must see dead people yourself once in awhile at work, don't you?" My mom says, getting up from the kitchen table where everyone is gathered, except for my dad. He's sitting at the peninsula so absorbed in the sports section that my mom has to ask him twice if he wants any more coffee.

"Sure. I have to say I'm mostly used to it now, but I remember the first time I ever saw a dead person I couldn't sleep for days after that."

"Who was it?" Kat says.

"An older man, a patient I had. It's kinda funny now, but at the time it wasn't the least bit funny. I had just graduated from nursing school and was working the night shift at the hospital. I worked on the medical-surgical floor, same as I do now. People come to the hospital to have surgeries performed for all sorts of things: gall bladders removed, bypass surgery, tonsils removed, or colostomies, like that Mr. Marcantoni. All sorts of things. When the surgery is over, we care for them while they recuperate. Unfortunately, some people don't recover; the sickness may have spread too much. Or the surgeries don't go well and they die."

"That's terrible! I don't know how you could work there. I could never deal with people dying all the time," Kat says.

"It's a fact of life. People don't live forever and as much as hospitals help heal people, sometimes people die in hospitals too. It's sad I know, but if you're going to be a nurse you have to learn to cope with it. I do."

I recall the conversation with Brady in school and the pictures he showed me. I'm trying to remember the word for the place where they put dead people in hospitals, when Kat fires off a bunch of questions.

"What do you do when that happens, Mom? What do you do with the bodies? Do the families have to put these people in their cars and drive them home?"

"No honey, that wouldn't be allowed. The bodies are moved to the morgue. It's usually in the basement of the hospital. It is, anyway, at the hospital I work at. The morgue is where people are kept until the families make arrangements for the wake and funeral. And that's what happened shortly after I started working there. A patient I was caring for, the elderly gentleman, passed away and I placed him on a gurney and wheeled him down to the morgue. I had never had a patient die on me before so this was the first time I'd ever been in the morgue by myself."

"What's it like?" I ask, beating Kat to the punch.

"It's a small room with the walls lined with what look like big metal drawers like on a bureau, but the drawers are metal and much bigger. They slide out just like a drawer in a bureau, except these drawers are more like table tops with no legs and they have bodies on them. Dead ones. And that's where I found myself at about two o'clock in the morning. All by myself."

"Oh my, gosh, you must have been scared out of your mind. If that were me I would have just rolled the guy in there and left him. No way I'd open any of those drawers," Kat says, pulling her legs and feet up onto her seat.

"I was scared, but I had a job to do. I knew from my training what I was supposed to do. When a person dies the nurse fills out a small tag with the person's information and ties it with a thin wire to one of the deceased person's big toes. It's called a toe-tag. I pulled open an empty drawer and carefully slid the man onto the drawer. They go in feet first on their backs, their head at the end of the drawer."

"And the guy's just lying there in his hospital gown?" Kat says.

"They're covered in a bed sheet, so you don't really see the person. Next, I grabbed the clipboard, walked down to his feet and began writing all the information off the toe-tag onto the morgue sheet. Mind you, I was creeped out. It was in the middle of the night. I'm in a room with no windows and who knows how many dead bodies hidden away in metal lockers.

"All I wanted to do was hurry up and get out of there, when suddenly the man sprung up like a jack-in-the-box into a sitting position. The bed sheet slid down off of him and he stared straight at me with his eyes wide open. Absolutely scared the heck out of me. I screamed and threw the clipboard and ran out of there like a demon."

"What happened? Was he alive?" Kat says.

"No, honey, he was dead."

"How could he sit up if he was dead?"

"It's called rigor mortis."

"Rigor, what?" Kat says.

"Rigor mortis. You see, when people die there's still all this heat in their muscles. The heat takes time to dissipate. When it does, different people can have different reactions, depending on how much heat was left in their body when they died. When the last of the heat leaves the body, the muscle will contract. When muscles contract, they move. For most people at the time of death it's usually just a small twitch that you may not even notice, even if you were looking. Or maybe their hand or a foot will make a jerking motion real quick and that's it. For others though, especially if there was a lot of heat left in the muscles, it can take longer and the contraction can cause a bigger movement. Like my guy who sat up into a sitting position. I thought the guy had come back to life, and wow, did that frighten me! I had nightmares for days after that."

No kidding, I had one last night.

"Speaking of dreams, I had one about Doug last night," Aunt Betty tells my mom.

As Aunt Betty is about to tell us her Uncle Doug dream, the door to the mudroom creaks open ever so slowly, as if some invisible person is trying to slip into the kitchen unnoticed. The strangeness of it silences Aunt Betty mid-sentence. Everyone, even my dad, look up in the direction of the door which is still moving.

Opening.

Noisily.

Slowly.

Creaking.

Opening.

Tension fills the room. Finally, the door, after it has opened almost all the way, comes to a stop.

Aunt Betty, attempting to lighten the tension, pretends to speak to the ghostly intruder and says, "Hey, look, if you don't mind, I was telling a story, can you close the door, please?"

BOOM!!!

The door slams as if the devil himself had shut it.

Chairs scrape on the wooden floor, shrieks of terror are launched like fireworks, and Aunt Betty's blood-curdling scream bounces off the kitchen walls and ceiling as everyone scatters a hasty retreat from the ghostly presence that has taken over the kitchen.

Everyone is huddled in a tight pack in the safety of the family room. Aunt Betty is hysterical and my mom is screaming about the house being haunted. I don't know whether to laugh or cry. Half-eaten bagels, clumps of scrambled eggs, soiled plates, coffee cups, empty juice glasses, and once-bitten muffins sit abandoned on the kitchen table.

"I'll tell you right now, I will not live in a house with a ghost. I'm serious!" Mom yells.

"There's no ghost. And we're not moving," Dad replies, though his voice is shaky as if he's not certain himself of what we all just saw and heard.

"You can't tell me there's no ghost. There's no way that door opens the way it did and then slams just when Betty said something. That's a ghost and you know it," Mom says, and she means business.

"It's probably the same ghost that Brady and I saw in that attic. I told you it was a ghost. See Mom, there are such things as ghosts!"

My dad takes a few steps into the kitchen then turns and says, "Everyone just relax. If it is a ghost then at least we know that it listens to directions." Everyone turns and looks at my dad like he's lost his mind.

"Look, when Betty asked it to close the door it did, right? It may have an attitude, but we can work on that," Dad says half-joking.

"This isn't funny, Brian," Mom says, beginning to calm down.

"I gotta go, Anne. Let me know if any other strange things happen." Aunt Betty turns to my dad, "Brian, would you mind walking me through the kitchen and to the door? I'd rather not go in there by myself. C'mon Kat."

"You alright?" Mom asks, putting her arms around Aunt Betty's shoulders. She walks her to the door with my dad.

I take a few pictures of the kitchen. But no ghostly apparitions appear in the images.

The key to convincing parents to approve sleepovers is timing and numbers. The best time to ask is when they're distracted or happy, best if they're both at the same time. And then there's no replacement for persistence. Even the most stubborn parents can be exhausted into a yes after twenty or so requests.

Another ghost event has my anxiety tuned to a high pitch, but the timing is perfect. My mom agrees that it'll be better if I sleep over Brady's house. Better to be safe than sorry. Besides, I'm glad to have someone to talk to about all this. A chance to try and make sense of everything that's happened.

"All this crazy stuff started after we found the dead man. It's like he's trying to tell us something, but what?" Brady says.

"We should have helped him; we should have done something," I say.

"Like what? He was already dead."

"Maybe he wouldn't be dead if we had gotten there sooner."

"Maybe we'd be dead if we got there sooner. You ever think about that?" He has a point, and I have thought about it. Having been followed, stalked, and chased, I'm not entirely convinced that someone doesn't want me dead.

"Maybe he just wants us to find out who he was," I say.

"And even if we figure out what his name is, so what? What's so important about knowing his name?"

As I recall last night's dream, I'm engulfed by a trio of twitches that clutter together.

"He must have a story to tell. A story that he wants us to tell," I say.

"What story?"

"I don't know. But we won't know until we find out who he was, first."

"I still think he was the guy who lived in that house with the attic. It was him that was rocking in that chair. He's probably still in that treasure chest. We should have busted it open when we were there."

"Well, there are people living in that house now and if they'd found a dead person in the chest, they'd have called the police already, there would have been a report in the police log. Besides, my mom knew the people who owned that house. She said the man would be nearly eighty years old if he were alive now. The guy we found wasn't that old. He was maybe in his fifties or sixties, but definitely not in his late seventies. It can't be him."

"Then how about the nephew who would visit?"

"Could be, but he doesn't live here anymore, and those people, the Browns, said they haven't seen him in more than twenty years."

"Well, I have no idea who that guy was and I don't see how we're gonna find out without a body. If you haven't noticed, the dead body hasn't reappeared,"

Before we can figure what to do next, Brady's mom shouts upstairs asking if we want to order a movie. The mystery of the dead man can wait. If there's one thing Brady and I love, it's a good movie.

"I just wanted to let you know that your dad and I are going out to dinner. So if you want to pick out a movie," Mrs. Hopper glances over at Brady's two little sisters, Alexis and Alana, "one that everyone can watch, go ahead. You got it, Brady?" Brady grimaces. "I'm serious Brady. I don't want to hear any complaints. And only call if it's an emergency. The last time Dad and I went out for dinner my phone buzzed with about twenty text messages you guys sent me."

"I didn't send you any text messages; it was all Alexis and Alana."

"Oh, no mister, you sent me text messages, too. Let me eat dinner without being interrupted with your nonsense, you hear me?"

"I won't send you any text messages. But what if the house is on fire? Is that an emergency?" Brady says.

"Only if you can't put it out yourself. And if that happens, don't call me, call the fire department."

"Where's Jake?" Brady asks.

"He's staying over a friend's house tonight, he won't be home. So it's you and the girls - keep an eye on them. Myles, will you promise me that you guys will all get along?"

"Sure Mrs. Hopper."

Parents can never leave kids alone in the house without spending fifteen minutes giving useless directions on stuff we already know about. When the Hoppers' car pulls out into the street Brady and I pick out a movie, one that we want to watch. Sorry, but eight and ten year old girls have no say, despite what Mrs. Hopper said.

The night has gone to dark and with all the lights off in the house, the large Hopper television glows like a cosmic orb giving the room an eerie feel. We settle in and are watching *The Shining*. It's one of those horror flicks that chase little kids out of a room, but Brady and I are pleased to see that his sisters are enjoying the movie as much as we are. There must be something about the Hoppers. They all have nerves of steel. The only interruption, which we didn't expect, is the Hoppers' dog, Maggie. She keeps jumping on Brady wanting to play. She won't sit still. My family has never had a dog, but even I can tell that she wants to go outside. Brady pauses the movie to let Maggie run around outside to her heart's content so we can watch the rest of the movie in peace and quiet.

That lasts only about five minutes before Maggie starts whining and barking.

Twenty minutes later Alexis whines, "Maggie's still barking, Brady."

"Yeah so, she's a dog. Dogs bark."

"She's been barking for a long time, and she doesn't sound right. She's scaring me."

"Just watch the movie. Forget about Maggie."

"She's right Brady. She's been barking for awhile, like something may be wrong. We should check on her." Something about her bark and how it's come and gone in spurts isn't normal.

"Ughh. Alright, let's go." Brady pauses the movie, throws the remote onto the couch, and he and I march toward the garage. Alexis and Alana, not wanting to be alone, follow closely behind. We descend the short staircase into the garage single file, Brady in the front, me behind him and his sisters in the rear. The garage, dimly lit with a single bulb, can hold three cars. With the Hoppers out for the evening in Mr. Hopper's car, only Mrs. Hopper's SUV is parked at the far end of the garage, its windows blackened like a casket. I've ridden in the car perhaps a hundred times, but something about it gives me an uneasy feeling.

Maggie lets out a sharp yelp then goes quiet. Her frantic barking which brought us out here in the first place doesn't resume. A few minutes ago we were annoyed enough by her barking to pause the movie, now we all wait and hope she begins barking again.

But she doesn't.

Fear burrows into me like a worm slithering into loose soil. Alexis and Alana whimper and whine. Dressed in their blue pajamas they remind me of the two little girls in the movie we were just watching. In the movie, these twin girls who've been murdered, wear matching blue dresses and roam the hallways of an abandoned hotel as twin ghosts. Only this young boy, and his parents who live in the hotel by themselves, can see the girls. In a scene we were just watching, the boy is riding his tricycle around the hallways of the hotel. It looks like fun until he rounds a corner and sees the two creepy sisters at the end of the hallway. This time, though, their blue dresses are smeared with blood stains. This haunting image prompts a couple of shoulder shrugs and rapid eye flutters that do nothing to ease me. The scuttling sound of a footie pajama scraping the cement floor nearly ignites a full-scale twitch attack.

Mrs. Hopper's car continues to hold my attention. I pray that I won't see anything moving inside of it. Reflections on the windows from the glare of the light bulb hide whatever may be inside. I can't decide if we're safer in the garage, or if we're trapped in the garage and just don't know it.

Brady's heavy breathing tells me he's thinking the same thing.

Please, Maggie, bark. Just one time, girl, please.

Brady retreats to the garage door opener taking each step like it may be his last. "I'm gonna open the garage door," he whispers, "you guys ready?"

Ready for what? I want to ask. But I can't because my mouth feels like someone has just baked a loaf of stale bread in it.

I turn my gaze from Brady's hand as it nears the white button, to the bottom of the garage door. At the touch of the button the garage door opener thunders above me. The mechanism that lifts the door sways and rattles. The door begins its climb. Without warning, a crazed animal wearing a skeleton skull bucket over its head squeezes under the door and charges full speed towards us. The scream of Brady's sisters practically peels the skin right off of me.

It's Maggie.

She bolts past us and scurries up the steps into the house. We race up the steps, chasing the Halloween dog into the family room, still aglow with the TV screen lit up. Then I realize that no one closed either door behind us. Brady and I run back as fast as we can, once more push the white button to close the garage door, and then the door that leads to the garage. We lock that, then run and dive into the couch.

"Jayzuz H. Christ, what's going on!" yells Brady over the hysterical screams of Alexis and Alana.

"Maggie, come here." I try to get her to settle down. She's tucked herself into a corner, growling and fighting madly to remove the Halloween bucket from her head.

Brady has to wrestle and pin Maggie down, holding her legs tight, before I can get two hands on the bucket and yank it off of her. She scampers down the hall and disappears into one of the other rooms.

"Recognize this?" I ask Brady.

"Yeah, where'd that come from?"

"The riverbank, that's where."

"Who would do something like this?"

CHAPTER FIFTEEN

Sunday, September 21st

Patches of late morning sunlight flicker on the walls in imaginative shapes and sizes. Sleep still in my eyes, I resist the temptation to fully wake, and bury my head into my pillow. I slept fitfully last night, as I expected I would. Another bad dream.

It began nice enough. I was enjoying a day filled with my usual activities at the river. Swimming, hiking, and exploring. The only annoyance was the chirping of a pair of birds. No matter how thoroughly I searched the woods, they remained hidden from me. I soon tired and sought sleep in the dusty comfort of the brick storage shed at the river. It was in a large room filled with rusty machines and a high ceiling that the two mysterious birds, one red and one brown, appeared to me, transformed into two young girls, wearing matching blue dresses. They poked and taunted me every time I was on the verge of sleep. Angry, I kept swiping at them, but it was useless. Flickering in and out of my dream they frustrated me beyond the ability to relax.

I reach to pull up the blankets, which are all clumped in a heap at the bottom of the bed. Too lazy to retrieve them, and now, more awake, I decide I'd better get up and go downstairs. Brady is digging into a bowl of cereal and Mrs. Hopper is sipping hot coffee from a blue mug when I sit at the kitchen table. The drowsiness hasn't quite worn off. Apparently, I'm the last one up. A cartoon blasting in the family room entertains Alexis and Alana, each with a bowl of cereal perched in their laps. Like my dad, I'm usually an early riser, so I feel out of sorts getting my day started long after everyone else.

"Myles, honey, turn around please," Mrs. Hopper says. Her expression looks as if I have a large, hairy spider crawling on me. I turn my back towards her.

"For crying out loud! What's on your back?" she exclaims.

Now it's my turn to be concerned. I'm not afraid of spiders, but I can't say I want one on my back, either.

"Brady, did you do that?" Mrs. Hopper says.

"Do what?" Brady starts giggling and I fear the worst.

I've been had.

"You know very well, what. I know your artwork when I see it."

"Brady, you mind telling me what's on my back?" my voice is heavy with defeat.

"Go look in the mirror, see for yourself," Brady says, unleashing a madman's laugh.

The mirror reveals that sometime during the night, for the brief time when I was thick with sleep, Brady used different colored markers to draw an exact replica of the Colorado Avalanche hockey shirt on my back. When Brady isn't gaming on XBox, the other thing he loves to do is draw and paint. He's really good, too. The best I've ever seen. And he knows I hate the Avalanche, most of all, their uniforms.

"This had better come out," I say. Either way, Brady won last night's battle in a playful war of sleepover pranks that's years old. He may have won last night's battle, but I'll win the war. I have a few tricks up my sleeve too.

"Brady Hopper! A dog has more manners than you. Is that any way to treat your guest? Myles, honey, I'm sorry, hopefully that comes off," Mrs. Hopper says giving Brady a scornful look. "I know you kids like to play jokes on each other once in awhile, but I worry that one of these times it won't be so funny."

"It's just a hockey shirt, mom," Brady says with a chuckle, "I didn't use a permanent marker. It's washable with water, it'll come out."

"It better."

"It's just a silly prank. Myles and I do stuff like this all the time. Has anyone ever gotten hurt?"

"No, but you have to be careful with pranks. Sometimes a prank goes too far and someone does get hurt. Like you kids claiming you found a dead body over by the river. Stuff like that is serious, Brady."

"It wasn't a prank. We found a dead body. A real dead body. Ask Myles."

I don't wait for Mrs. Hopper to ask, "It's true, Mrs. Hopper. My parents don't believe me either, but we did."

"Talking about pranks. If it was a prank, then it was probably Jake. So go ask him about it," Brady says raising his voice.

A look of doubt creeps onto Mrs. Hopper's face. She curls her lips and looks out the kitchen window. "I've already talked to Jake and he swears he had nothing to do with this."

"And you believe him!?" Brady shouts, disbelief in his voice. Mrs. Hopper doesn't say anything in her defense. "You always believe Jake!"

"How could Jake pretend to look like a sixty-year old man from India?" Mrs. Hopper counters.

"Maybe someone he knows had a grandfather that died. And Jake and his friends borrowed the body to play a joke on us. You don't know Jake, Mom. He does stuff. You have no idea what he's capable of!"

That sends a chill down my spine. My shoulders slam into my neck like a thunderclap.

Brady's younger sisters, Alexis and Alana shuffle into the kitchen, curious about the commotion. "Who died, Mommy?" Alexis asks.

"No one, pumpkin, go back in the family room and watch TV," Mrs. Hopper tells Alexis. Both girls trudge back to their cartoon.

"He does not. You let your father and I manage Jake. I'll talk to him when he gets back from the gym."

"I just want him to leave me and my friends alone. I know he's involved in this and some other things that have happened that you don't even know about. And that man was real!" Brady scuffles out of the kitchen. His footsteps crash up the stairs, followed by a door slamming. I stand there awkwardly for a few moments, then make my own way upstairs. More quietly than Brady.

I wait until Brady calms down and I'm able to quiet my anxiety before I leave. Nothing spoils future sleepovers like coming home sick, or in my case, coming home all wired up and anxious. I don't want to have to walk home through the neighborhood alone, so I ask Mrs. Hopper for a ride which she kindly agrees to.

When I walk in the door, Dennis is eating a sub sandwich he made himself. My brother takes his food seriously. I just slop my sandwiches together, but not Dennis. His sandwich is sub-shop caliber. It's topped with all the fixins, chopped tomatoes, onions, pickles, and hots, on top of three different types of meats and two types of cheeses.

"Where's Mom and Dad?" I say.

"They're out. By the way dude, someone called here looking for you."

A lump lodges in my throat. My neck stiffens.

"Some woman you sold raffle tickets to called." Relief washes over me as a near anxiety attack has been averted. My mind scrambles to think of what woman Dennis is talking about. "Wants you to come by her house after school tomorrow, says she wants to buy more raffle tickets. I wrote her name and address down." Dennis slides a small slip of paper across the counter.

Mrs. Brown - 209 Mountain Avenue.

"Any other phone calls?" I ask, trying to sound casual.

"For you? No." Grateful that the mysterious phone calls have stopped, for the moment anyway, I relax. "But did you try calling here this morning?"

"No. Why?"

"Someone called here a couple of times and hung up. I thought, maybe, it was you."

"It wasn't me. How many times did they call?"

"Twice, I think."

"Were Mom and Dad here when you got those calls?"

"No. They were already gone when I got up."

That's good. If they'd been here for two more hangups they would've gotten suspicious that something's not right. Probably would have called the police. Although, maybe the police should know about this. I can't pretend that this isn't serious. Maybe Mrs. Hopper was right. Sometimes things go too far and someone gets hurt. Right now, I need to make a phone call of my own.

Before I make my phone call, I spend an hour searching online one more time. Same as before, I don't find a single ring that looks anything like what I have. Then to be sure, I twitch through another shattering hour of searching - nothing, again.

I decide that if Jogesh hasn't been able to find out anything about the ring that I'll give it back. How to do that safely I'm not sure of. But I'll figure something out. I usually do.

Then I make that call.

"Hey, Jogesh, it's Myles Walsh."

"Hey, Myles, what's up?"

"Not much," the words stutter out awkwardly, this isn't the kind of phone call I'm used to making. "I was just wondering if your dad was able to find out what that ring is?" Several twitches tumble together, so that one twitch leads to another. I wait and hope for good news. Any news at this point, actually.

"Yeah, I was gonna tell you in school tomorrow."

"So, is there anything special about the ring?"

"My dad said he's never seen one before, but he's heard about them. It's a long story, let me get my dad on the phone."

A long story? I knew there was something special about this ring!

A voice crackles on the other end, Mr. Dhruv's. "Hi, is this Myles?"

"Yes, sir," I answer.

"So you're the boy asking about the ring."

"Yeah, I was wondering what it's for, if it means anything."

"When Jogesh showed us the picture I was surprised. Rings like this are very rare. I've never seen one myself, but my grandparents would talk about the existence of rings like this one. There really isn't a name for them, not that I know of anyway. Like I said, they're very rare, but one can still find them in some parts of India. Very remote villages where people still follow the old ways."

I hear him pause on the other end, then start again, "The Kavaad is an ancient storytelling tradition in India. The ring, like the one in your picture, is worn by the elder in the village who is known as the Kaavadiyas, or storyteller. Some say that the ring holds mysterious powers. Not magic or anything, but more like a power that connects stories to the Kaavadiyas.

"That's the meaning behind the composition of the ring. No two of these are exactly the same, but they usually share a few common features. The six small circles represent stories that need to be told and the elements of Kaavadiyas: storytelling, poetry, music, drama, dance, and philosophy. The three ropes that intertwine around the ring and through the circles represent how stories, storytellers, and listeners are connected to each other through the experience of storytelling. And then the large door in the center of the ring represents how, through the telling of stories, doors open for us, teaching us about the world we live in. The door also invites us to partake in this storytelling experience."

I stare at the precious ring, a portal to the world, with wonder and respect. It's meaning soaks into my bones. The events of the past two weeks, as crazy, frightening, and mystifying as they've been, now make more sense to me.

"Thanks, Mr. Dhruv. I appreciate you doing all this."

"I'm glad I could help. It was actually neat for me to see a picture of the ring. I've lived here now for many years and had forgotten about the tale of the Kavaadiyas. If you don't mind me asking, how did you come across it? I can't believe that one has made it's way here to the United States - I don't think anyone has ever heard of these rings outside of India and I'm surprised that one is here in Caldwell."

I stumble for an answer. As much as I'd like to tell Mr. Dhruv where I really got it from, I decide it's safer for everyone if I stick to my original story, the same one I told the helpful librarian. "It's my grandfather's. He bought it at a yard sale."

"Well, your grandfather has a very special ring. But I need to tell you Myles, that this ring belongs to the Kavaadiyas. It's part of an ancient tradition that must be respected and followed. Please remember that."

"I will Mr. Dhruv. Thanks."

What I must do next becomes clear to me.

CHAPTER SIXTEEN

Monday, September 22nd

Not taking any chances, I walk to the corner of Mountain Avenue and take the bus to school for the first time this year. In fact, it's been so long since I rode the bus, that I'm not sure where I'm supposed to sit. Everyone looks at me like I've made a mistake.

At school I open my locker on the third try. With the progress I've been making I could be opening this thing on the first try by Halloween. Spotting Brady, I hurry towards him with urgent news. But halfway there, I bump into Jogesh.

"Hey, Myles, what's up?"

"Hey, Jogesh." I try to step past him, not wanting to engage in a lengthy conversation, but Jogesh is too friendly to avoid and I'm too nice to be rude.

"That's pretty cool about the ring, huh."

"Yeah, it is. I really owe your dad big time. Listen, Jogesh, can we not talk about the ring for a few days?" He looks perplexed. "It's just that I don't want anyone to know my grandfather has it. He kinda feels like he shouldn't have bought it. He's trying to find the rightful owner and that might take a few days. Okay."

"Sure, no problem."

"Thanks. Look, I gotta talk to Brady about something before home-room, can we talk again later?"

"Sure. I'll see you in homeroom."

"Thanks, man."

I hate to ditch Jogesh like that but this is important. Brady has disappeared into Mr. Agostinos's homeroom, but I should have just enough time to talk to him. Then suddenly, Mr. Curtin hollers behind me, "Myles, can I see you for a moment?" His arms are folded across his chest. A stringy twitch shudders through my shoulders and neck. Now what? I backtrack to see what I've done wrong this time.

"I just wanted to tell you that I sent your mom an email this morning letting her know that you're doing well so far. You got an 82 on the chapter one test for *Where the Red Fern Grows*."

Relieved that I haven't forgotten a major assignment or bombed a quiz, I smile and relax.

"Thanks."

"I'm looking forward to seeing your story. That's the first double-test grade of the term, but from what I've seen so far, your story should be fine."

Lake Placid has just taken a few steps closer to becoming a reality. The thought of it sends a juicy buzz that I can feel all the way to my fingertips.

"You kids make any more progress with that thing you were asking me about last week?"

For a moment I think he's referring to the ring. My shoulders tighten as I consider how to respond.

"You know. The man you guys found?" Mr. Curtin says.

"Oh, that...a little bit."

"Let me know if I can help in any way." Mr. Curtin winks at me, then walks into his room without waiting for a reply. My plan to talk to Brady is cut off when the homeroom bell rings.

What I need to talk to Brady and Kat about has to wait until lunch because of the chaos of a typical McFarland morning. Later, when I see them in the hallway I drag both of them down the corridor that leads past the music room. It's the longest route to the lunchroom giving me the privacy and time I need.

"What's going on?" Brady says.

"There's something I need to tell you guys. I probably should have said something a long time ago, but..."

Mr. Jarrett, the music teacher, steps out into the hallway. He's tossing an apple in the air. Seeing Mr. Jarrett eating an apple during lunch is as predictable as homework. Teachers help out as aids in the lunchroom twice per week and today must be Mr. Jarrett's day.

"Let's go guys, you can have your conversation in the lunchroom," he says, chasing us away.

The lunchroom is crowded with noise levels that would rival a band of bagpipers on St. Patty's Day. There's nothing I can tell them here without twenty other people butting in. If that weren't enough, the principal, Mrs. Bishop, is circling around the lunchroom like a hawk.

As long as it's not too cold or raining, Mrs. Bishop lets us outside after we've eaten. I eat my lunch in half the time it usually does and motion to Brady and Kat to meet me outside when they're done. The morning's sunshine has given way to gloomy skies. Short gusts of wind push brown leaves along the pavement. It's chilly and feels like it might rain. I holler when I see Brady and Kat looking for me, then holler louder to carry my voice over the wind.

Brady plods through the parking lot with his hands jammed deep into his pockets. Kat tries to keep her hair out of her face. I can tell by their mannerisms that they would rather have stayed inside than be standing out here on a blustery day.

"So what do you have to tell us?" Brady says.

"Is this about the math test tomorrow?" Kat says.

I shake my head. "That day we found the dead man, remember?"

I take in a deep breath of air and draw in closer to them. "The guy was wearing a robe and he had some beads hanging around his neck. But he was wearing something else that caught my eye. When I went back to get your bike, Kat, I took something from him."

They look at me with shock in their faces.

"What did you take?" Brady says.

I dig into my pocket and take out the ring. "I took this." I display it openly in the palm of my hand, feeling its weight and significance. The dread that I had about keeping a secret from them is released in a twitch of surrender.

The ring captivates them. Mesmerized by the uniqueness of the ring and the unlikely source of its theft, Brady's eyes meet mine. He asks for permission to handle it.

"I can't believe you took this. How'd you do that?" he says.

"I poked a hole in the plastic, near his hand. Then just reached in and slid it off. It was loose, so it was easy, actually."

"I can't believe you took a ring off a dead guy's finger! You're usually afraid of your own shadow. Was his hand cold? What does a dead person feel like?" Brady says.

"That's gross. I don't even want to touch it," Kat says, stepping back.

Brady rolls the ring around in his palm, then twirls it between his fingers, studying its arrangement. "Why'd you take it?"

"I don't know. Just something about it. When I saw it, I just wanted to have it. Needed to have it. I thought it looked important, somehow."

"You can say that again. It looks like it belongs in a museum. What are you gonna do with it? You gonna keep it?" Brady says.

"That's the other thing I need to tell you. It's not just an ordinary ring. There aren't many of these things. They're worn by people in India that are storytellers. I went online last night and got all this information about the history of these rings. You see these doors and ropes and how they're all kinda connected?" I point to the features of its design. "It means something. It represents the power of stories and storytelling. The dead man who owned this ring was a storyteller. And I think I know how we can find out who he was."

"Myles, this is unbelievable," Kat says, impressed. "But you have to give this back. This ring doesn't belong to you."

"I know. And I will. I just need to know who the guy was first."

"The guy it belonged to, or the guy following you?" Brady says.

"The guy it belonged to. The dead man."

"How you gonna do that? Don't forget, someone's after you because you took this. Took something that doesn't belong to you. You don't know who this person is, or what they'll do to get it back, Myles," Kat says.

"Look, it's hard to explain, but ever since I took the ring, all these crazy things have happened. You guys know how I am with my twitching and with my anxiety attacks. Even with all the crazy stuff the past two weeks, I haven't had one meltdown, have I? There's something about this ring. That's why I've held onto it this whole time, even though someone is after me to get it back. I think everything has happened for a reason and that reason is that it's up to me to tell the dead man's story."

"We don't even know who the guy was. Or who killed the guy. And what story are you talking about?" Brady says.

"I know. But I think we can figure who this ring belonged to. I have no idea who killed him or how he died, but I think we have enough clues that we can solve the puzzle of who he was. Plus, those old people, the Browns, want us to come by after school today. They want to buy more raffle tickets. We may be able to get more information from them while we're there."

"Alright, cool. We'll meet after school, then," Brady says, handing the ring back to me. We both look at Kat.

"What? Alright, me too. But I'm not sure about this, though."

"Awesome! But you guys have to promise me that you won't say anything to anyone about the ring. Nothing. I'm serious."

This time it's Mrs. Brown who answers the door. Wearing another shower curtain, this one even more colorful than the last one; she looks like she just came from the beauty parlor. Her hair is swooped up in several wavy curls. "Hey kids, c'mon in." Her cheery invitation is a good sign that we're here for a visit rather than a simple purchase of raffle tickets.

"Larry! The kids are here," She yells up the wide staircase lined with family photos in a variety of frames. "C'mon in and sit down." She directs us into the kitchen where we sit at a simple round table. She offers us a drink which we each politely decline. Mr. Brown scuffles into the kitchen a moment later explaining that he naps at the same time every day. Being polite, I take out the raffle tickets that have been in my back pocket, but Mrs. Brown stops me before I have a chance to say anything.

"We have plenty of time for that, dear. Larry and I asked you kids to come over because the last time you were here we were talking about the people who used to live next door. Well, that got me to thinking, and I remembered something you kids were asking about." Her voice has a high pitched tone that reminds me of women who sing in church choirs.

"Larry and me got to remembering the time that family lived here. They were lovely people. Very educated with lots of college, both of them. A family relative, a nephew I believe, would come visit once in awhile. He didn't live there, would just visit, usually for a weekend now and then. He was a nice young man, very friendly. We'd see him in the yard or on the porch and he'd always say hello or wave. But.....sometimes, there were arguments. You could hear them yelling clear over here, even with the windows shut. Isn't that right, Larry?" Mr. Brown nods in agreement as if it's the only thing to do.

"The arguments were always the same. The uncle felt that the young man should not have come to this country, that he belonged back home in India. Something about a duty he had, tradition, stuff like that. And the doors! My heavens I thought they were gonna come right off the hinges. We could feel the house shake from all the way over here. You remember that Larry?"

"What doors?" I ask, thinking of the the mud room door that slammed a few days ago.

"Just doors in the house. But he'd slam them with such force. And that would really get the uncle going. He'd be yelling about how important it was to be opening doors and not closing them. That it was his duty to open doors. I remember him saying that. I thought it was good advice, myself."

"Do you remember what the nephew's name was?" I ask the question that has brought us here.

"Well, that's the other thing I wanted to talk to you kids about. That fighting business went on for awhile and then we didn't see much of the nephew. It was around that time, that Larry had his knee surgery. You can see he's fine now, but it landed him on bed rest for a month. Just when we didn't think we'd ever see the nephew again, we weren't sure what happened to him, and naturally Larry and I were too polite to ask, he showed up one day asking if we needed any help. You know, to mow the lawn and take out the garbage, things like that. I needed all the help I could get so I put him to work straight-away. He was a lifesaver for us that summer. The last time he was here we sat on the back deck together and shared a pitcher of iced tea. And then he told me the most beautiful story. One that I had forgotten. That is, until you kids came by selling raffle tickets. Then it came to me. I remembered."

"What was the story about?" Kat asks.

"It was about...two brothers. Haarsha was the older brother of Kamran by two years. Haarsha was creative and energetic. Kamran was good-natured but lazy. Both boys admired their father who, although not wealthy, was a successful merchant who was respected by everyone in the village. Sampat loved both his sons very much, as any father does. He owned a store that sold grains and feed supplies to the farmers in that region where they lived. Sampat's father had run the business before him, and his father, before him. It was expected that Haarsha, being the first, would one day take over the business from his father. Sampat would frequently boast about the proud history of the small business and the importance of family tradition. He would do this at mealtime, after evening prayers, and when the family swam in the cool waters of the nearby river on those rare days when they rested and leisured.

"Even in the company of others the father could be heard talking about Haarsha'a future. It was his way of gently reminding his son of his obligation to continue that which was expected of him, and that which would rightfully be given to him. Haarsha would listen politely and never objected when this matter was discussed, for he was a good boy. Kamran would listen politely too, but he would grow jealous and resentful that just because he was born of a different moon, the business would one day belong to Haarsha, and not to himself.

"But Haarsha's dreams lied elsewhere. He loved and respected his father, as all sons do, and he appreciated the comfortable life the business had provided for himself and his family. But Haarsha dreamed of a different future. From a very young age he had shown an interest in how things were built. This particular region of India, though not prestigious, was blessed with many temples. Haarsha would notice small details that would make one temple glorious to behold, while another, lacking those same details, would be plain and ordinary. In his spare time, Haarsha drew pictures of dazzling temples that he dreamed of one day building. A teacher at school was the first to recognize Haarsha's talent. Entry into the leading universities was reserved for the very privileged in old India. The teacher, although he held no powerful connections, was able to secure Haarsha a spot at a respected university based on his recommendation. An uncle, a successful doctor, generously paid for Haarsha's education.

"It was difficult for the son to tell his father that he did not wish to be a merchant as his father was, and his father before him. Sampat was angry and hurt, as fathers sometimes are. He reminded his son, as persuasively as his powers would let him, of his obligation to the family. But he could not win out over Haarsha's passion and determination. Kamran, seizing this unexpected opportunity, exclaimed his devotion to his father and to the family business. The father hesitated briefly, then accepted things as they were. Haarsha went on to university and became a leading architect. Temples he designed and built can still be seen all over India.....each loved and adored by their worshippers.

"And Kamran? What happened to Haarsha's brother? He took over the business after his father, poor faithful Sampat, several years later was struck ill and died, likely from exhaustion. Under Kamran's direction the business prospered at first, but sadly, Kamran discovered after a few short years that he did not have the passion for business that his father had before him, and his father before him. The business suffered from Kamran's inattentiveness, was eventually swamped in debt, and closed. Today it is nothing more than a distant memory, while Haarsha's temples continue to inspire those who seek their dreams."

"Wow, that's an amazing story," I say.

"The young man who told me that story was a very good story-teller." Brady and Kat turn to look at me. "He told me that story as a way to explain what he and his uncle argued about. You see, he wanted to be a teacher. His uncle would remind him about some obligation he owed to his family back in India. He wouldn't tell me what that was, though. But he was determined to be a teacher. It was his passion. And that was the last time I saw him or spoke to him."

My heart sinks. Not another dead end. Not only is this guy dead, but he doesn't seem to ever had a name.

"I felt I needed to tell you that story." She pauses, closing her mouth. She looks at each of us. Seriousness etched into her face. Then bending her head sideways and rolling her eyes, she says, "You may think I'm crazy, but I had a dream the other night and in the dream it wasn't the young nephew who told me that story.....it was you."

"Me?"

"Yes, you."

I wasn't expecting this. I'm undecided whether Mrs. Brown is for real, or a lonely old lady who's a quack. But now's not the time to be quibbling about details.

Without fully thinking through my response I say, "Did he ever tell you what his name was?"

"That was the other strange part about my dream."

There's another part?

She hesitates, uncertain of what words should come next. "I'm sorry, but I don't believe I know your first name?"

"Myles, Myles Walsh."

"That's right, you're the plumber's son," she slaps both hands on her knees. "But that wasn't it. That's not the name." She seems disappointed, though I'm not sure why.

"In the dream you told me your name was, Adheer."

"Adheer?"

"Yes. Adheer. That I am quite certain of." Her expression becomes grave. She leans towards me and says, "Adheer was the name of the nephew who would visit next door."

Jackpot!

"How would you spell that?"

"I have no idea. I suppose spelling it the way it sounds would be best." Her gentle laugh lightens the mood.

"Excuse me, ma'am. In your dream, did, Adheer, or Myles, tell you a last name?" Kat asks.

"No sir, he did not. We never learned his last name."

"Mrs. Brown, we can't thank you enough," I say this so enthusiastically that it surprises her.

"Thank me? What for?"

"Well, just...." I struggle to find the right thing to say.

"For crying out loud, Martha, can't you see what the kids came here for? As delightful as your little story was, the kids came here to sell us raffle tickets, remember?" Mr. Brown seems bored by all this and must think his wife's dream is nothing but nonsense.

"You don't have to remind me, mister, I know why they're here, I asked them to come, remember? Now you go get twenty dollars for these nice kids. My pocketbook is in the family room."

"Never mind him. He's always cranky after he wakes up from his nap," she says after Mr. Brown slouches off on his errand.

Once again, we're racing our bikes through the neighborhood.

We explode through the door and sprint upstairs to my room. Brady belly-flops onto my bed, Kat plops into my bean-bag. I remain standing, pacing, twitching, thinking, trying to unscramble a dozen thoughts at once.

"Oh, crap!" Brady shouts, tossing his phone onto the bed.

"What is it?" I ask.

"I just did a search for 'Adheer' and got 461,000 results."

"I got the same thing," Kat says, showing me the page on her phone.

"Alright, let's just stop and think about this." Needing to think more clearly, I don't bother to fight off a barrage of shoulder shrugs and eye flutters, but instead, let them ripple freely on their own.

"What was the last name of his aunt and uncle?" Kat says.

"That's right, that's probably his last name. Bingo. That was easy," Brady says.

I check my phone, where I keep notes, and find the last name.

"Harakatha."

I give the spelling and Kat does a search using - Adheer Harakatha. That brings 2,470 results. Still a lot, but between the three of us we can manage that. Brady doesn't waste anytime getting started.

"Wait a minute," Kat says. "Your mom and dad are my aunt and uncle, but my last name isn't the same as yours. How do we know his last name was Harakatha?"

"That's true," Brady says, his thumbs still busy with the search results.

"Yeah, but technically my mom and your mom are cousins, not sisters, so my mom and dad really aren't your aunt and uncle," I say.

"I suppose. But how about your mom's brother, your Uncle Walter. What's his last name?"

"Luro."

"That's not Walsh, is it now?"

"You have a point."

"We could spend the next three hours searching for an Adheer Harakatha and that may not even be his name," Kat says.

Why does everything have to be so hard?

"Have you found anything yet, Brady?" I say, hoping for good news.

"Nothing. Should I keep going through these?"

"How many results are there for just, Adheer?" Kat says.

"461,000," Brady answers.

"That's too many, we'll never get through all those," I say.

"When Mrs. Brown was telling that story today, she said Adheer wanted to be a teacher, it was his passion. And he was going to college to be a teacher. What if we searched for Adheer teacher?" Kat says.

"Try that," I tell Brady.

"47,900. A lot, but not bad."

"A lot better than 461,000," I say.

"How are we going to do this? We can't all be going through the same results," Kat says.

"There's three of us, we'll divide it up. Brady you take searches one through 15,000. Kat you take 15,001 through 30,000. And I'll take 30,001 through the end. Let's get started. If anyone finds anything, let the others know right away. That way, we're not wasting our time."

"And what are we looking for exactly, Myles?" Brady says.

"Anything that looks like it could be the man we're looking for." But that's a good question.

What are we looking for?

How will we know when we've found it?

"How long do you think it will take to go through 15,000 results?" Brady says.

"A couple hours at least. I guess we'll find out," I say.

"How late you planning on staying up doing this?" Kat says.

"I don't know. Hopefully we find something before midnight. There's no hockey tonight, but we have school in the morning."

"What if someone finds something after midnight?" Brady says.

"No one has to stay up that late. But if you do, send a text. No matter how late it is."

Back in my room after eating dinner and completing my homework I lay on my bed, frustrated and done in. The thrill of the search, energized by Mrs. Brown's story, has drained out of me. The reality that going through all 47,900 search results still doesn't guarantee that we'll find out who the dead man was festers in me like a blister.

What if he isn't on any social media sites? What if he has no presence at all on the internet? If so, then this would be a colossal waste of time. I sink into an ocean of despair, feeling doomed. Why is it that nothing is ever easy? I'm wallowing in self-pity when my phone buzzes with a text from Kat.

How far have u gotten? Anything?

It's not exactly a halftime speech by Vince Lombardi, but it's enough to get me back online, resuming the search.

For a dead man.

A ghost.

The ghost of a dead man.

A ghost more real than a person. One with a curious past, a missing ring, and an uncertain future. For these reasons and for others I feel connected to him, and he to me. For the first time since my theft, I place the ring on my own finger. The contours of the ring's silver metal feel peculiar, like its past might leak into my bones.

I reply: - 1 / 4 - nada

I'm still wearing the dead man's ring after midnight when I get my first break.

A game-changer.

I hope.

I click on a search result that takes me to a website that rates teachers. It's a place where students can anonymously write comments about their teachers. I find a teacher named Adheer Kathavyas at the Coyle Middle School in Alexandria Township, New Jersey. What gets my heart rate fired up though, are the comments written by former students. It seems he is loved for his great stories.

Without a picture I can't be certain this is the Adheer we're looking for. Using the name of the school I search and find the Coyle Middle School website. Hopefully there's a picture of Mr. Kathavyas somewhere on their webpage. I spend half an hour scouring every corner of their website and can't find a single teacher in any picture that looks anything like the dead man.

Now what do I do.

He must have a Blog. Sure. All my teachers have Blogs - that's how we get our homework assignments every day, and Mr. Curtin, Mr. Agostino, Mrs. Glennon, and Mrs. Thompson all have their pictures on their Blogs.

I go back to the school website and find a link to his Blog. No picture. Anywhere. I find out that he was an eighth grade language arts teacher, though. It's obvious reading his Blog that he loves teaching, he does what he is passionate about. Out of curiosity I click on the homework tab and notice that homework had been assigned the first few days of school. On Friday 8/29 he posted: No Homework - Enjoy the holiday weekend! Then nothing. No homework is assigned or posted after Friday. We found his body a few days later, Monday September 2nd. No homework has been assigned since then

- that's nearly three weeks with no homework. No teacher would ever do that, especially in September. Of course, how could he post homework if he's not alive to do it!

But I still need a picture. Impatience, anxiety, nervousness, buzzes through me. Think. Think. Someone must have reported he was missing. The report of the missing person call would be in the.....police log.

I find the Alexandria Township police log.

No one has been reported missing.

I check and double-check, going all the way back to August 29th. How could that be? I've twitched so relentlessly all night that my twitch tank is empty. My brain is telling me to twitch, it'll relax me, but I'm completely unable, as hard as I try, to shrug, crunch, or flutter. This only adds to my irritability and frustration. I thought for sure this was the man.

The clock reads 2:05. That's A.M. My alarm will be ringing just 4 hours from now. I'll be exhausted in the morning. Getting through my school day tomorrow will be impossible. I'm so tired. I bury my head in my hands. And then, I have one last idea.

The newspaper. The website that hosts the police log gives the name of the local paper as the Hunterdon Independent. If he was never reported missing then chances are there's no article in the newspaper. But what I see in the online edition from two weeks ago jolts me like a cattle prod:

Popular Teacher Dies,
Adheer Kathavyas, 62

And there he is.

His picture is under the heading. I've found him.

Again.

This time though, he's more than just a strange man with brown, wrinkly feet. I know who he is. A last final tremor shudders through me. The clock reads 2:11am.

I text Brady and Kat about my discovery, including a snapshot of the newspaper article with the picture of the dead man, Adheer.

Belief and disbelief.

Elation and sadness.

Energy and tiredness.

A whole range of conflicting emotions wash over me. I can hardly believe that the tumultuous events of the past few weeks have finally drawn to a close. I savor my accomplishment. The dead man's face stares back at me.

Adheer Kathavyas.

Mr. K to his students.

In the picture he's smiling, happy, and alive. I wonder, when he posed for the picture, if he ever expected to wind up in a plastic bag on a weedy, gravel path where a couple of kids would find him? Sadness lumps up in my throat. He was a teacher for more than thirty years who was beloved by his students, some of whom have gone on to become teachers them- selves. He never married, his students were like his own kids, with whom he shared his zany and amazing stories that always had a lesson in them. A relative, visiting from India, discovered Adheer sitting in his favorite rock- ing chair with a book in his lap. The article goes on to say that he suffered a heart attack at some point during the early morning hours.

The exact reason for his appearance at the riverbank is still unclear to me, but I have a hunch about that. I gaze at the Kaavadiyas ring, the one Adheer had worn for more than a quarter of a century. I feel ridden with guilt that I so thoughtlessly took something that meant so much to him. But I'm glad that in my own small way I can now help Adheer. Through the mystery of the ring, I can reclaim its history, tradition, and meaning, and give it back to its rightful owner.

But my work is not through.

The ring has one more Mr. K story to tell.

CHAPTER SEVENTEEN

Tuesday, September 23rd

I sleep like my old self for the first time in many nights. A summer vacation sleep. All four hours of it, anyway. I gulp down a ladle of cod liver oil before I realize, too late, that I've made a mistake. One that I can't take back. It doesn't matter though, I'm so relaxed that not even a mouthful of fish oil is going to spoil my day. Most parents will never admit that kids are sometimes smarter than they are. My mom and dad are no exception. Seeing the looks on their faces when I show them what I found will have to wait until after school. Mom has left a note on the kitchen counter about an early meeting she had, and Dad had to handle an emergency call from one of his best customers.

"Guess what?"

"What?"

"I opened my locker on the first try." Brady gives me a fist bump to celebrate.

"Did you show your parents the article on the dead man?"

"Not yet, they'd already left for work before I got up this morning. How 'bout you?"

"I'm gonna show them at dinner tonight, when everyone's there. I can't wait to see the look on Jake's face," Brady says. "That was awesome last night when you sent that text. It woke me up and I was like, Myles wouldn't be sending a text at two o'clock in the morning unless he found something. But I thought it was another clue. I wasn't expecting that you'd found the whole enchilada! Did you get any sleep last night?"

"I think I got four hours. But I'm not tired, believe it or not."

Kat bounces down the hallway, a smile gleams in her eyes.

"My gosh, can you guys believe we did it? We found out who that guy was. Or should I say, Myles, you did it. You must be psyched."

"I am. I still can't believe it myself."

"What are you gonna do with the ring?" Brady says.

"I was thinking of mailing it to Adheer. It's his ring after all."

"Do you have his address?" Brady says.

"I can get it and mail it there. Probably someone from his family back in India will get all his stuff. They should have the ring."

"That guy who's been following you will probably want the ring. What are you gonna do about him?" Brady says.

"I'm not sure. I'll tell him that I shouldn't have taken the ring. That it belongs to Adheer and that I mailed it back to where he lived. It's his ring."

"I don't know, Myles," Kat says. "Maybe you should give it to the police, let them handle it. Whoever's been following you around wants that ring pretty badly, and they may be the person that killed that man, Adheer. You don't know."

"I don't think anyone killed him. The newspaper said Adheer died of a heart attack."

"But we don't know that for sure. The newspaper also didn't say anything about him being found dead here in Caldwell."

"Yeah, I guess you're right. I'll just put it in an envelope and get rid of it."

My stomach is boiling with this morning's fish oil. The vapors of an oily fish-burp float invisibly through the classroom. I've belched three times so far today. Once I was able to time it so that I was in a crowded hallway. I've already excused myself once in Mrs. Thompson's class to use the bathroom, so I doubt she'll let me go again. I was hoping to hold this one off until the bell rings, which will be in just five minutes, but instead it rumbles out on its own. I try to breathe the fish-stink back into me like a vacuum cleaner. It's no use.

Jogesh, sitting two seats to my left, is the first to make a scrunch-face. He reacts to the eye-watering odor of the cod liver oil. Please, bell... ring, just one time...ring, please. Jogesh is too polite to say anything, but the same can't be said of Bobby the Beast. The top of his head may only reach my chin, but what he lacks in height he makes up for in girth. His barrel-shaped chest sits atop legs that are each as thick as my waist. He's a fullback on the football team and I've heard that trying to tackle Bobby is like trying to tackle a Mini Cooper. His nostrils flare open and his eyes dart around the room seeking the culprit.

"Who's eating a fish sandwich?" he yelps. Turning around he glares in my direction.

I shrug my shoulders, "Fish soup is always better the second time around."

A handful of kids laugh, even the Beast nods his head and smiles. I glance over at Kat, she giggles and shakes her head at me.

Mrs. Thompson can't hide a big smile. "Did you have a cup or a kettle? Wow! That must have been some oily fish you had!"

"Fresh off the boat. The best kind!" I reply, just as the bell finally rings.

Despite my objections that nothing is going to happen, Kat insists on riding home with me on the bus. Even the threat of unleashing another fish bomb doesn't deter her. Once in the driveway I see that a note is taped to the front door. Expecting it's from my mom, I'm surprised when I don't recognize the handwriting.

Panic comes crashing down on me. The note's handwritten words are simple and clear.

'Meet me at the river.'

"Who's the note from?" Kat says.

"Guess who?" I can barely utter the words. I show Kat the note then explode with a sequence of shrugs and crunches.

"Oh, my gosh!"

"It's okay. I'll go, you can stay here. He just wants the ring. I guess I'll have to give it to him. Once he has it, there should be no danger. I can always run for it if I have to."

"No way, Myles. You're crazy if you go down there. Just mail the ring to New Jersey like you said you were gonna do. But please, don't go down to the river. If the guy knows you don't have the ring then he'll just leave."

"The guy knows where I live, Kat. I don't think he's going anywhere until he gets the ring." But Kat isn't convinced. "Look, I can place it on the ground far away from where he is and run away. It'll be alright. Trust me."

"I'm calling the police, Myles," Kat says whipping her phone out.

"No, wait." I grab Kat's hands and the phone. "What if you and Brady come with me. You guys can stay and watch from the woods where he can't see you. You can always call the police then, if you have to. They'll be there in less than a minute."

Kat hesitates, thinking it over. "Myles, this is crazy, and you know it. What if it's that creepy property manager guy? You don't know what he'll do!"

"It'll be alright. Trust me." But Kat just glowers at me. "If he was going to do anything bad he would have done it already. Don't you think? Whoever it is just wants the ring. Trust me, okay? Plus, I really don't think it's the guy from Cedar Gardens."

Kat nods her head. "You better be right about this."

"Text Brady and tell him to get over here right away."

About fifteen minutes later the three of us ride our bikes to the river-bank. Just like we've done dozens of times this summer. Only this time..... someone is waiting for us.

When we pull into the gravel driveway we see the dark-colored car parked off to the side. The presence of the car, the same one that's been looking for me, reminds me that I better be right about my hunch.

"Do you see anyone?" Kat says, her voice edgy and shaky.

"No. But he's here. Probably down by the river. That's where the note said to meet him." I fire off a flurry of shoulder shrugs and side crunches, hoping they'll last me awhile.

"Follow me Kat, I know where we can hide," Brady says.

"Wait. Put your phones on vibrate. It's better if he thinks I'm alone." As was our habit, we leave the bikes at the edge of the woods where the path leads to our hangout spot.

Our familiar path, unused since our morbid discovery, is overgrown with weeds. The comforting smells of the trees and the river help to relax me. Going the rest of the way myself I proceed cautiously, ready for any-thing. When I reach the edge of the embankment where the path veers downward in a steep pitch, I look for Brady and Kat. I know my friends will call for help, should I need it. I'm unable to see them, but I can hear them burrowing into a thicket of bushes about twenty yards to my right. I slide down the embankment, loosening rocks and sand under my feet which announces my arrival. A voice calls out to me.

"Be careful."

Finding my footing I crouch behind a shrub and observe the man from a safe distance. He's seated on the large boulder with his legs folded and crossed. He looks to be as old as my Pappy. His face is creased with deep wrinkles. Dark splotches stain his aged skin. His hands, resting in his lap, remind me of the rough-hewn timbers that hang from my Nanna's kitchen ceiling, full of character, gnarled, and aged by years of use. His shirt is a simple, white tunic with a deep v-cut at the neck and no collar. Plain leather sandals are strapped onto his ancient brown feet. His garments give him the appearance of a priest.

"You don't need to be afraid. Thank you for coming." He waves his hands, encouraging me to come closer. His Indian accent is heavy but understandable.

I climb up onto the rock, keeping a safe distance. "I have the ring," I tell him.

"He used to love to sit here. That's why he'd come visit for the weekend. My wife and I lived nearby, on Mountain Avenue, for many years. He enjoyed his aunt's cooking too, but mostly he visited for the peace and solitude of the river." He turns his head toward the river, his melodic voice drifts out over the water. "It reminded him of our village in India."

"Adheer."

"Yes. Adheer," the old man replies, startled.

"My name is Amar Harakatha." He extends his hand to me.

Hesitating, I take his hand and we exchange a friendly handshake.

"I'm Myles Walsh."

"It was very brave and very foolish of you, Myles Walsh, to take the ring."

I suck in a deep breath of remorse. "He was a teacher."

"Yes, he was." A smile creases his mouth. He bows gently in a gesture of respect. Under his tunic, I notice beads similar to those Adheer was wearing.

"He taught language arts," I add.

"Adheer was also a storyteller. A storyteller in the Kaavad tradition. Its history goes back more than 400 years in India. The storyteller is known as a Kaavadiyas. Adheer's father was a storyteller, as his father was, and his father before him, going all the way back to the beginning of the tradition. Adheer, however, was restless. He was a great storyteller himself, but when he came here to this country to visit us, he discovered his passion for teaching. He believed that through teaching his stories could reach more people.

At first, I did not agree with him. But, I must say, he may have been right." The old man's eyes sparkle with life, and death, and renewal.

"How did he die?" I feel twitchy for the first time since climbing the rock.

The old man hangs his head. With eyes that are heavy with sadness he says, "He learned several years ago that he had a weak heart. Lately he'd been having chest pains, he knew his time might be near. Wanting the ring to go to a person who would carry on the Kaavad tradition he asked that someone from back home come and claim the ring. Having lived here and being familiar with this area, I came to see Adheer. We had dinner at a restaurant and afterwards, while we sat in the car and talked of old times.....well, his heart just gave out. I dressed him in the ceremonial robe of the Kaathadiyas and brought him here." He pauses, gazes at the river, its calm waters in no particular hurry to get anywhere.

"You were going to wash him with the river water," I say, as the man pauses.

"Part of a simple but necessary ceremony to pass on the ownership of the ring. The river water is symbolic. Poured over his feet, it blesses his journey to the next life. I'm an old man, now. I wasn't strong enough to carry him to the river. I was going to bring him part of the way and then bring the water from the river up to him. I thought I had picked out a quiet place where we would not be disturbed, but then I heard someone coming. It was you and your friends. I didn't have time to put Adheer back into the car. I had no choice but to leave him as he was. And that, unfortunately, is when you kids found him. I'm sorry if it frightened you."

"It was weird to find.....a dead body like that...but, it's okay now. I guess."

"When I saw you kids leave I went back and got Adheer. I returned him to his home in New Jersey. It wasn't until then that I noticed that a hole had been poked in the bag. The ring had been taken. I figured it was probably you kids, the ones I'd seen leave on bikes. I thought the ring was lost forever."

I reach into my pocket. "Here's the ring." I place the Kaavad ring into the outstretched, withered hands of the priestly uncle.

"Thank you," he says, bowing his head. "I saw to it that he received a proper burial. He had requested to be buried in a simple wooden casket. He wanted to get back to the earth as soon as he could. He always loved the outdoors."

"I'm glad."

"You kids are a tough bunch to catch up with. I'm getting old. I spent part of my time here to visit old friends. Occasionally I'd drive around the neighborhood hoping against hope to spot you kids. Hoping to get the ring back. I thought I saw you several times, but I didn't want to alarm you, or the police. I wasn't going to hurt you. I'm sorry if I scared you. But the ring is important. It's needed to carry on a centuries-old tradition."

"I know the meaning of the ring." The priest looks surprised. I lean forward to view the ring which he holds in the palm of his hand. "It has to do with the Kaavad, a storytelling tradition, like you said. The small circles symbolize stories that need to be told; the ropes that weave in and out symbolize how stories, storytellers, and listeners are connected through the telling of stories; the large door symbolizes how stories open up new worlds for us. It's through stories that knowledge and traditions are passed on."

"Then you know how important it is that the ring belong to the Kaavadiyas; to a storyteller." The man bows his head.

"The ring got me thinking about something. My pappy is the nicest person I've ever known. He's the kind of person who would give you the shirt off his back. I asked him once why he was so nice all the time. He told me that when he was nine years old his father died. His mother worked hard and sacrificed to make sure that he and his sister had what they needed, but more importantly, that they were raised the right way, always appreciating what they had.

216

"His mother met and married another man, who was divorced, with three kids of his own, two boys and a girl. His mom and stepdad worked hard to bring all of them together as one family. He once said that memories come by the truckload when you grow up in a family with five kids like he did. But for him, one memory stood out the most. His stepdad, Richard, came from a large family and the first time my pappy and his sister, along with his new brothers and sister visited Richard's family it was to decorate the tree for Christmas.

"My pappy was surrounded by many unfamiliar faces. He was in a strange place and wouldn't talk or even smile at anyone; but everyone went out of their way to welcome my pappy and his sister. And then it was my grandfather who was given the honor of placing the star atop the tree, courtesy of one of his new step-cousins who hoisted him up to do the honors.

"My pappy has never forgotten that moment. It changed his outlook on life. The lesson it taught him, and the one he has passed on to me is - to be a giver, not a taker. I want to give the ring back because it's the right thing to do. Its past, the stories it's told, and its future belong to the Kaavad."

"You have learned much, Myles Walsh. You are very bright. And a good storyteller yourself. A very good storyteller."

"I'm sorry that Adheer died. And that I took the ring."

"You are wise to learn it's meaning and generous to return it." Once more the old man bows his head in a gesture of respect. And then with much effort, he stands up straight and proud, like a man who has come to the end of something. "And now it is time to go. Your friends have been waiting patiently in the bushes."

When I get home I tell my mom everything. About meeting Mr. Harakatha. About a teacher from New Jersey named Adheer Kathavyas. About the ring he owned and it's meaning. I show her Adheer's teacher Blog and the newspaper article with details of Adheer's death and his picture.

"Myles, I don't see how you expect me to believe this. I don't know whether you're a gifted storyteller or a lousy liar."

"But, Mom, can't you see. Mr. Kathavyas used to visit the Harakathas, his aunt and uncle, at 211 Mountain Avenue. The same house where Brady and I saw a ghost in a rocking chair in the attic. He was back here in Caldwell to give his uncle a 400-year old ring. The uncle, Mr. Harakatha told me everything that happened. How he died. Everything. The website with the news of Mr. Kathavyas's death proves that we're telling the truth, that he's the dead man we found. We didn't make this up."

"And where is this mysterious ring you supposedly took from the man who was dead? Can I see it?"

"I gave it back to Mr. Harakatha."

"Very convenient. And where is Mr. Harakatha? May I speak to him?"

"He's probably on his way back to India." I feel like a thief, a liar, and an uncertain storyteller.

"Again. Very convenient."

"Mom!" I scream.

"Myles, I have to say you've done a great job trying to convince me. It must not have been easy to find an article about an Indian person who died the same weekend that you discovered a dead body. But it doesn't prove anything. Besides, the article says the man was found dead in his apartment in New Jersey - that means he died in New Jersey and not in Massachusetts. And he certainly didn't put himself into a plastic bag and appear here in Caldwell just so you and your friends could find him."

"I didn't just find anyone on the internet who died that weekend, I found the person we saw at the river!"

"I'm not buying it and I doubt your father will either. I'll let him decide about whether you can go to Lake Placid, or not."

CHAPTER EIGHTEEN

Thursday, September 25th

Mom is working at the kitchen table, her head buried in her laptop when I walk into the kitchen for breakfast. I'm about to gulp milk straight from the container when my mom alerts me to an envelope on the counter.

"This is for me?" I say.

"Has your name on it."

The envelope has no postage on it, no return address. It's heavy, like there's a small stack of quarters in it.

"Who's it from?" Mom asks.

"I don't know, there's no name on it, other than mine."

I rip a corner of the envelope then slide my finger along the sealed ridge, opening it to find a note inside. Confused and surprised I read the note:

Dear Myles,

Enclosed you will find the Kaavad ring. I believe that the ring has found its way to you for a reason. Though the exact reason may be unclear to you now, I entrust the ring to you with the certainty that it will help you to help others, as it did for Adheer. The ring will lead you on a journey of discoveries which may appear to be accidents, but are the result of the ring's power and your willingness to tell its stories. Honor and respect the tradition that has been bestowed on you, and the ring will always be your guide.

Sincerely,

Amar Harakatha

Reaching into the envelope I take out a familiar object.

The Kaavad ring.

Talk about responsibility! I feel the weight of 400 years of history as I roll the ring between my fingers. Gazing at the door symbolically centered at the head of the ring, I wonder, how many stories the ring has told?

What stories lie ahead for me?

Will I be able to tell them?

"What's that?" Mom says, enchanted with the ancient ring.

"It's the ring. Mr. Harakatha has given it to me. Here, he wrote a note with it." I give the ring and the note to my mom.

"Mr. Harakatha?" Mom says, her voice shaky with disbelief.

"He's the uncle of the dead man we found. Adheer."

"I know who Mr. Harakatha is. Why is he giving you a ring?"

I shrug my shoulders. "He explains in the note."

Mom's lips move in slow motion as she reads Mr. Harakatha's note.

"I'm not sure what this is all about. This is quite an unusual ring, that's for sure." It's Mom's turn to gaze at the intricacy of the ring's design. Feel its weight and ponder its meaning.

"I guess he just wants me to have it. Probably because I was able to find out about…..the dead man, his nephew."

"Well, that's very nice of him. I'm sure the ring is old, probably a family heirloom of some sort." She hands the ring back to me. "Take care good care of it." And then her head is back in her laptop and she's back in work mode.

But there is one other matter.

"So you believe me now?"

"Myles, you got me worn down to a stub with all of this!"

"So, do you believe me now?"

She looks at me. Guilt and surrender are quilted into her face. She bites her lower lip.

"I guess so."

"That means I can play in Lake Placid? The All-Star game, too?"

"Just get all C's or higher on your report card, then I guess you can go to Lake Placid. You hear me mister? No D's."

Right here in the kitchen I do my best hockey celly ever!

We write in a personal journal almost every day in Mr. Curtin's class. He'll put several prompts on the board and we respond to the one that interests us the most. Yesterday's choices were:

Is it better to have good manners, or to get what you want?

What do you like and dislike about your name?

Describe a time that you helped a parent solve a problem.

I chose that it's better to have good manners than to get what you want, because in the long run having good manners will get you more of what you want.

Today's prompt is: How do you know when you're grown up?

I don't know when it'll hit me that I'm grown up, but I'm definitely feeling more grown up since everything happened. My parents are always nagging me about being more responsible.

Put your dirty dishes in the dishwasher, Myles.

Don't leave wet towels on the floor, Myles.

It's not our job to go around cleaning up after you, Myles.

Like any normal thirteen year old I'm guilty of all these kid mistakes and more. And even though my room often looks like a locker room after a championship celebration, I do feel more mature, more responsible. After all, how often does a thirteen year old kid figure something out that the police can't?

Mr. Curtin is pleased when we tell him that we identified who the dead man was. "So, who was the man you found?" he says.

"His name was Adheer Kathavyas. He was a Language Arts teacher, like you."

"He lived in New Jersey," Kat adds.

"What was he doing here in Caldwell, then?"

"He used to live in Caldwell and he was here to meet his uncle," I say.

"Should we tell him about...you know..." Brady says.

I dig into my pocket and show Mr. Curtin the Kaavad ring. "He was wearing this when we found him." I give the ring to Mr. Curtin who sits up in his chair and inspects it as if it were a rare and priceless relic.

"Wow. This is very interesting. I've heard of the Kaavad tradition and the existence of these rings, but I've never seen one before. Not even a picture of one. It's beautiful. It could be a hundred years old, or more."

"It's more than 400 years old," I tell him.

He lifts his head and looks at me with a quizzical look. "So, Adheer was wearing this ring when you discovered him and now you have it?"

"I took it. I poked a hole in the bag. It just....well... it was like it wanted me to take it. So I did. I know I shouldn't have. I did give it back to Adheer's uncle, Mr. Harakatha, a few days ago after school. But then he gave it back to me. He said that I should have the ring, that it had found me and that I should carry on the tradition."

Mr. Curtin nods his head. He pauses for a moment. "Remember when I told you, Myles, that stories have a way of finding storytellers?"

I nod my head, remembering the conversation we had when I was stuck on my writing assignment.

"I think a very important story has found you."

"I know."

"I can't wait to read your story."

"I'll do my best."

"I know you will. But come to think of it, there's another story that needs to be told. One that you kids just might be perfect for."

"What story is that?" Brady asks.

"I, too, many years ago, discovered a dead man; that unfortunate man in the city who got too close to the radiator. Unlike you kids, I never found out what his story was. Kaavad rings are very rare. They work in mysterious ways. Maybe this ring will help you to uncover his story. You never know. One story always leads to another."

Mr. Curtin hands the ring back to me.

"What I do know however, is that there are many more stories in your future, Mr. Walsh."

Loose gravel crunches under the the tires of my bike as I make the turn into the parking lot. The brick shed with its boarded-up windows looms over the parking lot with its discarded rusty items, like an old grandparent, broken and weary, but still standing. I draw in the sweet odor of pine cones as I walk my bike around the Keep Out sign, ignoring its harmless warning. The weeds where the dead man once rested stretch upwards like proud sunflowers. I spring down the path and leap onto the large boulder, my fingers just catching the rim, I hoist myself up. The giant rock, warmed by the afternoon sun, massages my achy back as I lay and rest.

I take in the view from where I've spent countless hours relaxing with my friends. Summer is hanging around a little longer. The trees that line both banks of the river are still thick with forty shades of green. Birds, hidden among the foliage, sing happy songs.

Brady and Kat are on their way, Jogesh too, giving me a few minutes to reflect on the past few weeks. With all the craziness, I haven't had much time to fret about school the way I normally do. I've just gotten into a groove with it. All in all I'd say things have gotten off to a good start.

I take off my shoes. I pour a cupful of river water over my bare white feet. Taking the ring out I admire the simplicity and meaning of its design. I slip the ring on.

It fits perfectly.

CHAPTER NINETEEN

Monday, October 13th

I didn't turn in the story I'd been working on since the first week of school. The lonely man who died-by-radiator story. After thinking it over, and with Mr. Curtin's encouragement, I decided to write a different story. This first story that the ring reveals is one that is unexpected. Not quite as unexpected as finding a dead man inside a clear plastic bag on an old gravel path. But almost. It's a story that begins with a young boy from a small village in India who left his ancestral home to see the world.

His father was the latest in a long line of Kaavad storytellers, though with progress coming to their corner of the world the need for storytellers had diminished. Although Adheer had two older sisters, it was he who was his mother's favorite. She taught him how to roll rotli for dinner, and he ate all his meals on a special plate just for him. A bright boy, he excelled in school and was advanced a grade ahead several times. Right from the start, it was evident Adheer had a talent for telling a good story, but as he grew older he worried about eking out a meager living following a dying tradition. Plus many of his friends had left India to live elsewhere, places such as Canada, England, or Hong Kong.

Adheer's dream, however, was to live in America. But first he made stops along the way in Fiji, South Africa, and then England. He delivered newspapers and worked in a shirt factory in Fiji; made Bunny Chows and washed dishes at a restaurant in South Africa; and completed high school while living with relatives in London. He stayed with an aunt and uncle in America where he attended college, still unsure whether he wanted to become a doctor or a teacher. But teaching allowed him to pursue his love of literature and reading, while still honoring the tradition of the Kaavad. And of course, the ring was always with him wherever he went. He often performed Kaavad services in Indian communities all over New Jersey and New York where he taught.

He was born to be a storyteller and was a good one. He made a positive impact on the lives of thousands of people, mostly students who loved to listen to his exotic and fascinating tales. And not surprisingly, his life and death became a story itself.

You see, some of his former students had created a message board where hundreds of people posted pictures and descriptions of their favorite Mr. K stories. I enjoyed reading through them. That's where I got the details for my assignment. But the the story I liked best was about a man who owes his health and life to someone he'd never met before...

Steve's health problems began when he was just twelve years old, after tests following a summer's long illness revealed that he had only one, very enlarged kidney. It took two surgeries to drain and repair his kidney, but after that, he was basically back to normal. Over the years, he'd receive periodic check-ups to make sure everything was working well.

Life went on.

He graduated from college where he was a good student and played on the soccer team. He moved to Ohio and became a teacher, where he met his wife, the school nurse. Young and healthy, he continued to play soccer in various men's leagues. He mostly forgot about the one kidney.

Soon though, he started experiencing mild headaches that wouldn't really go away. Tests showed that his kidney was only functioning at fifty percent. Steve's doctor put him on a special diet, which helped for a while. But as time went by, he found himself tiring more easily, frequently falling asleep while correcting papers at his kitchen table. His wife was worried - she was aware of the dangers Steve faced. New tests revealed that

Steve's kidney was functioning at just twenty percent. A donor was going to be needed.

Soon.

A living donor.

No one in Steve's family was a match. None of his friends were a match, either. Time was passing quickly. Just when Steve was nearly out of options, a hero came to the rescue. A stranger had responded to an article about Steve on a teacher website that told Steve's story. This person went to his local transplant center for his donor work-up.

He was a match.

The surgery was finally performed.

Today, Steve is healthy and coaches soccer. He and his wife have three growing kids of their own.

The donor, the hero, was Adheer Kathavyas.

But the best part is when I showed the story posted on the message board, with a picture of Steve to my parents. It turns out that the person, that teacher who had saved my dad's life all those years ago, was none other than Steve. Dad remembered him as the teacher who had alertly given him the epi-pen that saved his life on that field trip to Washington. Even though he says he still doesn't believe in ghosts, I now know what serendipity means.

Steve wouldn't be here today if it weren't for Adheer Kathavyas who donated a kidney and saved Steve's life.

And my dad wouldn't be here today if Steve hadn't gotten that transplant and been there to save him.

And that means that I wouldn't be here today. But I am.

I'm glad that I found out who that dead man was. And what his story was.

And that's the story I wrote.

The Dead Man Story.

Or rather, The Adheer Kathavyas Story.

I got an A-, meaning I'll be playing hockey in Lake Placid just six weeks from now. I'll play my best in the all-star game and hope it's good enough for the St. Michael's coach. That's all anyone can do - the best they can.

My mom called the police and made me tell everything to the two policemen, Officers Lema and Mathias, the same two who had come to the house last month when we first discovered Adheer. Their investigation uncovered that one Amar Harakatha had purchased a round-trip ticket from Delhi to Boston. He also rented a vehicle at the airport on Sunday, September 1st, and stayed at the Holiday Inn in Caldwell until Friday, September 26th, when he returned the rental car and flew back to India. Officer Mathias also told my parents that as Mr. Kathavyas died in New Jersey and is already buried in New Jersey, and was never seen in Caldwell, at least not by them, it's out of their jurisdiction.

Their investigation also determined that Mr. Harakatha had not done anything illegal. Unusual perhaps, though he claimed he was just observing a 400-year old tradition, but nothing criminal.

Brady and Kat went with me to visit Mr. and Mrs. Brown. We thanked them for their help in solving the identity of the dead man. Mrs. Brown was pleased to learn that Adheer did indeed go on to fulfill his dream of becoming a teacher. But she was saddened to hear that the young man who once sat on her deck and shared an unforgettable story with her had passed on.

Brady and Kat and I still go to the riverbank, at least on the days when the weather cooperates. I'm still twitching as crazily as I ever have, but everyone is getting used to it and hardly seems to notice now. I am feeling a little less anxious though. The presence of the ring is a source of comfort, though the words of Mr. Harakatha and Mr. Curtin have been on my mind a lot lately. What the next six weeks, or the next six months, bring is anyone's guess.

As for Mr. Curtin…

Well, this has been the best start to a school year I've ever had. Can't say I've ever had a teacher like Mr. Curtin before. I don't think any of us have. Can't say I'll ever have a teacher like Mr. Curtin again, either.

He promised us on Friday that because we were so good last week that he'd tell us a Mr. Curtin story today.

He told us we'd like this one..

"As you guys know, Mr. Curtin used to live and work in New York City. And as you recall from an earlier story, my grandfather worked for many years on the subway system in New York. Well, the subway is the best way to get around the city and I used it all the time when I'd be out and about working.

"My office was downtown, near where the World Trade Center towers once stood. Whenever I needed to go uptown I'd use the Number 1 train. And that's the train I was on when I witnessed the strangest thing I've ever seen. This is a true story by the way.

"It was summer time, perhaps August if I remember correctly, and it gets mighty hot in the city in August. And with all the tourists that flood into the city from all over the world every summer, the subways are often jam-packed. Being a New Yorker I know that the best place to be on a crowded subway car on a hot day is leaning against the door that leads from one car to another. Now, if you've ever been on a subway before, you know that right outside that door is a small platform, perhaps two feet wide, just large enough for a person to stand on, and it sits about half a foot from the same platform connected to the next subway car. So you have this gap of 6-8 inches that you have to be careful to step over.

"I was leaning comfortably against the door minding my own business when I thought I'd heard someone knock on the door behind me.

There's a good size window on the door and I stepped aside and looked through the window to see who was walking through. In New York, people, usually teens, will walk from one end of the train to the other so as to be closer to the exit when they reach their stop. I thought it was a kid that was cutting through, but there was no one there when I looked.

"I went back to leaning against the door, tired from a long day's work, when I heard the knocking again. I quickly swung around to see who it was that had knocked on the door, but again, there was no one. I could see right through the window into the other subway car, and there was no one outside the door. I noticed none of the people in the other car seemed to be paying any attention to someone who might be playing some kind of joke. I looked around to the people standing near me, hoping they had heard the knocking too, but they were all busy reading the paper or talking to each other.

"Thinking now that I may have just 'heard' the banging and clattering of the train as it was speeding over the tracks I went back to leaning on the door. Just then I could feel the door moving, someone was trying to open the door. Again I spun around quickly to see who this person was that kept bothering me, and once more there was no one there. But I noticed that the door handle was moving, someone was definitely doing that, and it wasn't me.

"I slowly opened the door and the deafening noise of the train blasted into my face. To my surprise, there was no one standing outside the door. But something made me glance down...and there I saw something that I never expected to see. Something I did not want to see."

"What was it Mr. Curtin?" asks Brady.

"A man. A man fighting for his very life. Somehow he had fallen, and he was literally pinned up to his waist between the two steel platforms of the subway cars. What I was looking at was a man being severed in half. As the train was screaming, bumping, and bouncing down the tracks, the poor man was being grinded into two pieces."

229

A chorus of moans echo through the room. "What'd you do?" Someone in the back row belts out.

"I didn't do anything. I froze. I couldn't believe what I was seeing. Here right before my eyes I was watching a man die a painful and excruciating death. Because he was being sawed in half at the waist, all I could picture was his feet and legs being dragged along the splintery wooden tracks. For a moment I wondered if his feet were still attached. I figured it was highly probable that they had been scraped right off of him and that the stubs of his legs were slowly being scraped down to the bone. All this while the two subway cars were gradually slicing his upper body from his lower body. I kept waiting for that moment when the speed and power of the train would just suck him down underneath and chew him to pieces. I felt sick to my stomach. I wanted to cry, but was too much in a state of shock to do so. I just wanted the whole thing to end, to be over with, for me and for this poor, unfortunate person."

"You didn't do anything, Mr. Curtin?" Jogesh asks.

"I thought about helping him, I really did. At one point I even extended my hand down to him thinking I'd try and pull him out from between the steel platforms. He managed to raise an arm and a hand up to meet mine, and I noticed that his arm was large and powerful. I hesitated to grab his hand because the thought occurred to me that if I pulled too hard I might actually rip his upper body right off from his lower body. I wasn't sure at this point how much of him was still left, you know what I'm talking about? All I could picture was me yanking as hard as I could and that I'd be the one to separate him into two pieces.

"The other thought I had was that I was the only hope the guy had of surviving this horrific ordeal. His arm was muscular, huge. I was afraid he'd get a death grip on me and when that moment came when he'd finally be sucked down under the train, that he'd bring me down with him, and I didn't want that to happen."

"So, what happened to him?" Arian says, fidgeting in the front row.

"Like I said, I didn't do anything. I didn't know what to do. I was just waiting for the whole thing to end. And that's when he did something that just blew my mind. Despite his terrible situation, the unbelievable pain he was enduring, probably aware that he was dying an unimaginable death, he looked up at me and said, "Are you just gonna stand there, or are you gonna get outta my way?"

"I was stunned he could even speak. I didn't know what to say. So I said nothing in return. And then he yelled at me, "Get outta the way, would ya!" I stumbled back a few steps and got out of his way. I thought that he just wanted to die in peace with a little privacy, without me standing over him, gawking at him. But then he reached behind himself and pulled out two small wooden blocks that each had a thick rope attached to them, like handles. He wrapped his hands tightly inside the blocks. I was thinking, 'where did he get those from?' when he hoisted himself up in an odd way, and using the blocks like crutches, he walked himself right by me into the subway car.

"It was then that I could see that he was a man with no legs. Was a man who perhaps never had any legs, was in all likelihood born without legs. He scooted quickly to an old woman sitting in the nearest seat and stopped before her as if he were on his knees in prayer. He reached behind his head with one of his powerful arms and presented a rumpled and stained brown paper bag tied around his neck to the woman.

"She reached with steady hands into her pocketbook resting on her lap, and dropped a few small coins into the bag. The man accepted the donation then scooted from person to person, the wooden blocks clumping noisily on the soiled floor, until he had visited everyone in the subway car. A middle-aged businessman standing at the far end kindly opened the door for him. Using the blocks with the thick, twisty ropes he once more hoisted himself dangerously out onto the small platform. The screeching of metal and a warm blast of air whistled into the train. The door closed behind him muffling the noise.

"And the man with no legs disappeared."

Mr. Curtin continues.

"A few moments later I saw the door of the next car open and the man repeated his performance for another captive audience."

"Wow, Mr. Curtin! How do you have all these crazy stories?" asks Emily, the smartest girl in the seventh grade.

"I suppose I'm just one of those people for whom strange things happen. Question is, if you should ever find yourself in a situation when someone is in danger and needs your help, how will you respond? What will you do?"

Mr. Curtin looks directly at me.

Uh, oh. I've seen that look before.

I just knew this was gonna happen.

THE END

AUTHOR BIO:

Marty Conley has been telling crazy stories his whole life – mostly because crazy things always seem to happen to him. Born in New York, Marty grew up in Massachusetts where he played hockey, baseball, and football. He now teaches at a middle school outside Boston where he lives with his wife and four teenage children.